T0278736

SESG EXPLORER

CHRISTOPHER LORIC

DORRANCE
PUBLISHING CO
EST. 1920
PITTSBURGH, PENNSYLVANIA 15235

Dorrance Publishing Co
585 Alpha Drive
Pittsburgh, PA 15238
Visit our website at *www.dorrancebookstore.com*

ISBN: 979-8-8860-4324-2
eISBN: 979-8-8860-4572-7

CHAPTER 1

CAPT Shura looked around his bridge. All he could see through the smoke were electrical fires, smashed monitors, control boards, and worse of all, dead crewmembers. He looked down at his own smashed and bloody leg where a bracer had collapsed onto it. A flicker of light up and to his right brought his attention back to the space battle. He looked at one of the few monitors left to see the Admiral's ship make the jump into hyperspace as he felt his own ship being torn apart by the Kammorrigan's fire. He set his lips in a hard, defiant grin knowing that his own ship's destruction enabled the rest of the SESG to escape. The space destroyer erupted into a ball of fire as the Kammorrigan laser bursts and missiles slammed into it, destroying it utterly.

Vice Admiral Brannigan sat back in his command chair aboard the *USS Intrepid* and closed his eyes as he thought about the sacrifice of the crew of the *USS Scimitar*. Slowly he stood up and departed the command deck and went to his cabin. He went to his head and splashed water onto his face and looked at himself in the mirror....

•　　•　　•

In a secured room, within the National Command Center of the Pentagon, with the Top Secret sign lit, sat three general officers around a table with a group of service records before them.

"Why in the world do you want him?"

"Because not only can he command the strike group, he has practical diplomatic experience."

"But he just got picked up for Rear Admiral. There are more experienced admirals..."

"Yes, yes, Steve, but Admiral Brannigan is the right man for the job."

"Look, he isn't even part of Space Force."

"That is the Navy's own fault for being stupid, Steve. They could have placed him into Space Force long ago after his command of the DESRON. Look, after six years in the Sudan working with the United Nations, African Coalitions, and the Marines to relieve the suffering, Admiral Brannigan has a unique perspective. Plus, he has successfully commanded a destroyer, a cruiser, a DESRON, and now returns after a successful deployment of a Carrier Strike Group. Even before the Sudan mission, he deployed with a Marine Expeditionary Unit and understands how the Marines operate. Who better to command this group? Another admiral or general who will have indiscretions with his female officers?"

"Hold it right there, John! You know that these men are top notch. And we know about the Sudan incident he caused."

"Yes, you're right and I apologize for my comment. But these men don't have the same experience as Kevin. Not only can he command but he will think in the diplomatic and scientific realms. Only a few of those generals can or will think along those lines."

"I disagree. Many of our generals understand science and technology."

"Yes, but very few if any of them will have the practical diplomatic skills that Admiral Brannigan has. Don't forget, I saw firsthand what he can do. I was a colonel in the Sudan when he was a Lieutenant Commander dealing with the Darfur issues."

"Enough." Said the third man, "We will add Admiral Brannigan to the list and the President will choose. We, as the Joint Chiefs, will recommend these five equally. Just ensure that he has their complete service records, Steve."

"Yes, Sir."

• • •

MaryAnne stepped quickly across the sunlit room, taking off her gardening gloves to pick up the ringing phone. She listened quietly to the voice on the other end and replied, "I'll get him. It will take a few minutes." The voice on the other end acknowledged. As she put the receiver down, she let out a small sigh and slowly turned towards the door.

MaryAnne stopped at the railing on the deck and looked out over the green lawn and spotted her husband near the tree line. She watched him working around one tree when she caught him looking at her. She motioned with her hand that there was a phone call. She watched him approach thinking to herself how long this time before she would see him again.

"Hello."

"Kevin, this is Ralph Nabum."

"Hey Ralph, how is it going?"

"Sorry to interrupt your leave but we need you to come to D.C. right away."

"What's up?"

"Tell you when you get here. We have a plane waiting for you at Tulsa and we are sending a helo to get you."

"That soon, okay."

Kevin hung up the phone and noticed MaryAnne in the room. "I have to go to D.C. now. A helo is on its way." She just nodded and managed a smile as he walked by giving her a kiss.

The plane taxied to a stop while the landing crew brought the ladder to the plane. While the crews were opening the hatch, a sedan drove up. Kevin stepped out of the plane to a humid and wet day at Langley. He quickly stepped down the ladder into the waiting sedan as an airman put his luggage into the trunk.

The sun was setting as the sedan was coming to a stop at the Pentagon. Kevin was both glad and disappointed at their arrival. The two-and-a-half-hour drive from Langley was both uneventful and smooth. During the ride he thought about his wife and wondered what job he was going to get. They had talked about retirement and what they desired to do but now all that was dust. Being called like this meant that the Chief of Naval Operations had made up his mind about an assignment.

Two Naval officers came down the steps and greeted him as he got out of the car. They told him that boarding arrangements had been made and that the sedan was at his disposal. They continued letting him know about the various items around D.C. if there was time as they led him to the Navy side of the building. Finally arriving at the CNO's area, the officers ushered him into a small office where a yeoman had prepared coffee and hot water. They inquired into his needs and when he said that he was fine they made their excuses and departed. Kevin made himself a cup of coffee, looked around the room at the pictures while waiting. That is how Vice Admiral Ralph Nabum found him.

"Aaah, hello Kevin."

"Hello, sir."

"How is MaryAnne?"

"She is fine, thanks."

"How was the plane ride?"

"Normal." Kevin took a drink from the cup, looked at Nabum and said, "So, what is going on? Why did I have to get here so fast?"

"Sorry, no details from me. But it is an important job." Ralph looked at his watch then back at Kevin. "Shortly, you have a meeting with the Joint Chiefs. Its classification is at the Special Category level. You can decline the mission if you so desire, but..." After a short pause Kevin said, "But I either accept or decline now." Ralph nodded. "No other details unless I accept." Another nod. Kevin turned away and looking at a rendering of a WWII destroyer in action, finished his coffee. Ralph waited watching him. Kevin put down the cup and turned towards him.

"Well, let me hit the head and let's see the Chiefs."

Ralph and Kevin entered the briefing room, around the table sat the Joint Chiefs with a Space Force officer and two other Navy officers with briefing materials.

"Gentlemen, Rear Admiral Upper Half Kevin Brannigan," stated Ralph.

"Long time since Darfur," said General Malcolm as he came over and shook hands with Kevin. "General, it's good to see you again."

General Malcolm grinned and motioned to a chair at the table and took his seat.

The CNO looked at Kevin, "Ralph told you this is a SpeCat?"

"Yes, sir."

"And you accept the assignment without any knowledge of the mission."

Kevin looked him straight on, "Yes, sir."

The CNO looked at the Chairman "RADM Brannigan is your man, sir."

General Armstrong of the United States Army, the Chairman of the Joint Chiefs of Staff looked Kevin over. He surveyed his dress blues, rows of ribbons, Surface Warfare Device, and noticed that he wore the United Nations ribbons.

"Admiral, you were one of five names presented to the President. He chose you to lead this mission. You are the second person in this job. Your predecessor was relieved. We lost confidence in his ability to lead."

Kevin nodded in acknowledgement.

The Chief of Space Operations (CSO), General Rodriquez, motioned to one of the three officers standing by. He walked over to Kevin and placed a package in front of him.

The Chairman continued, "You are now transferred from the Navy to Space Force and will be leading an expedition into space."

Kevin looked at him slightly stunned and then at each of the Chiefs. "Is this the mission to Mars that is rumored, Sir?"

"No."

Kevin looked down at the package before him. Space, and not Mars. Another planet? Deep space? He wanted to rip into the package just like he used to at Christmas when he was a boy back in Norman. He looked back at General Armstrong, "Where?"

The Chairman responded "A long way. You have been chosen for this mission for both your military and diplomatic skills. This mission is an expedition of science and diplomacy with a heavy military emphasis." Contact with extraterrestrials. At long last, Kevin could hardly resist. The Chairman continued, "Our scientists have finally cracked the code on hyperspace. We have successfully tested a hyperspace drive. We have successfully sent both a chimp and a man through hyperspace. A golden moment in history that very few know about. You mentioned the Mars mission. While that is a real mission, it is a cover mission for the one you are going to lead. Congratulations." The Chairman motioned to the Chief of Space Operations of the Space Force.

General Rodriquez said, "SETI has actually paid off. Two years ago, it received an interstellar broadcast. It took a team of mathematicians, linguists, and crypto types nine months to crack it. The broadcast was *not* sent to us. We figured that it is a general broadcast to anyone who can pick it up. The race that sent it call themselves, the Kammorrigans. We want you to take a team out to make contact with them. No matter what, you are not to let them know where Earth is. Under no circumstance are you to let this info out. You are to establish contact, determine their intentions. If they are peaceable, then you can negotiate diplomatic and possibly trade ties. If they have hostile intentions, well we are giving you hydrogen bombs to launch. But only, if necessary, understand?"

"Yes, sir."

"Oh yes, collect any other information on any systems you come across. Any questions?"

"Plenty!"

•   •   •

"Hello, Love."

"Hi, honey."

Kevin was still reeling from his meeting with the Chiefs. His driver drove him to the Westin where Ralph had set up a room for him. He said goodnight to the driver after making arrangements to be picked up at eight in the morning. Now in his room he called room service and then his wife.

"Interesting meeting. I will be here for three weeks then I have some traveling to do."

"When will I see you next?"

"I should be able to get home in two or three months. I will have workups for about a year and then deploy. So, I will be able to get home a few times before deployment."

"Okay. You get anything to eat?"

"I ordered up something from room service."

"I was thinking about a golf tournament in Tulsa."

"Sounds good. When is it?"

"Next week, I'll be home when you get here. How long will you be able to stay?"

"A week. The next couple of weeks should give me a good status of what needs to be done."

"Okay, well enjoy your meal."

"Win the tournament."

"Love you."

"Love you."

Kevin quietly disconnected his device and sighed. He hated not being able to tell MaryAnne but that had been the way of it for years. While he missed her now like he always had he was also jazzed about the mission.

He sat back against the headboard of the bed and his thoughts drifted back over his life.

The smoke was pitch black. The smell of burning vehicles, tires, gasoline, and people seemed to drive all the air away. People were screaming, the children's screamed in fright as the women were being gunned down. The sound of weapon's fire was incredible. No one could think. Kevin continued to pour fire down onto the raiders as they killed the Sudanese civilians. His Marines were being hit by them.

Kevin screamed as he woke up. He was sweating all over and felt extremely hot. He threw the covers off him and sat up, swinging his legs over the edge of the bed. He dropped his head into his hands.

Damn, another nightmare, he thought. He rubbed his face and ran his hands through his hair. He looked at the clock and saw it was four A.M. He got up and went into the bathroom and turned on the cold water. He ran cold water over his face and head to include the back of his neck.

The Darfur region of Sudan was a bit of a nightmare for him. He was a U.S. representative to the United Nations in 2025 attempting to bring a lasting peace between the Christians and Muslim militant Arabs and Africans. After several engagements like the one, he just dreamed about there was some semblance of peace.

He was on an assessment mission to determine the engineering and medical requirements of an area when they came under attack by one of the groups and the ensuing gun battle earned him the Bronze Star. But the cost to civilian life was incredible despite he and his Marines driving off the raiders.

He sighed and went back into the bedroom. He looked at the clock and then went to the window and looked out.

He hated these nightmares and the fact he would not be able to get back to sleep. With such a long day in front of him he had wanted every minute of sleep he could get. *Oh well, that is the way this ball bounces.*

He put on his gym clothes and went to the gym. At least he could get in a run, perform core strengthening, and stretches. That would help.

He was picked up at the hotel by the same people who had driven him the day before except one change; Ralph Nabum was in the car. During the drive, Kevin noticed they were not heading to the Pentagon. "Ralph, where are we heading?"

"Oh, did I not mention that we have to go to the White House first?" Ralph was smiling at him.

"No, why?"

"Well, I don't know, maybe the President wants to see his new Space Admiral right away."

"Oh, you're kidding me. I have work to do and I want to get this done."

"No way, POTUS wants to see you first and we are going to see him."

It turned out meeting the President wasn't as bad as Kevin had thought it would be. They had to wait fifteen minutes before being ushered into his presence. The President was an older man but still keen. He greeted them in a very friendly manner and asked a few basic questions. He then spoke about how excited he was about this mission and was looking for the day they could launch the ships and expressed his support. At the end of the meeting, he surprised Kevin by having him remove the two stars from both collars of his Khaki uniform and proceeded to pin on three stars. Kevin was informed that the promotion to Vice Admiral was already approved and from now on he was fully a Vice Admiral. The President was very proud to administer the oath of office. Then they left. The whole affair took no more than twenty minutes. To say that Kevin was dumbfounded would have been an understatement. Ralph just laughed at him and gave him a hearty congratulation and reminded him of the wet down that would have to take place.

Soon the now Vice Admiral Kevin Brannigan was on his way to the Pentagon for his briefings. When they arrived, Kevin was escorted to a room where he was briefed by the Security Manager for his new level of clearance. Once this was accomplished, he was ushered to a briefing room set up for Top Secret briefings. Again, his dread of briefings was precariously balanced with his kid-like enthusiasm for the fleet that he would be commanding.

Kevin entered the room with everybody standing at attention. He immediately told everyone to take their seats as he sat down at the head of the table. The three support officers from the previous night were standing by to aid with the technical side of the presentations and to ensure the refreshments did not run out.

Around the table were the Commanding Officers of the ships of the fleet along with the other commanders. The executive officers were still onboard the ships preparing for the voyage. While the officers and crews now belonged to Space Force, several came from the other services. This mission and ships required a true joint force. So, each of the other services provided officers and units to make up Space Expeditionary Strike Group EXPLORER.

The briefing room was rectangular with audio visual support behind the screens at one end of the room. Keven sat with the doors behind him, which were rated for top secret. The table was rectangular but slightly curved along the two sides so everyone could see each other and the various monitors along the walls. Along the walls were seats for additional personnel. Seated along the right-hand side of Kevin were the Commanding Officers of the seven ships that made up the strike group. Along the left-hand side sat the various other staff and commanders. To Kevin's immediate right at the head of the table sat Major General Paul Connington, his Chief of Staff and for all practical purposes the second in charge of the fleet. Along the right-hand side sat Captain Karen Smith, the Commanding Officer of the *USS Intrepid*, the fleet's flagship. Continuing along the right side of the table sat Colonel Johnathon Williams, the Commanding Officer of the *USS Chesty* which would be the command ship for the Marines. Next was Colonel Mike Krist, commanding the *USS Icarus*, and following him was Captain Robert Murphy, commanding the *USS Excalibur*. Next sat Colonel Mark Adams, commanding the *USS Defiant*, then Captain Ismal Shura, commander of the *USS Scimitar* and finally Captain Allen Strickland, the commander of the *USS Nautilus* which would behave as a submarine in space.

Along the left side of the table sat Dr. Jack Vance, the head of the Science Branch. Next to him was Colonel John Roberts the Commanding Officer of the 51st Marine Expeditionary Unit, the head of the Marines that would be going on this venture. Next to him sat Colonel Robert Cole, the Carrier Air Group (CAG). Next came CDR Paul Ramirez, commander of the special forces assigned to the strike group.

The remainder of the morning was taken up with briefings from each of these commanders on the capability of the ships or units that would be going along on the mission. The *Intrepid* was by far the largest of the ships. She would be carrying the Admiral and his staff along with a platoon of Marines called Fleet Antiterrorism and Security Team (FAST). This team being trained in security operations and hostage rescues would be the Admiral's own response unit. Also, onboard the *Intrepid* would be the CAG. Col Cole would command the entire wing from this ship. His capability included forty fighters spread out on three ships for space battles and if necessary, support to any ground units on a planet. An additional ten fighters were onboard the *Chesty* to provide close air support for the Marines should they be on the ground. Col Cole would also have at his disposal ten ships for reconnaissance missions and several transport ships of various descriptions. The munitions onboard this ship included ship to ship missiles and lasers, rail guns, hypersonic missiles along with tactical and strategic nuclear devices for use against large space vessels or planetary targets. The last weapons had been discussed briefly the night before by the Joint Chiefs, they were weapons at Kevin's disposal should he believe they were necessary.

The *Icarus* and *Excalibur* could best be described as battleships. They were smaller versions of the *Intrepid* and were designed to support her in a space battle or provide fire support from space to the Marines on a planet. The Intrepid would carry twenty of the forty fighters and the other two ships would carry ten each. The ship that resembled the *Intrepid* closest in both size and capability is the *Chesty*, the command platform for the Marines. She was equipped with the ten fighters and transports to allow planetary landings by the Marines. The majority of the two thousand two hundred Marines would be onboard her with company size elements on the other three large ships. Her munitions were specifically designed to support planetary operations.

CDR Ramirez had command of a company size element of U.S. Army Rangers, a squad of Marine Reconnaissance company and a SEAL team. The SEALs would be onboard the *USS Nautilus* and *Intrepid*. The Ranger company that was provided by the Army would be onboard the *Chesty* to support the Recon company of the Marines. CDR Ramirez would be onboard the *Chesty* to plan out operations and effect command and control of these units.

Both the *Defiant* and *Scimitar* were comparable to each other. The *Defiant* was slightly larger than the *Scimitar*. They were the cruiser and destroyer respectfully. Their main function was to provide what could be called air defense to the fleet or in this case space defense. On the battle formation of the fleet these two ships would take opposite ends to provide an electronic net designed to destroy incoming missiles or enemy ships. They were of sufficient size and firepower to enable them to engage larger ships if necessary. All these ships had a main body with two arms reaching out in front. The larger ships had tubes for launching the fighters and landing bays underneath each arm for recovery. The *Chesty* was specifically designed to launch their landing transports from underneath the arms. These transports could also perform the task of a helicopter, specifically the role of close support or engaging enemy aircraft inside a planet's atmosphere. Every ship could fire their weapons in a three hundred sixty-degree bubble. Amazingly enough they had electronic shields that had been developed. These shields could absorb and distribute the energy of energy weapons such as their own lasers. To some degree they were also effective against missiles.

The *Nautilus* was completely different from the other ships. VADM Brannigan instantly could tell the submarine community had their influence with this ship. It actually had the appearance of a submarine in space except its conning tower was sloped dramatically. While the conning tower of submarines stood straight up with bow wings, the *Nautilus* was sloped dramatically back and came down over the spine of the ship. While the other ships had running lights, the *Nautilus* did not and would be completely black in color. The other ships, except for the *Chesty* which had brown and green colors were painted with blue and gray colors. The ships all had radar dispersion or absorbing material to present a smaller target, but the *Nautilus* was specifically designed not to be detected. She would be the Admiral's primary eyes and ears in space. She was equipped with lasers, missiles, and nuclear warheads but her main weapons were the intelligence gathering equipment onboard. She was not to engage in open warfare if possible but rather intercept signals and study other ships in space. She did have a small platoon of SEALs onboard.

Dr. Jack Vance was the last presenter. His brief started at 1130 and ran until 1230 when they broke for lunch. His department was made up of scientist on every ship excluding the two smaller ships and the submarine. These ships were equipment with small labs, except for the *Intrepid*, which had larger labs. His department was made up of astrophysicists, astronomers, geophysicist, and a few biologists. He had a small group of engineers to support the ship's engine crews if needed.

Kevin listened to each brief in turn with his opinions forming but when he noticed the morning was gone and lunch was at hand he called for a break. He told MajGen Connington that he would meet him in the room at 1330 and the rest of the officers at 1400 to continue.

Kevin met Ralph outside the room, and they went to the cafeteria. Ralph had told him the night before to wear his khakis, which he thought was strange when he was driven to the White House, but it proved easier to pin the stars on his collars with them. When Kevin left the White House, he had asked Ralph to make arrangements to have his dress blues re-striped. Ralph let him know that they were back in his room with the new rank as they went to lunch to catch up on old times.

Paul Connington was waiting for Kevin when he got back to the room.

"Good, I'm glad you are already here." Kevin started. "The briefings gave me the basics, but I am not satisfied. I got the sense that the science department is woefully undermanned, and I didn't hear anything to lead me to believe there are any diplomats onboard. I am going to want to review the manning and training status of the fleet soon."

"Sir, I understand but I really think that you should reconsider. Your predecessor had picked out the manning numbers and we are set."

"What?"

"Pardon, Sir?"

"You didn't just say what I think you did, did you?"

"Sir?"

"My predecessor? The one that was relieved for cause? You don't mean that one, do you?

"Uh, yes sir."

"So, you think that since he picked out a crew that it is final?"

"Sir, I meant..."

"Enough! You and the others better get it straight now. Isn't it obvious who now is in command?"

"Yes, Sir."

"Then I will decide if the manning levels are correct or not and I will decide what those levels will be. Understood?"

"Yes, Sir."

Kevin stared at Major General Connington who dropped his gaze a couple of seconds afterwards.

"I see," breathed Kevin, "I am going to have trouble with you, and I wonder how many of the Commanders?"

"No, Sir," replied the general, "there won't be any trouble. It was my mistake to assume that a new Commander wouldn't look over every aspect of this mission. I will have every Commander pull their manning and training documents at once. Further I will have the Logistics officer pull all equipment shortages, casualty reports and material status reports for your review."

"Good," answered Kevin. "In two weeks from now I will be briefing the Joint Chiefs on the readiness of the fleet and all changes that I estimate are required to make us operational and ready for launch. I want you to make a schedule for going over these reports in detail. I will want to see Dr. Vance's stuff first. Following him will be the CAG, the Marines, and then each of the ships. We will begin with the smaller once first, they will be the simplest. Now, are there any diplomats assigned to us?

"No, Sir."

"Then I want one diplomat, career oriented and not politically appointed. I want someone that is independent but who will know that I am in charge. Give this person a support staff of three. That may be too many, but one never knows. I will want to see the staff assignments also."

"Yes, Sir."

"When the Commanders come in you will organize the rest of the week with them. I want to get started tomorrow with Dr. Vance."

"Yes, Sir."

"Now, I am going with Vice Admiral Nabum for briefings on these aliens and this hyperspace drive system."

"Yes, Sir. I will have everything ready for you."

"Good, see you in the morning."

"Good day, Sir."

Kevin left the room and found Ralph waiting for him again. "How did it go?"

"As we expected. He threw up Mike as if he were still in the chair. But no worries, I took care of it. By the end of the two weeks, I suspect that I will be making several recommendations."

"I figured you would. I don't believe that any of them will be turned down. Do you think that you can launch within six months?

"I don't know. I haven't seen the reports to allow me to gauge that, but my instinct says that it will be closer to a year."

"Kevin, you may be pushed on that one. The CSO wants this to launch."

"Yeah, but it isn't his hide or crew going out there. Anyway, where are we going for this?"

"Oh, you will see. I think you are really going to enjoy this one." Ralph proceeded to laugh and Kevin slightly amused joined him as they walked towards an exit.

CHAPTER 2

At the end of the first day with the new Commander, Paul sat back in his chair in the office provided by the Pentagon. He picked up the drink he had made for himself when he heard a knock at his door. He sighed heavily. After all day the briefs and developing the schedule for the next two weeks, he was tired and didn't want anything but some time to himself.

"Enter."

The door opened and Colonel Robert Cole, the CAG, entered.

Paul indicated for him to pour a drink and have a seat. The Colonel smiled his appreciation and did.

Col Robert Cole was a career pilot. He was tall and lean with bushy blond hair and a child-like charm. He joined Space Force when he caught wind of something in space for his talents. Soon, he proved he could handle multiple fighters in both tight and loose configurations. After several rounds of competition, he won the position and was looking forward to lift off.

"Okay, what is it, Rob?"

Colonel Cole just looked at his drink for a few moments then stirred. "The Admiral is really looking at us like we haven't done anything at all. Going to be rough, especially since everyone has worked so hard for the past year and a half on this project. But, well," at which point he looked down at his glass again.

"Well?"

Robert looked up suddenly, "Well, why do we have him? Since you came over from the Air Force you have been part of the project. The number two man. You've been part of the whole design and team. Leading us to this point. Why aren't you in command? You ought to be, you know!"

Paul studied the CAG for a few moments while running his finger along the rim of his glass. Robert started to get a bit nervous, maybe he went too far.

Paul sighed, "Let me ask you something, Robert." The Colonel just looked at him.

"You and everyone else knew, even me, how Mike was carrying on with his aide, a mere Captain. What did we do about it? Mmm, you, the other Commanders? How did you protect him, even more importantly, the captain? What did you do to protect the group, the Space Force? Worse of all, what did I do about it?"

Robert started, "What could we..." Paul held up a hand stopping him.

"What could we do about it or should have done? A lot we could have and should have done, especially me." Paul took a drink. "I did go to the Chief of Space Operations for the job. General Rodriquez told me squarely I would not be considered for the job since I didn't take care of my Commander. He told me I was fortunate not to have lost this position or my stars along with several of you. Get that straight, we all lost on this one. We embarrassed the Space Force." Paul got up and poured some more whiskey for himself. As he went back to his chair, "You see, Robert, as senior officers we especially owe it to our units, commanders, Guardians, or other personnel, leadership. For my part, I got so caught up in this project that I let my Commander down and thus the entire group." He shrugged his shoulders. "Well, get used to the new boss. He can decide to relieve us if he believes we are not up to the task."

Paul took a drink while he let it set in with the CAG. When he saw that it did, he continued, "VADM Brannigan is an experienced officer who knows his way around a group, how to get out of tight spots. He is an expert in military and diplomatic matters. Hell, he is a better commander than Mike ever was. Watching him today I am damn glad he now leads us and I'm determined to do the best job for him, the group, the crew, and for Space Force. I am expecting you and the rest to do so also. Is that clear Rob?"

Colonel Cole swallowed heavily. He had not realized he could have lost his career over all the issues till just now. Now, his boss told him the expectations he needed to meet or get out of the unit. He looked at Paul and with conviction, "Yes sir, my team and I will do our best. We want this assignment and we shall pull it off."

Paul just nodded.

•   •   •

VADM Ralph Nabum was the Chief of Naval Operations man to Space Force. As the Navy liaison, Ralph had a lot of pull since he was the voice of the CNO. He knew the CNO wanted a strong Naval presence and not just an Air Force one. Old rivalries. But both the CNO and Ralph knew the value of the Air Force as the key component of Space Force. They also knew the value of quality ship commanders. Space is a mixture of ships' technologies and would require talented commanders to lead the new Guardian team. The Marines also wanted space. The future could be bright and shared among each service. Such was his pull, Ralph Nabum was able to secure offices, a briefing/conference room and a lounge for Kevin and his new team. Two weeks Ralph had argued to the Chief of Space Operations for Kevin to get up to speed. Ralph smiled to himself as he went to one of his meetings knowing he had succeeded for both the Marines and Navy on their presence, shoot, he even got a company from the Army to go along.

Kevin met up with his Chief of Staff first thing the next day. They reviewed the schedule for the next two weeks and Kevin made one adjustment. This would delay his meeting with Dr. Vance for about an hour. He then asked Paul to accompany him to see Ralph Nabum.

"I am surprised to see you so soon." Ralph said as they came into his office and took the seats that were offered. Ralph's secretary brought in coffee for all three men and discreetly departed.

"Did you like what you saw?" Ralph asked.

"Somewhat, today will begin our two-week review which will cover the entire crew billet structure and see who and what is in the billets along with the ships' design." Kevin started. "The briefs told me that the previous Commander had made this military centric to the point that there is no diplomatic mission. I want to change that. I plan on keeping a large part of the military piece but I suspect that I will be changing the mix of military, science, and most definitely diplomatic. I have two requests at this time." Kevin paused to take a drink of coffee while Ralph watched.

"The first is the difficult one." Kevin looked at Paul, "Are there any diplomats on any of the ships?"

"No Sir, your predecessor did not ask for any and I don't believe the Joint Chiefs even considered them."

Kevin looked back to Ralph, "That needs to be fixed. I am sure even before any changes are made, we could make room for a small cadre. I don't think we need many. Definitely I want a civil servant diplomat assigned to me. This person must understand that they work solely for me and not the State Department. As was briefed yesterday I am the responsible agent for this planet but I want an expert in diplomacy. This person will need a staff to assist but it must be small. Too many of them will cause them to lose focus."

Ralph frowned, "I don't think this request will go over well with the higher ups. You know that we have never truly gotten along with the State Department. Their lack of planning and incohesive manner of making decisions makes them very difficult to work with not to mention how self-serving they can be."

"I know but they come with skills that even I lack and you know my experience. Having a seasoned diplomat can aid in mission success for us. I will want a language expert on this person's staff along with experts in the science department."

Ralph started to interrupt and Kevin held up his hand to stop him, "I understand the objections but I insist on this."

Ralph sat in his chair considering for a few moments. He took a drink from his coffee cup and said, "Alright, I will see what we can do. The State Department knows nothing of this mission. The President has kept them out of it." Ralph sighed, leaning forward to put his cup down, "I think we can find a small, a very small, staff with a diplomat for you. What is the other request?"

"I need an Operations Officer for my staff." Kevin looked at Paul, "I believe there is no one assigned?"

Paul shook his head, "No Sir, your predecessor didn't see a need for one."

"Alright, well I want one."

Ralph smiled, "Who do you have in mind?"

"CAPT Ken Jorgenson."

Ralph really smiled then, "I will see to it. I am sure we can get him here pretty quick."

They got up, shook hands, and Kevin and Paul left.

Ralph sat back down and took a drink of coffee. He shook his head and frowned. He didn't like it that Kevin wanted a diplomatic staff, hell no one would. The Military and State Department have always had a rocky relationship. Oh, he knew Kevin was right; they were important and even needed but he didn't like it. He knew that the request would be approved but now he had to make sure that the State Department didn't have a clue what the mission would be and to pick the right person. This person had to have skills that would help Kevin, be a person that would help and not hinder the mission, and most of all not be too valuable to the State Department so they would be willing to give him or her up for over three years. What a sale this was going to be. After a few more moments of pondering this problem, he got an idea and picked up the phone.

•   •   •

Kevin maintained a stern disposition during his working groups. He wasn't leading a little experimental ship out of the system but a fleet of ships to establish diplomatic contact with an alien species and explore the galaxy. Sure, there had been tests done but no living person had actually left the system. The test demonstrated humans could survive the hyperspace drive system. The test ship went to the dark side of the moon and made a jump to Saturn, orbited the planet, and made a successful jump back to the moon. But he was to take a fleet of ships with thousands of personnel to another world, another system, and make contact. Yes, he would ensure each aspect of the ships and crew would be scrutinized. He had to make sure that he had the right capabilities to ensure mission success and bring his people back.

MajGen Connington had scheduled the two weeks as requested. Each of the Captains and Section Heads would be briefing the Admiral either one on one or two at a time pending the issues. Each person had to be prepared to discuss certain aspects of the crew, ships, and their individual missions. However, the Admiral had made it clear he desired to know everything about each section and ship in the group. From each Captain along with the flag bridge he desired to know how the ships would operate together and separately, how the MEU would be supported and how it would operate. Each of them was told to expect changes after the sessions.

The first briefer was Dr. Jack Vance, the Science and Political advisor. He was a tall man in his forties with a stomach, black hair and black eyes. He wore black rimmed glasses, which he would play with occasionally.

He sat down at the table and placed his books in front of him and opened them reviewing his notes. The Admiral and Paul just watched him and after a bit of time he looked up from his notes and said "I am Dr. Jack Vance, Sir. I am in charge of your Science and Political departments."

"Really? You are filling both the Science and Political?"

"Yes, Sir."

"Are you a diplomat?"

"No sir, I am only a scientist, but I do have the management skills to operate both departments."

"Okay, then the first item for change. You are only in charge of the Science Department. We will figure out the political or diplomatic department later." He looked at Paul. "I want the Political Department on the flagship and a station on the flag bridge for a diplomat." Paul nodded as he made the note.

"Okay, Doctor, let's go over the science department personnel and laboratories on each ship."

Dr. Vance opened to a specific page and proceeded with the briefing.

After a day of the science sections, the Admiral told both Dr. Vance and Paul there needed to be changes and he desired more science disciplines. Dr. Vance would put together a list of additional disciplines and recommended personnel and provide them to MajGen Connington. Meanwhile, Paul would have to consider their locations and how the ships would have to be modified to accompany them.

The following two days were dedicated to CAPT Ismal Shura, commander of the *Scimitar,* and Colonel Mark Adams, commander of the *Defiant*. The two ships were designed to be escorts. They did not carry any fighters; only transports ships that were capable of planetary landings. There main role was to integrate their fire systems into the protection of the fleet or act as scouting ships. They shared the same ships design as the flag ship but only smaller in scale. All the ships had shield generators, lasers, rail guns, various missile systems to include hypersonic missiles/torpedoes and had the capability to launch nuclear weapons against either space or planetary targets. Both ships had the same state of the art sensors and a communication system that could link with either the flagship or *Chesty* if required.

CAPT Shuma served in the U.S. Navy onboard cruisers where he received a nasty cut under his right eye leaving a scar. When this mission came up, he was picked to command the *Scimitar*. Col Adams had a knack of flashing his bright dark eyes at people and demonstrated a calm demeanor. He came from the U.S. Air Force and after a successful tour as a squadron commander was assigned to command the *Defiant*. Both officers demonstrated they knew their ships and crew inside out. Kevin quickly ascertained they knew their tactics and procedures and with only adding some engineering capabilities to them approved of their structures.

Next were the *Icarus* commander, Col Mike Krist and *Excalibur* commander, CAPT Robert Murphy. These ships made up the rest of the main fleet. They each housed ten fighters for the wing and supported limited transport and reconnaissance ships. They were designed to be able to provide temporary housing for the landing ships as well. Their two main purposes are to integrate their fire systems into the overall fleet protection and offensive systems and to provide Naval fire support to the Marines once they had landed. Their fire control systems were designed to deliver planetary bombardment and laser fire against multiple targets on a planet in addition to multiple targets in space. They had very limited science capability.

Col Krist joined the Guardians from the start of his career. He understood the workings of the Space Force. He had to take a tour onboard a carrier before accepting command of *Icarus*. He had an easy laugh to him but seemed to become frustrated at times with the Admiral and his questioning of the ship and crew. CAPT Murphy on the other hand, having grown up in the Navy, just went along as if he were answering any readiness question from a fleet admiral as he had plenty of times in his career. He actually ribbed Mike Krist during the briefing and discussions to distract him. During a break Mike approached him and almost violently demanded to know why.

"Come on, Mike. The Admiral just wants to know if we know our ships and crew. Don't get angry about it. I'm trying to help you by getting you into a better mood."

"Why is he going through this? We have worked all this out before."

Robert quickly looked about and seeing they were alone.

"Look, Mike. You know this and have it. You get frustrated or mad with the Admiral you could lose this command. He must know you can handle the pressure of deep space, contact, and even combat. You lose it here with him exploring your knowledge, the ship, and our missions then you've lost this chance. Calm down, think and don't take this personally. It has absolutely nothing to do with you."

Mike thought for a bit. "Well, you are a Navy man and of course he is going easy on you."

"Stop it! I know how admirals think since I have been around them. I can't tell you how many times I've been chewed out during a briefing, especially the morning turnovers. Damn, these guys know what they are doing. Besides, Admiral Brannigan has been there and done that, combat, diplomacy. He has commanded a Carrier Strike Group for heaven's sake. Now, just calm down and realize, he is doing his job. Answer his questions and find that famous humor of yours. I've done my intel on the Admiral. He likes calmness under pressure and even a good joke. Find the humor while giving him the information. You'll be fine."

"Ok, so it's not a Navy thing about the Guardians?"

"Nope, not at all. He is evaluating us on our ability to command. That is all."

When they started again, CAPT Murphy ensured he went before Col Krist. Afterwards it all seemed to smooth out.

At the end of the briefings, Kevin looked at the two COs and Paul. "Gentlemen, I see you know these items and your procedures. Expect changes though, especially for adding scientific experts and especially engineers."

"Paul, how much have these procedures been worked through with CAPT Smith and the other Commanders?"

"Individually sir, why?"

"Any actual ship exercises?"

"Very limited sir, mainly some simulations."

The Admiral rubbed his chin. "I see. Okay, when our Ops Officer arrives, we need to ensure these activities are tightened up. We will need to schedule some fleet exercises."

Paul took some notes, "Yes, Sir." He cleared his throat, "Not sure about the exercises. We may get a lot of push back on those. But I'll put together some proposals with the ship Commanders and present them to you."

"Thank you. Tomorrow, let's get started with the *Intrepid*."

The next day, CAPT Karen Smith, Commanding Officer of the *Intrepid* entered the briefing room. She noticed a picture of her ship was on the main monitor with information on others. The Admiral and Chief of Staff were already there.

"Hello, Karen," The Admiral said as he stood up and shook her hand and indicated a chair.

"Sir."

"It is good to see you again. I wondered what happened to you after your last carrier assignment. Glad to see you have been picked for this job and especially for the flag ship."

"Thank you, Sir."

The briefings started out pretty normal. The ship's shape was in the form of a giant horseshoe. The main body was circular in shape with two horns sweeping forward into points or what would appear to be points. On top of the main body was a thick disk that would house the flag bridge, flag offices, and quarters. Just aft of the disk was a short tower that is the bridge for the ship. Each arm of the horseshoe housed the Wing. Twenty fighters could launch simultaneously from them, ten from each horn. The underside of each horn also supported hangers for maintenance and storage of the fighters, reconnaissance ships, and transports. Further, the ordnance would be stored in these horns. The weapons array started at the point of the horns and spread along them at various points and the main body to provide an interlocking fire system. The *Intrepid* housed twenty strategic nuclear devices and accompanied by smaller tactical nuclear weapons. The fighters would carry missiles similar to the fighters that he was already familiar with but instead of the normal bullets for close in dog fighting these ships would carry explosive tip rounds. The *Intrepid* and the other ships followed this general characteristic and could provide fire in a three hundred sixty-degree bubble. The main weakness to the ships' defenses is located between the horns themselves. For defense, the ships inner horn systems were designed with a much smaller system with less penetrating power to avoid damaging the ship itself. In addition to the weapons systems the ships also had several shield generators and the ships had an additional electronic shielding system. Whether these shields could withstand an opposing force weapon were yet to be seen.

At the end of the two days of briefings and discussions, Kevin looked at both Paul and Karen.

"Karen, prepare for some major changes to your ship. I'm adding science and engineering stations and laboratories to your ship. Further, the flag bridge needs to be redesigned to include one or two diplomatic stations."

As she and Paul took notes. "Yes Admiral, any idea how big those changes will be?"

"No. Dr. Vance is working up recommendations for me now. When completed, Paul and I will review them and upon approval you three with the dry dock will have to get to work immediately. I know. A lot of time will have to be spent. Overtime will be authorized but the ship is a great piece of military hardware but lacks what we need for mission success. So, start warning your crew."

"Yes, Sir."

"Okay, that is enough for now. I'm glad you are here, Karen. Your expertise and experience will be of great benefit to us."

With that, they departed the room.

The next day, Kevin and Paul met early in the briefing room.

"Well Paul, overall, I'm happy with the Commanders. Ships, well they need a lot of adjustments and unfortunately, we may have to swap some Guardians out for the additional science and engineering disciplines but I want to keep them ready and try and take as many as possible."

"Yes, Sir. I see how it will be difficult, but if we make adjustments in the size of the quarters for the crew, we should be able to squeeze as many in as we can."

Kevin nodded.

"I was getting a bit concerned about Col Krist but he calmed down finally."

"I think it may have been just some concerns with a new Commander. Col Krist is a Guardian, just like the previous Commander. But am glad he is staying with us."

Kevin nodded in agreement.

"Now will come some painful briefings."

Paul looked at him a bit confused.

"It's rare to see a MEU Commander get totally along with a ship's Commander. Has there been any flare ups or signs of distrust or feelings of being slighted or of competition between these two?"

Paul thought for a moment. "Not that I have seen, Sir, but then I haven't really watched the *Chesty* Commander's interaction with the Marines. In fact, not sure if there has been much."

Kevin nodded, "Let's be alert for any during this next session."

Paul nodded.

Colonel John Roberts, commander of the Marine Expeditionary Unit, entered the room followed by Col Johnathan Williams, commander of the *Chesty*. Roberts was a tall black man with square shoulders and possessed a presence. He made Williams look small even though he stood six feet tall but lacked the bravado of Roberts. He almost seemed despondent. Kevin made a mental note of this, seeing how they would be occupying the same ship and commanders of their own units. He understood how Col Williams must feel having floated with the Marines himself.

Col Williams knew his ship and how to support the Marines. He grew up in the Guardians himself but did a tour on an amphibious readiness group in support of a MEU in preparation for this mission. He saw how the Marines seem to get all the credit compared to the ships' commanders. Personally, he would rather have the flagship but tried to keep his feelings hidden so he could go on the mission. His future depended on it.

Col Roberts though was all bravado. Or it seemed to Williams, yet he proved to both Kevin and Paul, he knew his tactics and procedures and how his Marines would operate both onboard the *Chesty*, ship take downs or planetary assaults. Williams demonstrated he knew how to support them from his ship.

Both the *Intrepid* and *Chesty* housed the fleet's communication systems that would provide both the Admiral and the Marine Expeditionary Commander with command and control over both the fleet and landing force. Main differences besides the type of transports that the *Chesty* carried were the berthing for all the Marines that would make up the Marine Expeditionary Unit to include the new tanks and artillery batteries. The *Chesty* had the added responsibility of being the second command ship of the fleet. If something happened to the *Intrepid*, then the *Chesty* would become the flagship. Col Williams both liked and hated this thought. He was in command of a command ship but if the Admiral came over then he would have two different Commanders to support.

The *Nautilus* was truly the different ship along with her captain. CAPT Allen Strickland was a submariner specifically chosen by the Navy to command the *Nautilus*. He was brash with bright eyes and sported a scarred left hand from burns he suffered early in his career from a main space fire on his first submarine.

Like its predecessor, stealth was its main purpose. The *Nautilus* was shaped a lot like a submarine. Where the other ships had a metallic blue from the above the midline and gray below, the *Nautilus* was all black with various sensor absorbing material. Even the other ships' sensors (and a highly classified sensor system onboard the *Intrepid*) had difficulty even detecting her even if the crews were looking for her. She carried ten nuclear missiles, hypersonic missile systems and lasers along with two shield generators. Her sensors even beat the most advanced in the fleet. Her role was to disappear and range around the fleet to pick up the communications, disposition and activities of any other ship, station, or planetary system. She had the ability to launch two stealth landing ships capable of planetary landings in support of the SEAL platoon onboard. She was properly designed and had room already to add a few scientists that would aid in her mission.

After the briefs, Kevin had a clear picture that he had a fleet of seven ships, one of them being an independent surveillance craft, fifty fighters, ten of which could be used either in a space battle or for close air support for the Marines. He had several reconnaissance ships the majority of which were Unmanned Vehicles. He also had both ship to ship and planetary transport ships most of which were designed to carry assaults against targets that would include ships, any asteroid, and even planetary targets. He would command the most advanced fleet in every aspect of a ship from the engine room which housed sub light engines and the hyperspace drives. He even had the ability to drop nuclear missiles from space on planets if the situation would call for it. An incredible fleet with an awesome responsibility he now commanded. This fleet was truly designed to bring war to a space target and yet his mission was first contact. Diplomacy, as the primary means of contact to be supported by scientific and engineering disciplines and if necessary, a military might.

· · ·

After the two weeks of briefings, Kevin was ready to brief the Joint Chiefs of Staff. He spent the last day with MajGen Connington and Dr. Vance concerning the science department. He was unhappy with how few scientists and disciplines there were. Dr. Vance had a list of specialties and personnel that he would like to have along. Kevin told him to prioritize his list and was very happy to find that he already had. He rose and turned over the items to his Chief of Staff and left for the day. His new Operations Officer had not yet arrived but Ralph had told him that orders were being cut to transfer CAPT Jorgenson to him. Kevin knew that he would need his rest. He would have to either request for more time or has he hoped could present a timetable and changes to the Joint Chiefs of Staff for the launch but these changes were important and could mean the difference between success and failure. While scientists could be a pain in the ass, they also could save the day by discovering some fact that the crew would either overlook or not even have an idea to figure out the problem. But Kevin knew never to underestimate a well trained and disciplined crew; they could perform miracles when called upon.

Kevin arrived at his room and ordered dinner. He went over to the window and looked outside and thought of his home in Oklahoma and immediately called MaryAnne. He needed to talk to her. Once again, he was about to embark on a mission that was going to take him away from her over a long period of time and further than he had ever been. He would hate that but she was one of those wives who never complained about her husband's duty to his country. Oh yes there was the regret of being apart for so long and missing each other's life. Sometimes they wondered why they were even married since they were apart so much. But she supported him being away and he ensured that she could do the things she desired. Still, it hurt at these times of being alone and realizing how much of her he had missed. He hated it but what does one do when one's feet are set on a path? You bear the pain and hope for a long time with your loved one to complete your life with. He shrugged and brushed away a tear and dialed her number.

The day following the briefing to the Joints Chiefs of Staff found Kevin and Ralph sitting in Ralph's office.

"They really didn't like hearing another year was required for your recommended changes" Ralph was saying to Kevin as he handed him a cup of coffee, "Especially General Rodriquez, your boss, the CSO. But they found that your recommendations made sense."

Kevin sighed, "Thanks, I was hoping they would see the value in them."

"They did when they realized that the designs were solely military with very little scientific and no diplomatic capabilities. While they don't like the extra months, they think the capability set is more balanced between the three disciplines." Ralph took a drink of his coffee and added "The CNO was the biggest advocate for having a person from the State Department. That was rather surprising since he is the one who complains the most about them. But he really thinks that having a small cadre will aid in the mission, of course he likes having one of his admirals in charge. Besides, he feels he upped one on General Malcolm. After all he likes showing up the Commandant." Ralph chuckled and Kevin just sipped his coffee waiting.

"Oh yes, everyone agreed to freeze the personnel in their billets. No one will be transferred from this mission, which I suspect that most if not all will like that. They have trained very hard for this and would hate to transfer out. Dr. Vance's scientists were all approved and he is already moving to get them here." Ralph took another drink and reached for the pot.

"What about the diplomat?"

Ralph looked up and smiled. "Three members are already on their way to the training area. The State Department didn't like just giving up people without knowing what for. These three I understand are very good at preparing all sorts of documents and will work well with the linguists that Dr. Vance is procuring for you. The other two, well" Ralph paused and chuckled looking at Kevin with a mischievous look.

"Alright, spill it" Kevin said.

Ralph smiled, "The diplomat they have chosen is a civil servant, which is good in that he is a career person vice being a political appointee. No political agenda here. He is not well regarded though in the department. He is coming from a central African country, kinda exiled there if you would. He is very independent minded but very intelligent. I think you will have your hands full with him but since he always got the dirty jobs so to speak you will have a more adaptable diplomat."

"And the fifth person?"

"Now that is kinda weird, too. The diplomat would be enough of an issue but they're providing another person with a bit of a record. He is some sort of liaison officer who has a rather varied background. His security checks out but something seemed odd about him. Sure to provide you with an interesting diplomatic corp." Ralph just smiled and lifted his cup as in a toast.

Kevin just shook his head and smiled. "Well at least I get a diplomatic corps, a beefed-up scientific department, more engineers and support on the military, redesign on the ships for better efficiency, and my entire group of people won't be transferred. Looks good to me. Oh yes, what about the Ops Officer?"

Ralph frowned at this mention. "Oh yeah. Ummm, you won't like this. We were having him transferred when he was involved in an auto accident. He is in very serious condition. They have not transferred him from Germany yet and I don't know when they will."

Kevin was shocked at this news. He started to get up and Ralph held up his hand to stop him. "There is nothing you can do, Kevin, except maybe send some well-meaning card and flowers to his family but he won't be ready even in a year to go with you. I looked at his record and FITREPS to get a feel for what you liked about him. I have picked a substitute if you will have the officer." Ralph was studying Kevin. Kevin still looked a bit in shock at this news.

"Of course, I will send him flowers and wish his family the best." Kevin just sat there and thought for a bit. Ralph knew to just wait as he had seen a lot of officers have to take a few minutes at the news of some accident to take an excellent person out of commission.

"Who do you have in mind?"

"An excellent officer in my opinion. The person has served with the Marines as a fire liaison officer, been an XO on a destroyer, commanded a cruiser, served on three major staffs in the Operations Office.

Her name is CAPT Josephine Lindsey. I think you will find her more than satisfactory in this manner."

Kevin just shook his head, "I don't know her but if you think she will do the job, fine I will take her. Just have her report to the training site." Ralph nodded, "When are you headed back for your two weeks?"

"Oh tonight, I will fly right into Tulsa and MaryAnne will pick me up. After that I will proceed to the training area to inspect the Marines and soldiers. About two weeks after that I will go up and see the ships. I am planning on splitting my time between the two areas. The Marines are already making their plans with the changes in the ship's configurations. I want to see what they have in mind."

"Well, you better get out of here then and see MaryAnne, give her my best."

"Thanks."

They stood up, shook hands, and Kevin left for the airport. Ralph turned and looked out the window. He would like to go out into space but he had a sense from the intelligence and scientists that worked on the deep space communications that this job would not be easy. No, Kevin was really the right man to go out. He would find out rather quickly if the people who sent the message were hostile or friendly. If friendly then he could come to some equitable arrangement and if not, well Kevin could get the fleet back and if necessary, inflict as much damage on them as possible. But would the technology be there to enable him? Ralph took a deep breath and let it out, only time would tell.

•   •   •

Josephine was resting by the mountain river. Her hike up the river and back was doable but a bit exhausting. She lay on her air mattress while she watched her kids frolic in the river. She looked around to see her husband bringing back his catch of fish. She thought how good that would be once they were grilled up.

She shook her head then and took a sip of her wine. It felt good to be away from everything. While her last duty at Indonesia Pacific was challenging and rewarding it proved a bit much. A lot of issues in the pacific which kept her away from her family. Well, that is the life of a Navy person. She just smiled to herself. Best to enjoy her time on her transfer leave. She even turned off all of her communication devices in order to enjoy this time with her family.

She looked up towards her husband and noticed he was looking upward with a frown. She turned her attention in the direction he was looking just in time to see one of the new silent helicopters coming in for a landing. She recognized the Navy bird almost instantly. *Damn,* she thought, *there goes my leave.*

As the aircraft landed a crewman stepped out. As he approached, he saluted her then handed her a packet. She accepted and saw they were transfer orders but not to her command billet. Rather to a project called Explorer. The crewman asked where her items were and if he could help her with them. They were to leave immediately. She started to get angry but he quickly told her a team was already approaching for her family. That was all he knew. She nodded and went over to her husband and motioned for her children to join them.

She quietly wiped a tear from her eyes as she watched her family out of the aircraft's window as it took off.

•   •   •

Kevin's car drove up to the parade ground located on the Top Secret Space Force base. The Marines were already in formation waiting for his cursory inspection. Col John Roberts and party were standing by. As the car came to a stop the Marines saluted and a sharp looking Marine stepped up opening the door. When Kevin came out of the car and stood up, he returned the salute and approached the Colonel to shake his hand.

"Welcome Admiral, I believe you will find all in order." The Colonel said.

"Thank you, I am sure all is in readiness."

They proceeded to the area in the center front of the formation to begin the formality of an inspection of the troops. The entire morning was spent going through the Battalion, MEU Logistics Group, and the Air Squadron. It was impressive to the Admiral to see how the Marines were combat ready. His talk to them was brief expressing his gratitude for their readiness and desire to go into deep space to both explore and defend the planet that is their home from potential hostilities. He assured them that each and every one of them would go with him. The cheering was enormously loud from the Marines.

"Your men and women looked quite impressive, Colonel." Admiral Brannigan said.

"Thank you, Sir. They are ready and every one of them were volunteers and hand picked. I am glad to hear they all get to go."

After the Colonel left the office, Kevin sat down behind the desk in his office located at the Top Secret base in Texas. This would be his office for the next year while the fleet was prepped for the long space flight. He sat back in the chair contemplating the next year wishing that he could already launch but if he did then they would be woefully unprepared for either the political or military situations that could arise. He sighed heavily hoping that this would be a peaceful mission, he would really hate to lose any of his men or women.

In a few days he would be taking a shuttle to the ships to perform an inspection on each one. Already his Chief of Staff, Major General Connington was with the fleet preparing them for his arrival. His new Operations Officer, CAPT Josephine Lindsey, should be arriving in the next few days. He was expecting her to join him for the ride up.

CAPT Josephine Lindsey was at first shocked, then excited as she sat in the briefing room for her introduction into the situation. An alien race, called the Kammorrigans, had contacted them. Their transmission had drafts of a hyperspace drive. She was pouring over the technical details of the drive, the communiqué, and other technologies. Dr. Salvadore, a key member of the team that developed the hyperspace drive system on the ships, was watching CAPT Lindsey closely.

As she turned the notes back to the hyperspace drive schematics provided, she suddenly frowned. She turned notes and the translation pages over and over again then looked back at the schematics. Dr. Salvadore smiled to himself. He was pleased at her discomfort.

"The schematic and translation seem to be missing something," she said.

"What do you mean?" asked Dr. Salvadore.

"I'm not an engineer but even I can read a schematic and this one for the drive seems to be missing a key component to make it work."

Dr. Salvadore decided it was enough. "You are correct. The transmission left out several key elements to make the drive actually work. If we had time, you could review the other technologies, including medical, and you would find key elements are missing. As such, you can't produce any of this technology with this communiqué. We believe these items are a teaser so a civilization would send the Kammorrigans a transmission. We have not done this. Thankfully, we were already working on the theories to build a drive. This information from the Kammorrigans only speeded up our work and filled in our gaps. As such, we have built our own hyperspace drives and tested them successfully."

"Okay, I can see them leaving out key elements of a drive to protect their own planet and desire a dialogue. But, why leave out the medical technologies?

"It was exactly for this reason several of us and our political leadership decided not to send a message back, though they gave us coordinates to do so. Rather, it was decided to send our own delegation to visit them, so to speak." He smiled at her reaction.

"So, we don't trust they are good actors," she responded. He simply nodded.

CAPT Josephine Lindsey sat beside him on the shuttle up to inspect the fleet. Kevin noticed she was a strong and handsome woman. She kept her blond hair in a tight bun and her uniform was immaculate. They were heading for the flagship of the fleet, the *Intrepid*; CAPT Karen Smith the ship's Commanding Officer would be standing by the hatch. They would be arriving in a few minutes but CAPT Lindsey gave orders that they would first do a flyby of each ship of the fleet before docking with the *Intrepid*. Kevin appreciated her thinking this way and was peering out the port hole checking out each ship as they passed by them. They were beautiful to him. Every one of them save one had a circular body with two horns extending out in front of them. These horns held the launch bays and main weapon systems along with the new force fields. The top half starting from the midline was painted a ship's gray and the bottom half with sky blue, except for the *Chesty* whose top half was green and bottom half was brown in color. All the ships were in a superstructure showing them to be dry docked waiting for the day they could be launched.

They docked with the *Intrepid* and the seal proved to be a hard seal. The airlocks opened to the sound of the Boatswain's pipe, and Kevin saw the mandatory eight side boys. The Admiral's ruffles and flourishes played as he stepped across the threshold saluting while he passed through the side boys at which time the music stopped and he dropped the salute. He approached CAPT Smith and requested permission to come aboard. After granting him permission, CAPT Smith took Vice Admiral Brannigan and CAPT Lindsey to the engine room to begin the tour and inspection. Kevin was finding the ship to be impressive as they toured the engine room, cargo holds, berthing spaces, armory, ship's bridge and finally entering the flag section. CAPT Smith asked if he desired to go to his quarters or the flag bridge. Naturally the flag bridge was foremost on his mind. The bridge itself is circular with an extremely elevated command chair in the middle that Kevin had already desired to be lowered for additional equipment. Once the seat would be lowered the astrogation, helm stations, and operations station would form a semi-circle in front of him. The outer ring held several communication sections, weapons, flight command and control, electronic warfare, and various science stations, engineering, damage control, fleet disposition, and diplomatic stations or will once his changes to the bridge are made.

The conference room adjoined the Admiral's personal office and cabin. He sat at the head of the table as MajGen Connington was going over the status of each ship. Already shuttles were arriving with the additional computers and other hardware to add engineering and science labs to the various ships. Only the *Nautilus* would receive limited adjustments. The *Intrepid* and *Chesty* would receive the most upgrades but the vast majority would be done to the flag ship. The additional scientists and engineers would require training in order to be ready for the mission. But the hardest choices concerning who would be designated as extra crew members would be made by each Commanding Officer. They would be taken off the ships' rosters and made into a relief pool of people should the primary personnel became injured. Kevin wished he could take all of them, he would like to have the redundancies but he needed the new people.

After everyone left, leaving Kevin alone with MajGen Connington and CAPT Lindsey, he looked at them.

"Well, what do you think?"

CAPT Lindsey said, "They are efficient and this is just wonderful. I never thought this would happen to me but it is amazing. I only wish we could take her for a spin around the solar system." She beamed at them.

Kevin looked at Paul who looked back and just smiled.

"CAPT, I don't think these were built for joy riding but you will get the real chance to see how they fly."

After chuckling, "Okay, so what do you think about the fleet?"

They looked around at each other and Paul said, "This is a good fleet, Sir. They will not let you or Earth down. They are eager to launch so they will probably be working extra hard to get the modifications done."

"I agree with the COS in regards to this fleet. But I am not sure they will have the modifications done earlier than planned. I would like to meet my staff section in order to ensure that the fleet operating procedures are in place along with integrating the Marine planning process into the fleet's."

"Sounds right CAPT. Paul does the *Intrepid* have the various systems in place or does this have to be done back in Texas?"

"Unfortunately, not all the systems or programs are totally loaded onboard so we will have to do it on Earth."

CAPT Lindsey said, "I would like to get them working up here at the earliest possible moment."

Kevin looked at her, "Make sure you have Karen, Johnathan, Col Roberts, and Cole get together. I think the CAG has overly planned his support for the MEU rather than taking care of the fleet. Let's ensure it gets balanced out soonest." Kevin looked at Paul, "The main duty of the CAG is the fleet's protection along with being a strike capability. I want to ensure they can do this plus support the Marines. See to it Jo, alright?"

"Yes, Sir," she replied, "I would like to visit the *Chesty* to see their setup."

Kevin looked at them, "How soon can we visit the *Chesty*?"

Paul shrugged, "Tomorrow, Sir."

Col Johnathan Williams was nervous. He didn't quite know why but VADM Brannigan made him nervous with his cold stare. But he thought the real reason for his nervousness was finding out that Jo was now part of his staff. It had been quite some time since he dated CAPT Josephine Lindsey and now she would be the Fleet Operations Officer. That meant she would have a lot of power in the fleet. It also meant that she and Col Roberts would be working closely together and maybe on his ship no less. The crewman announced hard seal, the pipe sounded as the airlock came open. The Admiral and party stepped aboard rendering respect back to the honors provided.

"Welcome aboard, Admiral, to the *Chesty*."

"Thank you, Col."

"Should we start with the engine room sir and then proceed to the Flag Plot?"

"That sounds good"

The *Chesty* proved to be in the same shape as the *Intrepid* except it appeared not as shiny. This was definitely a troop ship designed to carry the Marines and prepare them for launch onto a hostile world or an enemy ship. The designers were deliberate in the way they designed her. They wanted it to be Spartan in nature to avoid the Marines from getting too comfortable in it but to know it as a safe harbor after a battle. There were already Marines onboard to ensure that she would be combat loaded for any general contingency. The *Chesty* holds the Close Air Support fighters for the Marines, all ten of them and the vast majority of Marine transports. While CAPT Lindsey looked over all the command and control and planning spaces, Kevin was checking out the launch areas for the assault vessels, transports and space tanks. He was in total awe of these devices.

· · ·

"Major Clark, the Commandant has some very specific orders for you."

"Sir." Major Jack Clark, the Officer in Charge of the Fleet Anti-terrorism and Security Team or FAST stood at attention in front of the Marine Expeditionary Unit Commander, Col Roberts. Col Roberts sat behind his desk and looked again at his computer screen. The Commandant's email to him was very clear.

"The Commandant is a close friend of Vice Admiral Brannigan. He was his Commanding Officer during the operations in the Sudan. While he desires the success of this mission, he wants to ensure that the Admiral is safe no matter what. Understand?"

"Yes, Sir."

"No matter what! He doesn't want the Admiral to be without one of your Marines or a group of Marines depending on the situation when he is off the ship. Clear?"

"Yes, Sir."

"That means if he is off the ship at all during this mission, be it on another ship, a planet, the planet we are attempting to get to, a friendly ship, or a ship in question. Understand?"

"Yes, Sir."

"I don't care if he gives you an order for you not to have a Marine at all with him. That is straight from the Commandant and the Admiral does not have the authority to give you this order."

"Uh, sir? Do you mean that if Vice Admiral Brannigan gives me a direct order not to accompany him I am to disobey him?"

"That is correct, Major."

"Sir, I do not believe that is lawful, especially since he will be the law out in space."

Col Roberts smiled. He sat back and was waiting for this response and was happy to hear his Marine Officer to consider the difficulties that he was being put into.

"You would normally be correct, Major, but not this time. The Commandant has the backing of the President and the Joint Chiefs of Staff. With those persons backing this makes it a lawful order; besides the Commandant is sending his own email to the Admiral. He is your primary mission. He will fully understand this as you do now!"

Kevin sat back from the computer slightly pissed off at his old friend. This limits his mobility having to always have one of the FAST with him. This team was designed to rescue hostages not be a personal security detachment. He reached over to his intercom and hit the button for the Colonel.

"Yes, Admiral."

"Get your ass into my office now."

"Yes, sir."

The Colonel stood at attention before Vice Admiral Brannigan.

"What is this shit?"

"Sir."

"What do you have to do with this email from the Commandant?"

"Nothing, Sir. I received it and obey."

"You what?"

"I obey the order from the Commandant, Sir. He and the Joint Chiefs of Staff have ordered the FAST to be a Personal Security Detachment."

"That is not their design, Colonel. I want to know why you have communications with the Commandant about this mission and not just for administrative reasons."

"Sir, the Commandant contacted me. I have no contact with him about operations."

Kevin stared coldly at the Colonel judging if this was the case.

"Make sure you don't. You screw with me and I will ensure you are busted, understand?"

"Yes, Sir."

"I am forced with having these guys as bodyguards now but I want them to be a FAST first and foremost. I need them in that role. Clear?"

"Yes, Sir."

"Now send me that Major."

"Yes, Sir."

•   •   •

The Diplomat, Michael O'Shea, stood in the shadow of the building in the heat of the day watching some children playing in the street. He was wondering what his life would be like if he wasn't always so outspoken with his superiors. He was still standing there when a messenger from the consulate approached him. He sighed and took the message offered to him and saw that he was to return to D.C. at the earliest possible moment. *Great, what now?* he thought as he thanked the messenger and tucked the paper away in a pocket. He just stood there watching the children wondering how their lives would turn out.

Mr. O'Shea approached the door in the Pentagon with his escort. He didn't like the military and now he found he was being assigned to them. His meeting at the State Department was like a chewing out when they hinted that he was worthless to the organization but they were giving him one last chance by assigning him to the military. *Great just what I need,* he thought, *why don't they just shoot me in the head?*

They approached the door with a sign that read VADM Ralph Nabum. The escort knocked on the door and then opened it ushering him in. The office was roomy with a desk at one end with a window behind it; two chairs were in front of the desk. To one side of the room were bookshelves and a door in the middle and on the other wall a small table with a coffee set. Behind the desk with his head in his hands reading something sat who O'Shea assumed was VADM Nabum. O'Shea approached the desk and cleared his throat but the man continued to read whatever was on the desk ignoring him. He stood there wondering what would be the most appropriate thing for him to do, *do I sit down or should I say something*? At long last the man looked up from what he was reading and regarded him with a cold stare. O'Shea knew he was being evaluated but not like the Admiral would be evaluating another Navy Officer. Finally, the VADM motioned for him to take a seat.

"Mr. O'Shea, I am Vice Admiral Ralph Nabum, would you like a cup of coffee?" The Admiral asked.

O'Shea thought about it and said "Yes, if you don't mind."

The Admiral got up and went over to the coffee set, "How would you like it?"

"Black, if you don't mind."

The Admiral filled a cup for O'Shea and one for himself. After handing the cup to him he sat back down behind his desk. He took a drink of his coffee while eyeing O'Shea over the rim of the cup. Finally, he set the cup down, sat back and said, "You don't know why you are here, do you?"

"The State Department didn't tell me. All they said was I was chosen for a job with the military."

Ralph nodded knowing why the State Department sent O'Shea. They didn't like him, they thought of him as a rebel, not a team player, and the sooner they were rid of him the better. He scratched his head thinking if Kevin would appreciate this man or just blow him out of an airlock.

"Personally, I think the State Department would love to get rid of you, either have you quit the department or just go away in some manner."

O'Shea saw where this was going. "Whatever. I am dedicated to this country and I will speak out when I see things are wrong. Yes, I differ with the Department on plenty of issues and I really dislike the military."

The Admiral smiled at him, "Yes, I know. I know they want you gone and they figure with your dislike of the military you would just quit and then you would be gone. Besides not liking you, they don't like us either and so, they win if you stay on the job with us since they both fill their requirement and get rid of you."

O'Shea just looked at him. He really didn't like this man behind his desk all smug. Just like the arrogant military to presume they know everything. Unfortunately, he was right about the State Department and himself. He sighed, "Okay, what is the job? What trouble does the military find itself in that they need a diplomat, even one as sorry as me?"

Ralph frowned at that. "A bit of a defeatist attitude, isn't it? I was hoping for more fight."

"That depends what the fight is about."

Ralph nodded his head and considered this man. Of course, he would sound a little bitter after all didn't Kevin sound that way at times when he thought about his life in the military and how much of his family he missed. He was away when his daughter died and his son won't even speak to him now. All because he served his country. Now he finds a man who has it rough in his own department because he wouldn't be a yes man. He nodded again.

"Okay, before we continue you must accept the job. I cannot tell you anything without you being committed to it and yes, I know you don't have a clue what the job is. This is very compartmentalized and I must have your buy in before I can tell you anymore."

O'Shea got that oh great I am totally screwed look on his face as he considered this. *What some black ops mission that I have to pull our collective asses out of the fire job.* But what real choice did he have? If he left this office his career was over and what else would he do?

"Alright, I am in," he sighed.

Vice Admiral Ralph Nabum smiled gently at him and nodded, then he moved closer to his desk and began briefing Michael O'Shea on the most secret and dangerous mission that O'Shea had ever heard of.

CHAPTER 3

After months of training, Marines making attack landings on the moon, the Wing making support runs for the Marines, attacking bogies around the asteroid belt. The ships themselves traveled across the solar system in exercises battling each other. They even had a few exercises in which the fleet attempted to locate and destroy the *Nautilus*. But this proved to be fruitless and the *Nautilus* took out three of the ships in simulated battle before she was killed.

All the crew had their leave periods and are as trained as possible. The ships were as prepared as they could be. All the storage holds were filled, ordnance onboard to include nuclear weapons. They even had additional storage facilities for samples that they may collect on their way.

The *Intrepid's* flag bridge was finally restructured. The Vice Admiral's chair was lowered by three feet but still stood one foot above the rest of the bridge. Vice Admiral Brannigan sat in his command chair waiting for all reports to come in. His chair felt quite comfortable enabling him to withstand shocks that may result from battle or atmospheric disturbances. It gave him maximum visibility of the bridge and all of its screens. The semi-circle stations in front of the chair now housed three stations; on the left, operations (where CAPT Lindsey and her ops staff would sit), the center console was helm and the right astrogation. MajGen Connington's station was to Kevin's right and slightly forward and Mr. O'Shea's was to Kevin's left almost in a direct line. Along the bulkhead were stations to aid the Admiral with the fleet's disposition and whatever tactical situation may exist. These included the main viewer located front center of the bridge, then to the right of Kevin, fleet disposition, engineering A (which monitored power plants, shields environmental, etc.), weapons, a doorway to the Admiral's section, Engineering B (which monitored the hyperspace and sub light drives). Next to it were the science stations to include astrophysics to support astrogation. Next to them was the planetary sensor station. The second access to the flag bridge with the diplomatic station next to it with the general sensor station and finally communications.

All around the rest of the bridge were screens for other fleet operations to include electronic warfare, missile defense, sensor readings, and planetary information. He could easily see the diplomat and he of course could see both the main screen and the Admiral. Kevin sat back in his chair and thought about what the next two years may bring. What a hope this mission could be, to travel to an intelligent life and hopefully a peaceful relationship with them. He glanced over at O'Shea, together he and the diplomat are the hope for the planet to find a new ally. If they are not able to secure a positive relationship then what could be the outcome? Total war with the civilization they are off to visit or planetary annihilation by them, not a situation that he really desired to contemplate. No, they had to be successful.

He looked over at the chronometer; the time was approaching for them to depart. His officers were busy ensuring the final checks were on schedule. He put on his head piece that was his private link to Space Control. He listened to the chatter from Space Control to the fleet. All the chatter was normal prior to a launch. He punched in a code that linked him to VADM Nabum.

"Hello, Ralph."

"Kevin, how is it?"

"All is sounding good; what about on your end?"

"It looks good down here. We still show ten minutes. I understand that all the readings are green."

"I don't see any problems from up here and we are all getting punchy waiting for the word. We are excited about getting started. This is definitely a pre-launch until we hit the coordinates for the first jump."

"How are the calculations?"

"Our Astrogators have already calculated the jumps all the way to the destinations with backups calculations just in case something does go awry. We are just waiting for our short flight to the jump off point."

"Well then, good luck and God's speed. I trust that you will have a successful mission and return home safely."

"Thank you, Ralph, and we will be seeing you."

"Ralph out."

"Kevin out."

The Admiral looked around his bridge and the chronometer, a few more minutes. He keyed the fleet mic.

"Fleet, your preparations are for this moment. We are about to launch on a fabulous mission. Soon we will be leaving these dry docks for our jump coordinates. We have been preparing for this day for over a year and soon, very soon we will start our mission. I know each of you are ready and you know it as well. Fleet Captains your ships are prepared. Now be ready to launch your ships and prepare for jump."

The chronometer sounded the time for launch. VADM Brannigan looked about the bridge, "Give the signal."

CAPT Lindsey punched in the code and seven ships left dry docks for the last time on start of their mission. All crew members are in their stations or secured in their berthing secured for the jump. The seven ships came into formation with the *Nautilus* moving out into the lead. The *Intrepid* moved into the lead position of the formation with the *Chesty* behind. Both the *Excalibur* and *Icarus* took up positions forming a circle with all four ships. The *Defiant* and *Scimitar* took up positions in orbit around the circle formation of the four ships. The *Defiant* positioned herself to the starboard and above the other below and to the port in a protective position. All seven ships made for the jump coordinates at full sub light speed.

The satellite was aimed directly at the ships as they moved off from their dry docks. The recording devices in Space Control were on. Ralph Nabum looked around at all the different workers in the control room at this Top Secret base in Texas. He sighed; Kevin was off and hopefully would return. Now they had to begin the next phase of the Space Fleet. They needed to complete the orbiting station and build several more ships. He was waiting around for the very first Human jump into deep space. He lowered his head in deep thought. He no longer could concentrate on the SESG, instead he had to build a space fleet. But tomorrow he had to return to D.C. to pick up his fourth star so he could start the work. This time however, the world would have to know about the new fleet. He shook his head and waited for SESG EXPLORER to reach its jump coordinates.

The strike group reached the coordinates, all hands tensed in anticipation. VADM Brannigan waited for each ship to check in stating their status was green for the jump. The *Nautilus* came in with their signal and she was given the go ahead. Kevin watched the viewscreen with the *Nautilus* on it. He saw the hyperspace well open and a flash as the ship entered. The other six ships signaled they were green; CAPT Lindsey looked up at the Admiral. With a nod of his head, she sent the signal for the jump. The hyperspace well opened again, and all six ships entered.

The entire crew could feel a strange sensation since they never experienced a jump before. Around the flag bridge the crew maintained their stations checking their instruments and consoles. VADM Brannigan looked at the main view screen and watched as the spinning wheel of the well was going by. He glanced at the communications board and could see all six ships sending signals to each other. He looked up to see MajGen Connington approaching.

"All the sensors are online and functioning within normal limits. We have all ships on sensors. We are scanning out into the well to see what we can."

"Very good."

CAPT Lindsey called out from her station, "Prepare to come out of the jump."

The entire bridge tensed again and within a few seconds they came out of the well.

The sensation of coming into normal space was just as tantalizing as entering. The well gave way to streaming stars that finally became the stars they were used to.

VADM Brannigan looked at the view screen to see the star known as Alpha Centauri. At long last, mankind has reached the closest star. He looked at the board for a status of his fleet. CAPT Lindsey and the rest of the hands were waiting for each ship to check in with a status after their first jump. VADM Brannigan sat back in his chair waiting. He knew that each Commanding Officer was checking their engine rooms and life support systems first, then they would move onto their weapons and shield systems before reporting in. After that they would continue to check systems just to make sure they were good to go. After a minute, seven green lights appeared on the board at the station in front of him. The crewmember announced that all ships reported a green status.

Kevin said to CAPT Lindsey, "If there aren't any contacts on any of the screens, allow our scientists to begin their scanning. "

She checked her board briefly, "No contacts, Sir." Then she flipped a communication switch, "Science stations begin your scans," she spoke into her mic. Another station that monitored the various stations reported that the scans had begun. He looked at the view screen with that warm sensation of success. They made their first jump and all appeared to be a success. He waited watching the star system that is Alpha Centauri.

"Any way to see Proxima from here?" he asked. One of the technicians looked at his scanner and replied, "No Sir, it appears to be on the other side of the star."

"Thank you." He thought, *what a shame. Well, the probe would take care of that.*

Five minutes later the ships still reported all green. Good they made their first jump without any mishaps. He got up out of his chair and walked about the bridge looking over the various shoulders of his people checking the systems. After he made a full circle, he turned to CAPT Lindsey.

"Captain, please have CAPT Smith deploy the probe followed by the relay station."

"Yes, Sir." CAPT Lindsey turned back to her station to execute the order.

He then looked over at MajGen Connington, "Have the ships begin computation for the next jump."

"Yes, Sir." The Chief of Staff then turned to his station to relay the order. VADM Brannigan took a deep breath and slowly let it out. He was about to accomplish the first mission of the SESG EXPLORER. Jump to Alpha Centauri to test the hyperspace drives of each ship and upon a successful jump deploy a probe designed specifically to map and perform exploration of Alpha Centauri. The probe would be sending back all astronomical and planetary information to Earth. The next phase would be to launch a relay station to be tested by each ship. This relay station hopefully would be used to transmit communications between the Strike Group and Earth.

He watched the screens as the probe was launched. Kevin knew that the scientists would be going ape over the launch of this system. He checked one of the stations responsible for monitoring the scientists' systems. Sure enough, they were checking all the systems as the probe sped on its way to accomplish its mission. He felt a pang of regret knowing that he would not be able to see the results of this probe. "The data link is good reported the crewman excitedly." He placed a hand gently on his shoulder, "Thank you." He then moved off to one of the communications sections. MajGen Connington joined him. They both watched as the relay station was launched into a geocentric orbit about the system. Immediately the crewman started testing the linkup. After a few minutes he signaled all was good.

Paul inquired, "Is the link picking up the signal from the probe?"

The crewman checked his board, "Yes sir and it appears to be a solid signal."

Both nodded and moved off. Kevin knew the probe would perform an orbit around the system and then proceed into the binary star system for more data. The relay station would relay the data back to Earth and hopefully be a relay for them.

VADM Brannigan took his seat and looked over at the Astrogation station.

"How far off of the mark are we on our jump?"

The Astrogator had anticipated the question and turned to the Admiral, "Sir, we are right on the mark. Having the modifications and the Astrophysicists and Astronomers onboard paid off. I hate to admit it but I think we would have been off of it if they didn't rewrite the program and lend their expertise."

That was more information than what was asked for but Kevin liked the justification for the extra year with the modifications. If anything could go wrong and cause total failure it would be in the jumps. A few decimal points off on the calculations could send the fleet into a different location and they would be lost.

"Have you compared our position to Earth's?"

"Yes Sir, we are where we are supposed to be."

"Excellent, thank you. Is the next jump calculated and double checked?"

The Astrogator turned to his station to verify the data and turned back, "Yes Sir, all we are waiting for is the signal to make the next jump."

Kevin nodded and leaned back into his chair. The next jump was supposed to take two days to travel and would take them truly away from home. Oh yes, Alpha Centauri was away from home but in the relative notion of space travel and hyperspace, it was a neighbor. If need be, they could get home if there was a problem but the next jump was going to take them to an area they could not get back if anything went wrong. The crew was waiting; the probe was already starting its orbit and transmitting data.

VADM Brannigan looked at his primary Communications Officer, "Please open a channel to Earth via the relay."

LT O'Hara motioned her compliance and opened a channel and nodded to the Admiral.

"Space Control, this is SESG EXPLORER. We have made a successful jump to Alpha Centauri and have deployed both the probe and the relay station. We are about to make our second jump. SESG EXPLORER out."

He then looked over to CAPT Lindsey. "CAPT Lindsey send the signal for the second jump."

"Aye aye, Sir."

Within a few seconds the *Nautilus* opened the well and moved into it followed by the other six ships. The second jump was underway.

VADM Brannigan, MajGen Connington and CAPTs Lindsey and Smith sat around one end of the flag conference room table. CAPT Mulligan, the ship's doctor sat next to CAPT Smith. Kevin looked over at Dr. Mulligan; he was a tall man with a head full of white hair. His green eyes were sharp and clear as they looked at each person around the table. His specialty was Internal Medicine. One of Kevin's other modifications was to increase the medical staff on the *Intrepid* and *Chesty*. The surgical teams he had onboard the *Chesty* to receive any wounded. He ensured she was outfitted with the latest and best surgical suites, Intensive Care Units and a fine ward. A lot of the diagnostic systems were also onboard the *Chesty*. But he also ensured the *Intrepid's* medical area had state of the art diagnostics and flight medicine. Of course, every ship had Battle Dressing Stations along with their main medical spaces for wounded suffered in battles or accidents.

He looked over the Doctor, yes this was a man that could be relied upon in a pinch. "Well Doctor, what can you tell us about the sensation of traveling in the well?" They had completed one day of the two day jump to their second position. Not only did the sensation stay with

Kevin, but there were reports coming in from all seven ships indicating the sensation. The Doctor looked at him.

"Obviously the sensation is due to being in the well but I don't think there is anything serious happening. This is new to the human body and we may just have to adapt to the hyperspace environment."

The Doctor picked up a report that was in front of him and studied it for a few moments and looked back at the VADM.

"The tests that we have run so far and will continue to run are inconclusive. We don't believe anything harmful is happening to anyone but it will take a few days to figure it out. I do not recommend that we stop our travels but we should monitor the crew. We already have a baseline on every one onboard to include DNA samples. We now have another set of samples on a good sampling of the population and will be comparing the results. My instinct tells me that we are just experiencing a new environment that we will have to adapt to. Of course, I will let you know of any finding that is contrary right away."

VADM Brannigan sat back in his chair with his hands in a steeple in front of him and lightly tapped his lips with his fingertips in thought. Just a new environment to get used to, that is quite an assumption but what else did they have to go on. No one seemed fatigued over the travel; they had freedom of movement about the ship and could continue to work. No reports of hyperspace sensitivity or psychological problems were coming in.

He looked up at the Doctor, "Is the Psychiatrist reporting any crewmember with undue anxiety over the sensation?"

The Doctor shrugged, "He has seen a few people that are worried about it and what it may mean as we all have. All hands are good to go though. What he is seeing is more preventive in nature rather than an issue. I think the main thing will be to send an education message to each ship for all hands. We should let them know that we are aware of the situation and monitoring and will take appropriate action if there is a situation that require it." The Doctor then rubbed his chin in thought. MajGen Connington picked it up right away.

"Yes Doctor, you have something else?" he said.

The Doctor shrugged again and looked a little indecisive and said, "We were just wondering if this is a medical issue at all."

Paul responded, "How can it not be? You are responsible to the CO and the Admiral for the health of the crew and we are feeling a sensation. It is your job to figure it out and take care of it." A sharp tone was entering his voice showing irritation at the Doctor. The Doctor shrugged and continued.

"We are thinking that we are seeing a symptom with a cause that we cannot fix."

Paul started, "What do you mean? Of course, you can take care of the crew."

At which time Kevin held up a hand silencing him. In a relaxed state he looked at his COS for patience and then looked at the doctor.

"Please, let us know your thoughts."

The Doctor nodded and continued, "We are traveling in a hyperspace environment that we may not be meant to travel in. We never have truly explored this environment. True we sent one person for a short jump just to make sure the hyperspace drive worked and the person didn't turn into say a blob. But we never have really looked at this. We have one physiological sensation without a medical cause. What we have is an environmental cause that may or may not be detrimental to us. But should we wait to see a detriment to our health? Maybe it is from other scientific disciplines and engineering applications that have placed us in this environment. We think that the solution to this is an engineering solution. The crew and I believe yourself would like the sensation to end. The best way would be to take an engineering approach." He glanced over at the COS and continued, "After all, if we should take a step outside of the ship, we would have a medical condition of being dead not to a medical reason but an environmental reason of extreme cold, harsh vacuum and lack of oxygen. We use EVAs to survive the environment. This seems to be the same thing."

VADM Brannigan steepled his hands again and glanced at MajGen Connington who seemed to be mulling this over. Paul nodded and said, "The Doctor is correct in his assumption, I think."

Kevin nodded in agreement. He then looked at CAPT Lindsey.

"Have the Doctor's data given to the engineers and have them look into some form of shielding or ship modification to counteract the sensation. I think he is right and we need to explore this. I agree the sensation may be nothing more than getting used to it but then why wait for contrary information."

"Yes Sir, we will get them started right away," CAPT Lindsey said.

Kevin dismissed them and took a few minutes to think about the situation before getting up and going into his office.

VADM Brannigan sat in his office with MajGen Connington seated across from him. His office was pretty good. He had a small table near the bulkhead across from his desk that could seat six people; a bookshelf was actually against that bulkhead. To his right was the door that led into a short passageway with a hatch going into either the flag conference room and at the other end the flag bridge. To his left was an L shape couch around two bulkheads, one on the side of the porthole and his desk and the other to the hatch leading into his cabin. On the other side of the room and at the end of the table was a view screen. On his desk was a picture of MaryAnn, two computers (one for unclassified material and the other for classified). He had a miniature view screen built into the bulkhead just under a bookshelf so he could see what the main view screen on the bridge showed. He was looking out the window at the well which looked the same as it did on the view screen. The well was a blur of grayish black swirling along as if in a tunnel. He could actually see the *Excalibur* toward the starboard flank of his ship. Magnificent he thought. He turned back to MajGen Connington.

"Well Paul, what is the initial report from the Engineers?"

MajGen Connington looked up from the palm pilot that had the data on it.

"Encouraging, Sir. They have taken readings from each ship and transmitted the data to us and with Medical's info they think they will be close to a solution."

Kevin looked at him skeptically, "That is quick or are they optimistic."

Paul chuckled, "I think they are optimistic." He looked over his palm pilot. "They really need to perform some tests while we are in normal space but they theorize that we can modify the deflector screens to enable us to travel through hyperspace without the feeling. If so, this would give us added protection against any form of debris in space too."

Kevin nodded, he liked that thought.

A general announcement signal went off followed by, "Five minutes to normal space. Prepare for transition to normal space."

Kevin looked at Paul and got up to head for the flag bridge followed by MajGen Connington.

They entered onto the flag bridge and VADM Brannigan took his command seat as MajGen Connington took his seat behind the second semi-circle control center. CAPT Lindsey reported that all ships were at General Quarters preparing for the transition. Kevin had decided earlier in the day that his fleet should come out of hyperspace on this jump at General Quarters. He thought this would be a good drill for the ships and he wanted to be ready just in case there was an unanticipated threat. He checked the status board in front of him that showed all seven ships still reported green and another indicator showing all seven at General Quarters. He nodded in satisfaction and sat back in anticipation.

"Three minutes to transition." the crewman at the hyperspace station behind him reported.

They waited. This time VADM Brannigan had asked that the Astro Sciences maintain their monitoring of the well and to continue through the transition and into normal space. He had passed orders to the Astronomers and Astrogation to provide him immediate feedback to location and success of the jump, that is are they where they are supposed to be.

"One minute to transition." This time the crewman sounded a bit anxious. They all were, Kevin knew. *This is exciting* he thought to himself. The sensation changed as the engine room began to bring online the Ion drives and cut out the hyperspace drives. Suddenly the view screen showed the stars streaming past the ship and then turn normal. They came out of hyperspace. All seven ships went from a fast speed to a slow crawl. All stations on each ship were performing their systems check and scanning the space around them. Kevin watched as the board responded with seven green lights showing positive outcomes of the systems checks. He waited as CAPT Lindsey gathered the reports.

At last, she responded, "All ships report a successful jump. There are no contacts on tactical. We are in the clear and have room to maneuver. The *Nautilus* is moving out to a monitoring position. We are scanning the surrounding space."

Astrogation reported, "Sir, sensors and Astronomy confirm that we have made a successful jump. We are where we plotted to go."

"Thank you." He said.

"Sir, the system we have entered is a Red Sun with two asteroid belts and three planets." reported the crewmember manning a sensor station to his left responsible for scanning the surrounding space for planets in a system. "We are relatively close to one of them."

VADM Brannigan looked about the bridge at the crew. Most of them were at their stations ensuring the systems were running normal. But a few of them looked at him with eagerness at the possibility of checking out a planet. He looked over at the planetary system crewman.

"Planet system, are you able to scan the three planets?"

"Sir, we can scan the closest relatively well but the other two are a little difficult for our sensors."

"Scan them in as much detail as possible. CAPT Lindsey maneuver the fleet into a high orbit over the closest one."

"Yes, Sir."

The planetary station reported, "Sir, from the scans the nearest planet has a relative breathable atmosphere, may require filters, it is a desert world with high winds but we may be able to explore it. The next planet appears to have a lot of clouds possibly like Venus. I will need more time to get a better reading on it. The other one appears" he took a moment with adjusting his sensor, "yes, I believe it is more of a molten rock due to its proximity to the star. But the first planet is definitely explorable."

VADM Brannigan looked around the bridge and could see eager faces.

"Okay, let's see what we can find out about this planet."

The fleet moved into a high orbit about the third planet from the sun. Its orbit was between the two asteroid belts. The fleet had to maneuver up and over the outer belt to avoid the asteroids and meteors within it. The *Nautilus* did not go with the rest of the ships but maintained a higher orbit with passive sensors taking readings. Her primary mission was to maintain a silent watch of the space for any adversaries or other contacts which could threaten the fleet. The four primary ships of the SESG maintained their circular formation while the *Scimitar* and *Defiant* flew above them in a protective formation.

Colonel Roberts sat in his command chair in his flag plot watching his monitors as Force Recon prepared to shuttle over to the *Intrepid* to pick up the geologist and other scientists. He had one platoon as a quick reaction force in case they were needed and his pilots were in their attack ships. They didn't really think they would be needed on this desolate world but it never hurt to be prepared.

VADM Brannigan stood at his porthole looking out at the world they were orbiting. It didn't look hospitable in the least. Oh, the scientists were eager to get down there and check it out. They had been in orbit now for two hours taking sensor readings of the atmosphere. There definitely appeared to be traces of oxygen and nitrogen but they would need environmental suits nevertheless. There was sand

and other debris in the air driven by high winds. They finally found a place to land the landing party to perform exploration. He was as eager to learn what they would find out but he didn't want to spend too much time exploring a dead world. They had a long way to go for their mission but this would be a great test world. He had ordered the MEU to support the landing team with Force Recon. They would be the least intrusive of the Marines but could defend and call for help the quickest if needed. The scientists didn't like it but Dr. Vance ensured the grumbling was kept to the minimum. He told them that it was necessary.

There it is, Kevin spotted the two shuttles from the *Chesty* leaving and coming over to the *Intrepid* to escort the three shuttles bearing the scientists and all of their gear. The two Marine shuttles moved into position waiting. Finally, the other three shuttles joined their formation and they began their descent into the inhospitable world. Already the scientists wanted to name the world and CAPT Lindsey had reported the crew was already coming up with names. He shrugged his shoulders. Dirtball would work for him he just hoped all the people he sent down would return safely and with something interesting other than dirt. He kept going over with his CAG and the MEU the importance of safety. He knew the scientists would get reckless in their eagerness and it would be up to the pilots and the Recon Captain to keep them from getting hurt. He let out a deep breath and shook his head. All in the name of discovery and chuckled to himself when he couldn't see the ships anymore, he turned away from the porthole and sat down behind his desk. He looked at his wife's picture and then looked at his computer to see what the engineers were saying about the hyperspace environment and if they could counter its effects on the crew and the unknowns to the ships.

The shuttles made it through the atmosphere. It was a rougher ride than anyone had anticipated. The scientists were anxious and wanted to get started but the orders were clear. No one left the shuttles until his Marines gave the all clear. Capt Leroy knew the Colonel would have his ass if they lost anyone. His Marines were suited up and ready to go. He looked them over once more. His First Sergeant gave him the thumbs up. He took another breath and then sealed his suit. He gave the nod to the Marine at the hatch and the seal was broken. The two Marine shuttles opened up and the Marines made a quick exit forming up a perimeter and checking to see if there were any hostilities. Capt Leroy stepped out of his shuttle and was walking towards one end of the perimeter to ensure it was all clear when he noticed part of a structure. *Oh great,* he thought, *what is this?* He motioned for two Marines to follow him and headed for it. Yep, that is part of a man made or rather an alien made structure. He gave a call through the suit's communications to the rest of his Marines to encircle what they could and check it out. He knew the scientists would be busting at the seams to get started but this trip just turned out to be more than expected.

Col Roberts was annoyed but spoke calmly into the mic.

"Okay, you are sure there are no hostiles in the area?"

"Yes Sir, we are pretty sure. We did a sweep without any encounters. I have let some of the scientists out of the shuttles but am keeping them close to the shuttles just in case. They can conduct their experiments there." Capt Leroy reported. Col Roberts thought briefly and concurred with this action.

"Sir, there is an opening into the structures but it goes underground." Capt Leroy had to shout into his comm set to be heard. Col Roberts could hear him but there was a lot of static. Capt Leroy continued, "I would like to take the geologists and enter the structure to see just what is there."

That Col Roberts did not like. He didn't like losing contact with his party especially with an unanticipated twist. But they are Marines and scientists.

"You are sure there is no danger?"

"No, Sir. There are signs of some form of activity but no way to tell without entering the structure. My first impression is this is some sort of mine. If so, I would need the geologists to tell me what they are mining, whoever they are."

Col Roberts scowled but knew the Captain was right about this. "Alright but keep most of your forces out of there, only take what is actually necessary and be ready to bug out."

"Solid copy Sir, thank you, Sir. Team Alpha out."

"Bulldog out." Col Roberts turned to his Comm Officer, "Get me the Admiral."

"Thank you, Colonel, keep me appraised."

"Bulldog out."

"Thunder out"

VADM Brannigan looked around at his principals. "Interesting development. Place the fleet into a tactical alert. CAG have your fighters prepped but do not launch. Dr. Vance I want to know what they find. Dismissed."

Everyone around the table nodded their concurrence and moved to implement the orders.

Capt Leroy went into the entrance they had found first. He didn't want anyone else to precede and get hit with some trap. He was followed by two of his Marines and three Geologists. They turned on their helmet lights and flashlights on their rifles. After entering the structure through a hatch and a couple feet in they found a ladder heading down into the structure. There were not any visible signs of booby traps so they headed down the ladder into the structure. Twenty feet below they reached a landing and after going through a short tunnel the area opened up. One of the geologists made a comment that the people that made this area had to be bipedal like humans. This made Capt Leroy feel a little better, at least these people were about the same size and shape as them and therefore no big ass monster would be coming at them. They fanned out with the Marines setting up a security perimeter and the three geologists started rooting around the various items that they were finding. Three tunnels headed off into other directions. The Marines positioned themselves at each one shining their lights down them. The geologists meanwhile were finding records in an alien writing and containers of crystals. The signs of a mining camp were definitely here but where were the inhabitants?

The 2nd Lieutenant stayed at the shuttles where he could have the best communications and watched as the other scientists were gathering soil and air samples. In and out of one of the other shuttles they were moving. They apparently had brought some equipment with them to do initial analysis of their samples. The Lieutenant was slightly nervous. Here he is on an alien world and his Captain was in some hole in the ground while there were obvious signs of intelligent creatures about. One of the Marines came into the shuttle reporting that the outer perimeter sensors were in place. The Lieutenant nodded appreciating having those sensors in place due to the sand in the air preventing any decent vision. He only had to wait a few minutes before one of the sensors tripped. He immediately looked at the screen to see what was happening. A body of persons had apparently tripped the sensor but no real details. He sent a communication to the Marines in that sector to keep their eyes open while attempting to contact his Captain. He couldn't reach him so he sent two Marines into the structure to alert him and then notified the *Chesty* about the trip.

The Marine moved slowly towards the tripped sensor using the ground and dust saturated air as cover. He finally saw a body of creatures, humanoid in appearance starting towards the shuttles. One of them saw him and fired a shot but fortunately it was in such a hurry that it missed him. He immediately radioed in the event.

The *Chesty* went onto immediate alert. The ship's sensors detected a large body of creatures moving in on the structure and shuttles. Col Roberts could not reach his Captain on the ground but his Lieutenant had sent a hurried message that they were under attack. VADM Brannigan had ordered the *Chesty* to take a planetary assault position. Even now *Intrepid* was moving into a protective position above her while the Marines readied for a landing.

VADM Brannigan sat in his chair watching as the *Chesty* was positioning herself for a landing if it became necessary. Already the ships' sensors showed a large body of creatures moving toward the shuttles. Suddenly a klaxon went off alerting the crew. They looked up to a screen showing nothing but space. Kevin looked at the tactical display to see a number of ships moving in their direction. At this time comms reported that a message from the *Nautilus* was coming through. The report identified that there were five ships, apparently escorts, and a rather large ship for a total of six were on an attack approach to them. *Great, we are under attack at our second jump point.* One could argue that this was way too close to Earth. But what was attacking them? He ordered that communications attempt to establish a link with the approaching ships and had Mr. O'Shea prepare a greeting. Meanwhile he turned his attention back to the planet and picked up his headset indicating that he wanted to talk with Col Roberts.

"Colonel, you appear to be in position."

"Yes Sir, I figure to launch the Quick Reaction Force and take out the opposition."

VADM Brannigan thought briefly and stated, "Let's not make an assumption of quick victory here. I want you to assume that you are facing a technologically advanced enemy. Use the space here as Maneuver from the Sea but instead as from Space. I would rather you overestimate this enemy and use maximum firepower."

"Yes Sir, I understand. I will then change to use the QRF as a reinforcing one to the Recon unit and land my forces behind the enemy and use surprise and their rear as an advantage."

"I approve, meanwhile we will keep these other ships off of you."

The fleet had maneuvered so the *Chesty* was over the landing party's position to launch the Marines and use their batteries from space. *Intrepid* was positioned directly above her to protect her. Meanwhile *Excalibur* and *Icarus* positioned themselves along the bow and aft of the *Intrepid* to provide fire support against the attacking ships. Both *Scimitar* and *Defiant* were moving along the x axis to them preparing to move out to meet the oncoming ships. The *Nautilus* had disappeared into the darkness of space to monitor and advise. All hands were at battle stations and all ships reported their shields and weapons systems were online. The CAG reported that all pilots were in the tubes ready for launch. Meanwhile, the *Chesty* launched her ten fighters to provide Close Air Support to the Marines.

One craft would remain circling in the upper atmosphere to provide the communications link while the other nine would form up into three squadrons. Capt Jolene Duncan took her squadron down towards the creatures moving into position against the landing party. As her squadron flew over their heads, they were shot at with ground type weapons. All of her craft were missed and they made another fly by sending pictures and reconnaissance of what they observed. The ground enemy was organized into three segments supported by some form of artillery and moving slowly towards the shuttles. Col Roberts ordered his three squadrons to take out the artillery type pieces.

Capt Duncan led the three squadrons into low altitude attacks targeting any piece of equipment that appeared it could launch rounds. Meanwhile *Chesty* launched the Quick Reaction Force to support the Force Recon unit. Capt Leroy already had the scientist inside the mine with half of his unit. The other half he had in a close perimeter around the entrance. The shuttles were to remain on the ground until he received launch orders. The pilots remained at their controls.

Capt Duncan made three passes with successful hits on each piece they aimed at. The enemy did not have the correct aiming devices to hit them she noticed. She was thankful for that. On each pass she noticed that each of the other units had a few hundred beings in them. Some of them seemed larger than others.

Mike O'Shea approached the VADM. "Sir, I have a message ready to be sent. I really think we ought to try and talk to them."

"We have already started action on the ground, Mike."

"Yes, but we may be able to stop if they will."

The Admiral thought for a moment.

"Communications, send to the approaching ships Mr. O'Shea's message. Ground monitoring, do we have any form of an identified HQ for their ground forces?"

"No, Sir."

"Okay, Mike, we will send to the ships and see what happens. If they don't attack and somehow able to stop the forces planet side, then we will continue talks. If not, oh well."

Mike nodded and moved back to his station.

Meanwhile the *Chesty* began her landing of the Battalion behind the approaching force lines. She was dropping the assault vehicles with the company of Marines for them and the space tanks. At last, they would be truly tested. Behind the assault vehicles, shuttles were landing to release the two other companies of Marines and their Weapons Companies. The Weapons Company would only be allowed to fire based on the information that Capt Duncan provided in order to avoid fratricide.

In orbit, the enemy ships were on top of the fleet. The enemy ships launched five missiles at *Intrepid* but *Scimitar* and *Defiant* each fired their laser weapons and destroyed the missiles. The two smaller ships moved out in flanking maneuvers while *Excalibur* and *Icarus* established their perimeter of fire. Once those two ships had their angle of fire, the CAG launched his forty fighters.

The enemy ships formed up around the larger vessel. Three of the escorts formed up in a wedge formation in front of it while the other two took up flanking positions. Both the *Excalibur* and *Icarus* targeted the wedge and before long had destroyed the lead ship. They followed up by targeting the other two ships while the *Intrepid* targeted the main ship. She pumped more power to her weapons impacting the larger ship's shields. Meanwhile the *Defiant* swooped under the flanking ship while *Scimitar* swooped up above the opposite ship. The flanking ships moved to intercept and both fired missiles directly into them. The first missiles shattered the enemy's shield and the remaining slammed into the two escorts almost simultaneously. The remaining two escorts fell to the fire of the *Intrepid's* escorts and all five ships concentrated fire upon the main ship. Her shields buckled under the concentrated lasers of the five ships and finally blinked out. At which point all five ships fired missiles into her aiming at the propulsion and weapons systems. In a short time, the ship fell dead to the firepower of the missiles. Only chunks of the six enemy ships remained. The fighters never had a chance to fire a shot. The CAG recalled thirty of his ships and sent the other ten to form a cordon. Later he would reduce the number to one squadron of five fighters.

The *Scimitar* and *Defiant* received orders to collect what debris made sense and scan for any databanks.

The land battle almost went as well. The tanks smashed into the rear lines supported by the assault vehicles along with the fighters. The two rifle companies supported by the weapons companies took up positions to keep any of the enemy from escaping. The Marines destroyed them in half an hour without taking any casualties. Col Roberts was thankful but concerned. VADM Brannigan was glad of the reports that were received but was wondering why such an easy victory. He knew that his crews were highly trained and well prepared but this should not have been easy. He got up out of his chair to head to his office.

"Give me any additional reports. I want to know who these people were."

MajGen Connington, Col Roberts, Mr. O'Shea, and CAPT Lindsey sat around the Admiral's small table in his office waiting for him to return. Dr. Vance came into the office and took a seat. A couple of minutes later VADM Brannigan came into the office out of his cabin and took a seat opposite of the screen at the table. He looked at each one of them.

"A good day. We engaged an enemy and came away victorious without any losses. Good job but why was it so easy?"

Each officer and the Science Department Head looked at each other. Col Roberts spoke up.

"Sir, it appears that this enemy," He paused, "well, they were pirates."

"Pirates?"

"Yes, sir."

CAPT Lindsey spoke next, "It appears that their ships had minor armaments like we would expect from any pirate ship on Earth. There wasn't anything too useful that we recovered but the analysis, Doctor."

Dr. Vance continued, "Yes sir, the metallurgical analysis shows heavily used ships and poorly maintained. I think they were pirates. Further on the planet the Marines found that there really weren't any true formations and definitely any uniform weapons and such. They were rag tag at best. The Marines could have won with less force but the precaution was correct with such a short notice. Further the Marines found another base. It appears that this was a pirate planet mining various items such as crystals that we found."

Kevin thought about it for a few moments. He steepled his hands together thinking about the information that he was presented.

"Alright, they were pirates and that is what we will log until evidence says otherwise. Col Roberts, what is your assessment?"

"I agree that they were pirates. The victory was too easy but it was also good to have this real-life experience for our Marines and ships. I think we were fortunate though."

"How so?"

"They were not organized and I and my staff underestimated them. We are looking at our procedures. The one thing that I think we should have done was to launch an Unmanned Ariel Vehicle when the shuttles went down. We would have had an earlier warning and been able to assess them better."

The VADM thought about this, "I agree."

"Dr. Vance, what about the superstructure and crystals, what are they?"

Dr. Vance looked at a report on his palm pilot that he brought with him.

"The structures that we have found were both living quarters and mining facilities. I think the pirates were in the ships and the miners with a few pirates lived and mined on the planet. They mined several different things but the primary was these crystals."

He looked at his palm pilot again.

"I would like to bring several drums of them onboard to figure out what they are but..."

They waited without saying a word. Dr. Vance read the report some more and then looked up at them and continued.

"We think they may be an energy source and if we can figure out how to utilize them then we can improve our entire power system."

"A power source," MajGen Connington sounded shock, "are they stable or explosive? What would happen if they went off?"

"If they are unstable, we lose it. But if they are stable and we can harness them, then the potential may be worth it."

They sat around the table considering what Dr. Vance said.

VADM Brannigan said, "Bring onboard several barrels of these crystals, keep them isolated from the main cargo holds. Perform your tests and if they work out then we have something worthwhile. Meanwhile let's bring onboard other of the materials and figure out what they are and if we can use them. Have CAPT Smith rig it where we can jettison the crystals if we need to."

They all acknowledged the order and started to leave.

"Hold on." the Admiral said and they sat down. "I am concerned about the proximity of this place to Earth. Yes, I know it is a great distance from Earth but it is only our second jump to get here. I don't want this place to be a pirate or enemy stronghold especially if this place has such a potential. It is obvious that we cannot leave anyone or any ships behind."

He looked around the room waiting for any thoughts.

CAPT Lindsey said, "We could drop a nuke at the site but then we lose all potential usage also."

Everyone shook their heads.

Col Roberts spoke, "All we can do is leave a relay station as a listening post and hope Earth can send ships at a future time."

The Admiral thought about it and nodded, "I agree that is the best we will be able to do. Ensure that the signal from the relay station sends short pulses only and that it scans the system and planet below in short periods only."

They acknowledged and the VADM got up and went over to his desk as the others left. He looked out the porthole instead of sitting down. *Wow we may have a new energy source. No more nuclear fusion or fission, no more oil now a crystal technology that may actually provide us with energy. I wonder if we can include them into our system and increase our shielding and weapons along with the drive.* Kevin almost did a small dance. This is an excellent discovery.

CAPT Smith had the cargo facility properly prepared for the crystals with an ability to jettison them if required. The engineering group along with a geologist was checking out a couple of the crystals. They were clear in appearance except for a few of them that had a yellowish or reddish color to them. They seemed happy but worried as they looked at her with expecting eyes.

She said, "You will be allowed to take one at a time to other labs and we will be setting up a small work station in here for you." That seemed to do the trick. She left to report to the Admiral.

Three days later around the planet and the Admiral was getting anxious. They had explored the entire planet to a level that he really desired to. The exploring teams had combed all the mines and the living areas that were safe to do so. The system was already scanned by his two escort ships, The *Scimitar* and *Defiant* along with the *Nautilus* and some very interesting data was gathered but he needed to move on.

He sat back in his seat and closed his eyes. No, he needed to move on. His teams have already had enough time and now he needed to recall them. He looked at one of his stations in front of him and estimated from their data that it would take three hours to reform his fleet. He turned to CAPT Lindsey.

"CAPT Lindsey," she turned to see him, "recall the ships and alert the teams on the ground that they have two hours to do anymore exploring and an hour to pack up and head back up. We will be depart-ing the system when the fleet is together and they are onboard. Also, transmit our logs and reports back to earth via the relay station at Alpha Centauri, ensure these coordinates are included."

"Yes, Sir." She responded. She turned to her board to send the appropriate messages.

VADM Brannigan then looked at Astrogation, "Astrogation, begin your calculations for the next jump."

"Yes, Sir." The young crewman responded and she turned to her system calling up the Astronomers and the jump program to begin the calculations.

Three and a half hours later the fleet was reassembled and the shut-tles were back on their way to the ships. Kevin was in his office waiting for word of their arrival, he wanted to be gone already but there were always delays. Meanwhile he was reviewing the engineering report on the various weapons from the pirates and miners. Some of them were projectile weapons that definitely made the Marines the state of the art. The projectiles were not able to penetrate the Marines' armor. But there were energy weapons that the engineers believed could be mod-ified to improve their entire firepower. This made him happy.

Major Clark was walking along the passageways in his own thoughts when he saw someone who he had seen on occasions but never had interacted with. He was approaching the VADM's Aide when a thought struck him and he veered into the Lieutenant's way.

"Good morning, Lieutenant."

"Good morning, Sir."

"Come with me, Lieutenant; we have something we need to do."

"Sir?"

Major Clark took him by the arm and steered him down the pas-sageway explaining his idea to him. They approached one of the FAST's berthing areas, rang the bell, and then entered.

"Lieutenant, this is Staff Sergeant Jones, your new instructor."

All the shuttles were onboard and VADM Brannigan sat down in his chair reviewing the status boards in front of him. All ships showed green. He turned to CAPT Lindsey.

"CAPT Lindsey, send *Nautilus* through and let's test the comms."

"Aye aye, Sir."

He watched as the hyperspace window opened up and *Nautilus* entered the well. This would be a short jump and they hopefully would receive a communiqué. The *Nautilus* would return through the well if they didn't receive any response from the fleet. They waited. An hour later the hyperspace window opened up and *Nautilus* came back through. VADM Brannigan nodded and waited for the report to come through.

MajGen Connington and CAPT Lindsey approached him. The CAPT said, "The report shows all clear on the other end. They sent a signal and obviously it hasn't reached us yet or never will. We will either have to wait or travel at the same time. I recommend that we travel together except on short jumps or high threat jumps. In which case *Nautilus* should go first to check out the security situation and come back to us." MajGen Connington assented to this recommendation.

Kevin thought about it for a few minutes. "We will see when the time comes. I don't want to commit to the procedure at this time. Thank you. Prepare for the jump."

The ships formed up and upon fleet signal the hyperspace window opened up and the Strike Group moved into the well.

CHAPTER 4

The Strike Group had just completed a week-long jump. They had spent the past three months performing multiple jumps. The Strike Group would make a jump and ensure they were still on track with the plotted course. The VADM maintained his insistence that they be careful with their jumping to ensure they did not get lost. He demanded that they jump, stop, and look around at the star constellations. Each time they entered normal space they would take a day to map the stars and systems. This data ensured that they could update their star charts and ensure their jump calculations were up to date. During one of their jumps, they found a similar planet with the energy crystals but it appeared to be untouched. The Strike Group had dropped another relay/listening station in orbit.

They had sent messages with the updated information and finds back to Earth but had not received any responses to their messages and therefore did not know if the information had reached them. This didn't really bother the Admiral or his Commanders since they had already planned that they would lose contact after the first jump.

They spent another day mapping the stars, updating their databases and calculations. They prepared for another week-long jump. The engineers had solved the problem of the hyperspace sensation by modifying the ships' deflectors. Doctor Mulligan reported that this helped the crew. The Commanding Officers were quite happy about this and the Admiral was thankful that he had added protection while in the well. The energy output was minimal. Meanwhile he was waiting for two reports from his various science and engineers concerning powered weapons and the crystals that they had found. The information on the powered weapons showed promise and they had developed a prototype that the Marines were testing. The only problems seemed to be overheating of the barrels and a quick drain of the energy supply. However, the weapons produced enough energy to kill an enemy and penetrate armor.

The reports on the crystals indicated that they are a power source. The geologists were studying them to see how they were produced by the planet. The engineers were delving into the ability to harness their energy and how to apply it to the drives and other systems. The Admiral was really interested in this aspect. The potential to increase all ships' efficiencies were vital in his mind to survival in this mission and future space exploration.

The window to hyperspace opened and the Strike Group moved into the well.

Life onboard the ships in hyperspace was like any ship of the Navy. They had their normal routine of eating, sleeping, working, and time off. Various watch stations would monitor systems and the tactical situation. They had no idea if they could sense another ship outside of the Strike Group and if they would be in danger if another ship was in hyperspace. Could they fire upon each other? The Admiral didn't care to test the thought that a battle could take place in hyperspace. The loss of one life over such an experiment would be one too many in his mind. So, the crew would maintain the ship and ensure all systems were operating nominally. Interaction among the crew was good. They didn't spend too much time in hyperspace in order to avoid boredom in addition to getting lost. The Marines and other units aboard performed sustainment training within the confines of the ships, the scientists and engineers continued their study of hyperspace or their other projects, the linguists and Mr. O'Shea and staff worked on the alien's language ensuring they did not make any mistakes when they finally reached their destination. The Admiral and his staff continued to monitor and make their contingency plans. All in all, this mission was going quite well.

Lieutenant Shapiro stepped out of the shower. He was sore and bruised and slightly frustrated. He just wanted to go to bed but he needed to get ready for dinner in the flag mess. People would start talking if he didn't show and that damn Major of the Marines would come looking for him. He was in his quarters and at first, he thought he could hide from Major Clark. But the Major had the code to the Admiral's cabin and his outer door. The outer door led to a passageway with a secure lock that only a few of the staff had the code to. On the other end of the passageway was the Admiral's office. The Lieutenant's cabin was directly opposite of the Admiral's. John felt lucky, he had an outer room for his office with all of the equipment he needed for the Admiral. Through a hatch at the other end was his bedroom and personal head. He was truly fortunate to have these quarters but it also meant he was at the beck and call of the Admiral 24 hours a day. He definitely had earned the quarters even now.

John Shapiro, U.S. Navy Lieutenant hand selected to be the Vice Admiral's Aide but not only Aide but with the additional duties of a protocol officer, flag writer and secretary. A load of duties for one man. A fleet admiral rated a separate person for each job but not on this mission. Not enough space on the ship and at times not enough work for each position. Then this major grabs him one day in the passage way and turns him over to his First Sergeant for additional training.

The Major explained that he wanted the LT to know how to fight, shoot weapons, be a personal bodyguard to the Admiral. When he tried to argue with the Major and remind him it was his job to protect the Admiral, he was quick to point out that a Marine just couldn't always be present. Especially once they were on Kammorriga. Of course, the Major would do his best but he wanted the LT prepared. And worse yet, the Major swore him to secrecy of the training. So now in addition to all his duties he was secretly being trained in a profession he never chose, a personal bodyguard.

He was happy to be part of the mission and being an Aide ought to make his career. Just not seeing the good of it all when every other day he gets beat up by a Marine or two. But he can now handle any weapon with the Marines and had become a good shot with a pistol and a carbine energy weapon. He even had achieved top scores in the various driving simulators.

He lifted his left arm and viewed the bruises along the left side of his chest in the mirror. Those hurt but was assured by the Corpsman of no broken ribs. His chest and stomach were a lot more fit and muscular. A grim smiled almost a grimace crossed his face. He was improving and in the best shape of his life but damn it was costly.

He proceeded to get ready and go to dinner. He knew Major Clark would be waiting for him.

They came out of hyperspace and found themselves with a sight that they marveled at. The Admiral couldn't take his eyes off of the main view screen for several moments. The Strike Group had moved into normal space with a large cloud in front of them. The sensors picked up a bluish light emanating from it. The cloud was approximately the same distance from the local star as Earth was from Sol. The sensors reported various gases indicating the sensors wouldn't function efficiently and shields would be inoperative. The Strike Group launched a probe into the cloud and dispatched the *Scimitar* and *Defiant* to the other side of the cloud to retrieve the probe since the signal was cut off when it entered the cloud. Meanwhile the ships began their scans of the surrounding space. They began their star mapping.

VADM Brannigan and his primary staff sat around the flag conference room table. Dr. Vance was reading the report from his department on his palm pilot while the others waited. As normal, the other officers were talking quietly among themselves. They had stayed in this system for over two days now taking various readings of the cloud. The probe had finally emerged from the cloud the day before to be picked up by the *Defiant* and returned it to the *Intrepid* for analysis of its data.

Dr. Vance looked up and gave a soft whistle, "This cloud is really amazing. It is huge, measuring several hundred kilometers across!" He was very excited over this find. "It is composed of several different gases such as hydrogen, nitrogen, helium, carbon, iron, plus many more."

CAPT Lindsey asked, "Could the ships enter it?"

"Oh yes, no problem but I seriously doubt if our shields would work, a lot of the sensors would be down if we entered it. We would have to stay close to each other or we would become lost in regards to our relative position towards each other. But no harm would come to the ships or the crew. This is a wonderful discovery, some of the speculations wonder if this cloud could have been a star if one or two other ingredients were in place. We really would have to perform a lot more studies on it to be sure of anything."

Dr. Vance scrolled through his pilot, "We don't know what is at the center of the cloud either."

VADM Brannigan continued, "So, we can enter the cloud with our ships without any problems but we cannot see with our sensors very far." He steepled his hands together in thought.

CAPT Smith spoke up, "Are you thinking this could be a sanctuary or something?"

He looked over at her, "Yes that is what I am thinking. If we needed some place to run to and hide this maybe it."

CAPT Lindsey said, "We could make a contingency plan just for that. But why not just head for Earth then?"

"Why take an enemy back to our home world?" asked MajGen Connington. "Would it not be better to hide out here and make repairs and hopefully whatever enemy may be pursuing us would lose interest or consider us dead?"

"I see your point." She said. "I will work with my people to ensure that we have these coordinates locked into each ship's astrogation systems but classified from other people."

Kevin nodded, "Yes, that should suffice. I think this would make a good contingency spot for us. The only thing it gives away is this is a sector that we came from, are aware of but in no way leads to Earth herself."

He looked around the room for any more comments.

"Alright then let's prepare for our next jump. I wonder what else we will be finding out here."

A month and three jumps later they arrived at another site to begin star charting. For some inexplicable reason the Admiral felt something was slightly off. He approached the console with the sensors.

"Crewman."

"Sir."

"Let's take a look way out. Take some extremely long-range readings and let's see what we might see out there."

"Yes, Sir."

Several hours later the Admiral was sitting in his office with MajGen Connington.

"The scans picked up an ion trail at the far edge of the sensor range. The decay indicates a line of travel."

"Were they heading away from us?" Kevin inquired.

"Yes, Sir. We have some coordinates that may make it worthwhile to send the *Nautilus* ahead to check it out."

"Alright, make it so."

Thirty minutes later the *Nautilus* made a jump in the direction of the calculated coordinates. Meanwhile the remainder of the strike group set up a defensive position with a Carrier Aircraft Patrol flying a protective circle with a ready alert squadron in the tube. VADM Brannigan was in his chair watching the view screens waiting for any ships. He could sense the tension onboard the bridge. Everyone was anxiously watching their systems. The comm system on his chair beeped. The Admiral looked down at it and picked up his headset. After placing it on his head he pressed the button.

"Yes, Doctor, what can I do for you?"

Dr. Vance sounded eager on the headset. "Admiral, we got it. We figured out how to harness the energy of the crystals. We believe we can integrate them into the system and would like to get started."

"Not now, Doctor. I don't need our systems offline at this time."

"But Sir, we can increase our energy output on all systems."

"Not at this time, Doctor. I will let you know when we can begin. Admiral Brannigan out." He killed the comm system and checked the screens. A moment later the hyperspace window opened up. The ships switched on their shields and waited. The *Nautilus* sent her signal. All hands on the bridge relaxed while Kevin watched the screens. A few moments later no other ships appeared and the Admiral picked up his headset and asked the communications section to contact the *Nautilus*.

"Well, Captain."

"Sir, we made the jump and found a space station."

"Make your report."

"We made the jump and went into silent mode immediately. We then approached within a kilometer of the station. We remained on passive sensors. We picked up several ships coming and going to the station. We identified several ion trails similar to the one we picked up. The station is rather large with several docking facilities. They did not appear to be hostile."

The Admiral thought about it for a few moments.

"I want you to send all the data to the *Intrepid* for analysis."

"Yes, Sir."

"Out here." The Admiral closed his mic. He looked over to Paul. When his COS approached the chair, the Admiral softly said, "Paul, we have found another set of intelligent life. This time it is advanced, a space station."

"We should jump to it and check it out."

"Ummm, we should check it out but I think we should go slowly."

"You don't trust this?"

"I don't know. This will be our actual first contact, besides the pirates and miners that is. We are a long way from home with no back up other than ourselves."

"Our intentions could be made clear to them." Paul countered.

"Yes, but how?" The Admiral sat back in his chair thinking about it. "I want a meeting with you, Ops, the CO of the *Nautilus*, Mike O'Shea, and Dr. Vance."

"Yes, Sir."

The Admiral got up and went into his office. He sat down and looked out the porthole. Wow, a true to goodness space station. Wonder what species owns it and if they are hostile or not. Way too many questions that require answers that could not be figured out sitting here.

The Admiral sat at his table with MajGen Connington, CAPT Lindsey, Dr. Vance, Mr. O'Shea, and CAPT Strickland. They were eating dinner together.

The Admiral looked at the Commanding Officer of the *Nautilus*, "CAPT Srickland, please tell us about the station."

The Captain took a sip of his wine, "Well Sir, it is huge. It is a kilometer in length from a north to south axis. It has three circular disks for what appeared to be habitable stations. The largest is on top. The other two disks are below it in decreasing size. After the bottom disk the spine of it continues down with various modules attached to it. We picked up several signals from the station which the scientists and linguists are analyzing at this time. They appeared to be signals designed to guide in ships to the station. From appearances this is a fueling station or a merchant station. The only thing we couldn't tell was what exactly it is, why they are here or who they belong to."

MajGen Connington nodded, "CAPT Lindsey what do you have?"

"Nothing at this time sir, we are waiting on the analysis." She said and took a bite of her food.

The Admiral continued eating his food so MajGen Connington looked over at Dr. Vance and waited for him to finish eating. "Doctor, any word from the analysis team?"

"Yes, there is. CAPT Strickland's sensors picked up traffic as he indicates. We are now deciphering it to see a couple of different things. One is the traffic patterns and how we can tie into them. The other is any other communications that may lead to answers with why this station is here and who it belongs too. But the analysis will only go so far."

"Meaning what?" asked MajGen Connington.

"We need to go and explore."

Kevin finished his class of wine and looked at them, "The crux of the matter."

The group looked at each other and then back at the Admiral.

"Yes, the crux of the matter. We are out here to explore and this is our second opportunity and hopefully not a hostile one. We may even be able to learn something about life out here. Of course, our primary mission is to reach our destination but we are to explore. The only executive order is to keep our origins and the location of Earth a total secret. Don't let anyone know where she is!"

Everyone nodded.

"Alright. Mike how best do you think we should make contact? I don't really want to appear as a military organization but our ships bristle with weapon systems."

Mike O'Shea thought for a moment. "Would be best to be explorers or traders. Trading would be difficult I think since our cargo is for us and our mission vice trading. So, explorers would be best with the ability for some minor trading. I can send one of my folks in with the team to help them. Perhaps we should send in a smaller ship."

"Alright, we will send in one of the escort ships to make the contact." The Admiral agreed, "We will bring the fleet into the same space but outside of the reach of their sensors and monitor the situation. CAPT Lindsey, make the preparations." The Admiral nodded at his guests.

MajGen Connington finished his glass, "Okay crew let's get with it."

Everyone got up and started leaving. VADM Brannigan nodded for MajGen Connington to stay behind. When everyone left the office, Kevin took his seat behind the desk with Paul taking the seat in front of it. Kevin turned on his computer checking the status reports across his screen. He scanned his email and didn't see anything worthwhile.

He looked up at Paul "What do you think about this space station?"

The Chief of Staff shook his head slowly. "I don't like it. It seems really strange to me to have it out here. It does make me wonder whose space we have or are entering. I wonder if they think our planet is in their space." He shrugged.

Kevin nodded, "I was wondering the same thing. So, we need to check them out and see what it is that they know and think. We will need to put a linguist with the team that goes onto the station." He paused for a moment thinking. "I like sending one of Mike's folks along as a negotiator. Also, I want to have an intel gatherer on the team. I think the most important things to acquire are their star maps and anything about who they are."

"Yes, Sir. I will make sure that we have them on the ship with orders to that effect."

"I don't want the CO of the ship leaving his ship. I need him to stay in total control of the situation. Place a platoon of the Rangers onboard the ship to be able to affect a rescue if required or attack the station if necessary. Let's be smart about this, proceed with caution but proceed."

The bell at his door sounded and Paul got up opening the door. A steward stood in the doorway. Paul looked at Kevin who nodded and he let him enter the cabin while he left. Kevin sat behind his desk with his hands together thinking about the station while the steward cleaned up the table and took away the dishes. He was thinking how many things could go wrong and how devastating it could be to the mission if he lost even one person let alone an entire ship. He sighed and turned to his computer.

The preparations took three days for the fleet. Twice the *Nautilus* was sent to the area where the station was located to monitor the electronic signals and explore the surrounding space. She was able to pick up several different signals that aided the analysis team on deciphering the best signal for a ship to use. They were able to separate several signals that showed a dozen different species of space travelers. The excitement was high across the fleet. CAPT Lindsey had chosen the *Defiant* to be the ship that would dock with the space station. The ship, the Rangers, and the party that would be going into the station were running drills on emergency break away, rescue, and even attack operations. The *Nautilus* was running drills that included inserting the SEALs onto the station if that would be required. Meanwhile the FAST and MEU were running various extremist hostage rescue operations. By the end of the third day, Kevin was very pleased with the performance of all teams. He sat in his office with his Chief of Staff and Operations Officer.

CAPT Lindsey looked tired from the endless planning sessions with her staff. The Future Operations Planning Team had different scenarios dreamed up with different solutions for each one. She had gone over each and every one of the options ensuring that the fleet had their maximum protection while being able to rescue the team that would be on the station. Both the flagship and the *Chesty* would be on the highest alert to receive casualties, attack the station, and even on an off chance fight a space battle. After all there were twelve different species with their own ships out there. Who knows if they would coordinate efforts to attempt to take out the Strike Group? She believed and even felt like she owed it to everyone to be ready for this. Kevin and Paul were watching her as she poured over her hand-held device reading through the plan again. The *Defiant* would arrive outside of the sensors and travel along one of the established routes to the station. She would then, hopefully, be granted permission to dock. Once she had docked or at least be allowed to send a shuttle, the team would go onto the station. The seven-man team which would include a team leader, the linguist, a diplomat proficient with negotiations, an intel officer, and three security men would go onto the station to acquire whatever knowledge about the station, this space, who owned the station and to acquire a star map. The *Nautilus* would stay close to the station to monitor all traffic and communications to and from the station and be prepared to deliver the SEALs if required. Meanwhile the rest of the Strike Group would jump into the area outside the range of the station's sensors and wait for the mission to be over. Their only role would be a quick reaction force if the team needed rescuing beyond the capability of the *Defiant*. All hoped that would not be necessary.

CAPT Lindsey had an argument with the Marines. They wanted the security portion to be all Marines and to place on the *Defiant* an entire company. She dissuaded them from this course of action. The Admiral wanted the Rangers to be the unit for a quick reaction force or QRF if the boarding team ran into problems. Like the FAST they were trained for the kick in the door and get the hostages or prisoners. It is true the MEU trained for the mission but it was one of twenty missions that they trained for. The Rangers are better suited since their training is more specialized. Besides there is only so much room onboard the *Defiant*. Dr. Vance had picked one of his best linguists for the job. The young man was flexible in dealing with most situations. The engineers and linguists were working overtime to provide him with a translating device to aid him with the job. She was impressed by the linguists with how they were able to pick out a basic alphabet and sentence structure from the signals that were collected. She found herself almost as excited as they were for this opportunity. In the end this could help them with their primary mission. If this device proved its worth then they could adapt it for the planet they are heading for.

Kevin took a drink of his coffee. "Well, are you satisfied yet?

She looked up at him slightly embarrassed. "We are ready, Sir. Just some last-minute details."

"Planning is important, Captain. Especially for contingencies, but don't over think this.

"Yes, Sir." She put down the hand pilot, flexed out her fingers on her hands as she sat straight up in her chair and let out a deep breath. "We are ready."

"Good, then let's everyone get a good night sleep and tomorrow we will execute."

The *Defiant* jumped into normal space and performed a quick scan. Nothing showed on the sensors except the station in the distance. She then banked for one of the approach routes and moved off smartly.

The *Nautilus* was already in the area but didn't show up on the scanners thanks to her stealth. Everyone aboard knew that she was out there monitoring. It was a form of comfort knowing that she was out there. The ship continued with its scanning while maneuvering onto the traffic lane. There appeared on the screens another ship making its way along the route to the station. The *Defiant* continued her path following the other ship but from a distance. While the *Defiant* was following the route the rest of the Strike Group jumped into the space.

Kevin sat in his chair onboard the flag bridge watching the screens. After brief moments CAPT Lindsey turned from her station and reported that all ships had made the jump in the proper formation. He sat there and thought, *now we wait.*

The *Defiant* entered the communications range and sent the station the signal requesting approach and authorization to dock. The bridge crew waiting in anticipation for authorization as the ship continued to travel towards the station. The Tactical Watch Officer watching his board began getting nervous and started to flip the switch to bring weapons online.

"Why do you desire to get us shot, Lieutenant?"

The Watch Officer suddenly jerked his hand back. "Sorry, Sir."

The Captain nodded at him and looked back at his screen. The Lieutenant shook his head at himself, took a deep breath, and slowly let it out steadying himself.

The Comms Officer let out a little cry of joy when her board lit up with the answer. "Sir, we have authorization to dock." She quickly read her screen, "They are telling us to come on a heading of 0016 and dock with the upper circle. Woo, this is great."

"Alright Ensign, thank you, Helm bring us about and follow the direction. Comms send to Helm their directions."

LCDR John Reyes, the *Defiant's* Executive Officer, looked up from the screen, picked up his jacket, and looked at his team. "The Skipper just sent the word that we are on approach and for us to precede to the airlock. We will need to pay a docking fee and that is being prepared for us." He then looked at the Platoon CDR, "Hopefully I will be able to get this team back and you won't have to come get us Lieutenant." The team picked up their jackets, the three Master at arms ensuring their weapons were properly tucked away hidden from view and all seven members headed towards the airlock with the two rangers that were in the room with them.

The Helmsman brought the ship around the station along the route that the station controller had provided. Col Adams watched the screens while traveling along the path. His science section maintained their scanning of the station gathering as much data as they could. The Tactical Watch Officer stations continued their scanning for the station's weapons and shield systems. The station grew larger in the screens as the ship neared the larger disk. From a distance the station looked like a long pole with three disks, the top one being the largest and decreasing in size to the lowest. The bottom part of the pole had various antennae looking devices with some appearing to be waste disposal centers. As the *Defiant* closed in on the docking section, the appearance of a smooth disk disappeared into various external docking stations and entries into internal docking stations. There were various items that appeared to be grappling hooks, cranes, antennae, weapons, satellite dishes. The *Defiant's* sensors were taking everything in. They could see several ships attached to the external docking stations. These ships took on various shapes and sizes. Some were smaller than the *Defiant* while others were slightly larger but the majority were about the same size. As they passed some of the openings, they could see smaller ships and cargo. They were being directed towards an external docking station on the far side of the disk just below its midline.

Col Adams was excited about this opportunity and wished he could go aboard the station. He could feel the excitement and anxiety on his bridge and knew that his crew felt the same way he did. He looked at his Helmsman and noticed that he was very intent at his station ensuring that the ship cruised into the docking station. Col Adams got up and walked over to the Helmsman and placed a reassuring hand on his shoulder, "Don't worry, you are doing a great job." The Helmsman took a deep breath and slowly let it out and Col Adams could feel the tension leaving him. He looked around his bridge.

"All hands, this is awesome being able to dock with an alien station, to meet another race of intelligent beings. Only a handful of us will actually be able to do this at this time. There still is a threat and a job that we have to focus on. Let us hope that the threat proves to be false but we still have to be vigilant and the ship needs our attention. Our brave shipmates will be leaving the safety of our ship and entering an alien world. We hope they will be able to foster good relations but we must be ready to save their lives if we have mistaken this station as a potential friend. Like you, I am extremely excited about this time. This is why we are out here but keep focused on your boards. That is all."

As he turned to go back to his chair, he could feel the tension of the excitement turn into the calm that a professional has performing his task. He took his seat and observed his bridge crew finish docking his ship to the station. Soon the hatch would open and his XO would be in another world. He looked over at his Communications Officer.

"Communications, did you perform the radio check with the XO?"

"Yes Sir, all loud and clear," the Ensign responded.

"Very well. Ops, do we have the payment at the hatch?"

"Yes Sir, we have three silver bars ready. I only hope the translation came across right," he shrugged his shoulders, "also, the Rangers are standing by if anything happens."

"Yeesss," breathed the Captain, "well let's hope both the payment is correct and we don't need the Rangers."

He sat back in his chair waiting for the status reports to come in.

LCDR Reyes stood by the airlock with the three silver bars and his team. The Rangers were there but out of sight around the bulkhead. He could hear the ship slide into the berthing station. He nodded in satisfaction at the smoothness of the Helmsman. He knew the young man would be nervous with this being his first alien docking, he had done several practice runs back at Earth station both in the simulation and practicals, but this was truly his first one. But it was a smooth operation. He could hear as the docking tube was sent to the hatch opening and hear the seals go solid. He checked the airlock status and saw a solid lock between the tube and the outer hatch. He pushed a main control button on the panel and the inner hatch cycled open. He and his team stepped into the airlock and pushed a button on the inner hatch control panel and the inner hatch cycled closed. LCDR Reyes thought about locking out this control which would effectively seal them off from the rest of the ship and keep any alien from just opening the hatch. They would have to blow it and by that time the Rangers would be in place to repel any borders and the Captain could get the ship away. But that action would sacrifice his team and he had two civilians with him. *No*, he thought, *the Rangers would be pissed if he did that since they expected to rescue them if need be. Besides they were trained to be able to rescue a team and keep any intruders off, just like his ship's Master-at-arms were.* He went to the outer hatch control panel and checked again to make sure there was a hard seal. He opened the comm circuit to the bridge before unsealing the outer hatch.

"XO to bridge."

"CO here," answered the Captain.

"We are ready to open the outer hatch and exit the ship, Sir."

"Proceed when ready."

"Yes sir, we are opening now."

He turned and checked his team one last time. They were all dressed in civilian clothes with their jackets on. His three Master-at-arms and himself were all armed with their weapons concealed beneath their jackets. The Linguist had his translator at the ready, the Intel Officer with his scanner and their Diplomat with a small bag he used as a briefcase. The scanner was designed to gather data that both the scientist and intelligence sections could utilize. He pressed the button and the outer hatch cycled open.

The air initially rushed out but the tube and airlock quickly equalized. The air felt and smelled the same, sterilized and made breathable by scrubbers. The station's tube was a hard tube that the XO felt was similar to an airport gate. He stepped onto it and it proved to be solid. The team entered the tube and the last man pressed a stub that cycled the hatch closed. To open the hatch would take a hand print and a code punched into the code pad. Both the code and hand print are necessary to open the hatch which is designed to keep any intruder from just opening a hatch and entering the ship.

LCDR Reyes and his team approached the far end of the tunnel and stopped. He scanned the hatch looking for a control panel when it opened. Standing or rather squatting on the other end was a four-legged four-armed creature. Its legs formed a square as it stood there incased in a metal suit that covered it entirely. It emitted a sound and LCDR Reyes looked at John Peterson, the linguist, for a translation. Mr. Peterson watched his translator then nodded at LCDR Reyes indicating the bars. LCDR Reyes handed over the three silver bars to the creature. It accepted them with one arm and with another one took a device and waved it over them. After looking at the device it emitted another sound and stepped aside indicating that they could enter. LCDR Reyes glanced at Mr. Peterson who said, "He said welcome." LCDR Reyes nodded at him and then he and the creature proceeded into the station.

This part of the station felt like an airport. There was a waiting area just outside of the tunnel section and a gate at the far end of the waiting area. They stepped through the far gate into a tunnel that ran along the perimeter of the disk. At regular intervals on the same side as they had entered through were other gates. On the other side of the tunnel at even longer intervals were open gates with a custodian. LCDR Reyes and his team approached the closest one and passed through. Just outside of it was a map of the facility. The disk apparently had a mall area consisting of five decks; beneath the mall were other decks that appeared to be service and cargo areas. The deck immediately above the mall had what might be administrative offices and the three decks above it did not indicate what they might be for. LCDR Reyes looked at Mr. Peterson.

"Can you scan the symbols into the translator and see what it shows these decks to be?"

"Yes, I can." Mr. Peterson then stepped up and scanned the names of the decks into his translator. The translator confirmed what LCDR Reyes thought from the general design of the disk. The bottom decks were designed for cargo and ship services, the middle decks are where the mall is located; the deck immediately above the mall was administrative, with the upper decks reserved for station personnel only. LCDR Reyes smiled to himself thinking how this spaceport was a lot like any port he visited so far. Why would he need an interpreter? He looked at the map but didn't see any sign of the other disks. *No big deal,* he thought.

"Alright, let's head to the mall area and make our way to the administrative level."

He then looked around and not seeing anyone watching him, keyed his communication device by pressing a button. "*Defiant,* Reyes here."

"Copy loud and clear, status."

"We are through the gate and about to enter a mall area where I expect to find various shops and then we will make our way to an administrative level."

"Copy."

"Reyes out."

"*Defiant* out."

LCDR Reyes looked at his team, "Let's go."

They moved towards the opening to the lowest level of the mall. *How convenient,* thought LCDR Reyes, *they had these openings open onto the lowest level of the mall. Obviously, they desired the visitors to spend as much as they could.* The hatch opened at his approach and the group was instantly assaulted by such a strong and overpowering smell of creatures, scents, spices, and other items that they could not identify. When they stepped into the mall the myriad of activity seemed overwhelming at first. Located in no particular order were several kiosks selling various wares by creatures beyond their wildest imagination. The creatures came in all shapes and sizes. The various dialects and sounds that they were emitting were beyond the capability of the translator, and Mr. Peterson looked both excited and complexed by it all. The lighting wasn't too bright in the entire area and seemed to come from high above. They looked up and could see that the mall did consist of five floors, with the roof actually above the top floor of the open mall. They began walking through the place, Mr. Peterson attempting to catalogue the various languages and Capt Andy Jackson, the Intelligence Officer, gathering as much data from the area as he could. The Security Team was astonished at what they were seeing but covered their backs and sides. LCDR Reyes, after his initial shock, began scanning the area looking for any kiosk that might sale star maps or any useful information. While he saw a lot of interesting items that he would love to explore, he kept focused on his objective. It was the only way he could see not to get entangled in the kiosk and the wares. However, he moved slowly along looking for any stairs, escalators, or elevators to take them to the next level. He knew the Intel Officer, Linguist, and Diplomat wanted to stay and gather information so he gave them as much of an opportunity as he could but kept the team moving.

• • •

VADM Brannigan was in his office when he heard his comm system beep. He keyed the switch, "Brannigan here."

"Yes, Sir," answered CAPT Lindsey, "we received a tight beam signal from the *Defiant*. They have successfully docked at the station and the team is inside. The payment of three small silver bars was accepted. So far everything is good to go. The *Defiant* has continued to scan the station and are cataloguing the data."

"Thank you." He keyed the switch off.

Good, first contact and so far, all is good. He started reading the fleet reports again waiting for the report from the *Nautilus*. Soon he would start reading from his personal library a book that looked rather promising but first had to finish these reports.

On the fringes of the station's sensors the *Nautilus* maintained a silent watch on the communications arriving and being sent from the station. Her crew finally picked up a frequency that they were attempting to isolate since it seemed to be beamed out to deep space. All other frequencies were normal space traffic and trade. But this frequency was a tight beam which made the *Nautilus'* crew curious. They were attempting to zero in on it to find out what was contained within the signal and where it was heading.

LCDR Reyes finally got his team up to the third floor. So far, he hadn't seen anything that looked like star maps and Mr. Peterson hadn't been able to translate anything that indicated such a place. They had noticed several different shops that sold what appeared to be food, definitely clothing and space suits, various equipment for ships, weapons, generators, food processors, and other items that they couldn't identify at this time. They stopped and looked at the generators and weapons stores. They were storing information on these shops in case they decided to buy some before they left for the engineers to look at. The weapons included projectiles and energy versions but were primarily individual type weapons. LCDR Reyes and Capt Jackson were interested in seeing if this station would provide upgrades to ships but didn't see anything in the mall to indicate this but they kept in mind there were two other disks to this station. One could be berthing and station servicing but what would the other one be?

The team reached the fourth level and noticed that these shops were slightly different. They appeared to be more of consultation type booths. After checking several of them out they determined these were the upgrade shops for ships. One shop focused on shielding, another on weapons, a different one on ship generators and reactors, yet another on medical capabilities, and another on environmental, and on and on. They came across a few shops with crystals being advertised as a power source. LCDR Reyes made sure they spent some time in these shops and had instructed Capt Jackson to ensure he got data on these. In one of the shops, they discovered they could place an order to upgrade ships with items purchased from these shops, if they desired them to be installed, they would have to make arrangements with the administrative level to have their ships transferred to the lowest disk for the upgrades. This disk was the station's space garage.

They finally found what they were looking for on this floor. Several stores that offered databases to include various star maps. The star maps could be bought for specific regions, trade routes, mining opportunities, galactic regions, galactic governments, and much more. They inquired about the various prices for each item and methodology of payment. Something they had discovered about the mall in regards to payment depended on what it was you wanted. Some items could be bought right there at the kiosk or store and others had to be arranged from the administrative level. LCDR Reyes decided he wanted to see this level along with the fifth level of the mall.

They reached the fifth level and noticed that there were fewer shops and they were larger. As they approached them, they noticed that some had stages and all of them had cages. Some of the cages were filled with various creatures and most of the shops had at least a few cages filled. They had seen what appeared to be pet stores on some of the lower levels but these were different. Mr. Peterson suddenly looked up from his translating device looking shocked and sick.

"These are slave shops." He turned to LCDR Reyes. "We have to do something about this, this is wrong!" The emotions in his voice started to rise.

LCDR Reyes looked around at the various cages in the one store they were standing in front of. The various creatures looked down trodden. Some were in excellent shape and others were being prepped, either for their new masters or to go on sale. But they all had that look in their various forms of eyes, at least the more mammal looking eyes, of hopelessness. LCDR Reyes started walking away from this particular location and heading for the administrative level.

"Wait, where are you going?" called Mr. Peterson, "I said we have to do something."

LCDR Reyes turned slowly towards him while scanning the area and said in a low voice, "That is not for us to decide. We will report this to our authority and let them decide what will be done." Mr. Peterson just gaped at him. "We need to act like we are not bothered by this. Remember this is neither our space nor our jurisdiction. Any interference on our part can get us killed and cause problems for those waiting on us. We will report all we find." He then turned and started heading towards the ramp. The team followed him and Mr. Peterson continued to look sick but didn't say anything.

LCDR Reyes had been to plenty of spots on Earth that still had human trafficking going on. The United States among other nations were attempting to stop it but it existed even in the U.S. He didn't like it at home but if they couldn't stop it there then how could they stop sentient beings from being sold all the way out here. Well one thing for certain wherever there was intelligent life then there were all the vices that went along with it to include this despicable act. No doubt then there were also various forms of mind-altering drugs to be had.

Dr. Vance and his Chief Engineer, Dr. Joseph, sat in the Admiral's office waiting for him to arrive. They had their presentation ready and Dr. Joseph's excitement could hardly be contained. He even got up twice now to pace the room. Dr. Vance continued to look patient. He was used to dealing with policy makers and the military types. Over excitement usually drove them into their ultra conservative mode but at times it could energize them. It just depended on the subject and if there was a good plan of execution for implementation. His view of Vice Admiral Brannigan was that of a reasonable man but a commander of a fleet on a dangerous mission and thus very conservative in what happens to the fleet. This may prove to be a tough sale. Dr. Vance was glad that he could get this one-on-one time with the Fleet Commander, especially with the excited Dr. Joseph. Damn engineers could get out of control once they had a pet project that was succeeding.

The hatch slid open and VADM Brannigan and CAPT Lindsey both entered the office. Damn, he was hoping it would just be the Admiral but now the Ops Officer was here. Dr. Vance maintained his blank expression as he had learned to do during the years. The two officers took respective seats, the Admiral at the head of the table and the CAPT to his left. This way everyone could see the view screen at the other end of the table.

"Well, Doctors," started the Admiral, "you have a presentation of the crystals I understand."

"Yes sir." Dr. Vance began, "we have been able to perform tests on the crystals and have figured out a way to harness their energies to our benefit. I hope that you will like what you see and perhaps we can make some modifications to improve our energy output."

"Very well, let's see what you have."

"Dr. Joseph, please show us your presentation." Dr. Vance turned over the meeting to Dr. Joseph.

"Thank you, Sir, for this opportunity to present these results." Dr. Joseph began while acknowledging everyone in the room. He then touched a pad to bring up his presentation on the viewscreen.

"As you know Sir, we saw a promise of increasing our output across all of our systems." Started the Engineer, "but we haven't implemented our ideas due to the operations of the fleet. We did acquire a spare generator from the Cheng or Chief Engineer of the ship to perform experiments. We were able to adopt the generator to the crystals and were able to double the output of the generator."

"Excellent news, Doctor," CAPT Lindsey interrupted. "I have already seen your report on the output of the generator. My question is, while your experiments are promising, can our circuitry support the output?"

Dr. Joseph looked a little perplexed but responded, "Yes Ma'am, the systems can handle the output. We could increase the shields, weapons, all categories of life support, sciences, and the hyperspace drive."

She continued, "How do you recommend we proceed with modifications."

The two Doctors looked at each other. Dr. Vance said, "You have already decided on the modifications?"

The Admiral spoke up, "No we haven't. I just don't really desire to listen to the whole presentation. I am more interested in the fact that the experiments proved that we can utilize these crystals. It seems the answer is yes. But I am not too inclined to take any systems offline for modifications. CAPT Lindsey was able to get an advanced viewing of your brief and is on your side for the modifications."

"Ah I see Sir," responded Dr. Vance. He looked over at Dr. Joseph and thought for a few moments.

"Dr. Joseph, I recommend that you skip to the schedule of modifications. I also think that we ought to show the projected results."

"Yes, Doctor." Dr. Joseph quickly keyed in the two slides that were requested and brought up the schedule on the view screen. "Admiral Sir, we recommend that we start with the drives so we can make longer and quicker jumps. Then we can move to the weapons and shields. The deflector in particular must be updated which will enable us to deflect any objects and it will be even more stable to aid in the elimination of the hyperspace side effects. Then we can move onto the secondary devices." He switched to the next slide. "Our projections show a twenty three percent greater output of the energy weapons, a greater stability for the shielding that should increase their effectiveness against energy weapons by sixty percent and even be able to stop missiles. And," Dr. Joseph stopped when he noticed the Admiral raised his hand. The Admiral continued to look at the view screen showing the results.

"Dr. Joseph, you have got to be kidding about these results." He looked at both Dr. Vance and CAPT Lindsey.

"Sir, we ran these results six times and noticed only a plus minus of one percent in any single results. These results are solid."

The Admiral looked at Dr. Vance, "Have you independently confirmed these results, Doctor?"

Dr. Vance smiled and handed his hand pad to the Admiral, "Yes Sir, I have."

The pad was not taken by the Admiral; instead, he motioned for the previous slide and said to CAPT Lindsey, "You think this should be done?"

"Yes Sir, this will increase our effectiveness and thus aid us in our mission."

"Umph." The Admiral sat there looking at the view screen thinking. *It would be good to increase their capability but at what expense? The designers and engineers worked very diligently to get this fleet this far and there wasn't a space dock that they could afford to put into for any upgrades.* Alright he decided; this is a good thing that these results showed but he didn't like the schedule.

"Gentlemen, I don't like your schedule. CAPT Lindsey, work with them on this. The deflectors can be the first thing to be upgraded along with the secondary systems. The Hyperspace drive is absolutely the last upgrade to occur. I don't want that offline until we know for sure that these upgrades will work. Work on the schedule by ship and system."

"Yes, Sir." Both the Captain and the Admiral left the room to go to the flag bridge.

"What was that about, how did she get my results?" Dr. Joseph inquired of Dr. Vance.

He smiled in return. "I sent them to her and had a private meeting with her. I already knew that the Admiral may like the idea but wouldn't approve of any upgrades unless we had her support. Sorry, but I needed to stack the deck in your favor. I know that you really desired to give the presentation but you will learn that a lot of times a presentation must be brief or they won't listen."

Dr. Joseph took it in and nodded, "Then thank you. I know this is the right thing to do."

"I agree, now you need to see CAPT Lindsey about setting a time to get the schedule right. Send her an email asking when you can meet. She will respond and let you know when and where. I recommend yourself and one other and no more." Dr. Vance then got up and Dr. Joseph followed him out of the Admiral's office.

. . .

LCDR Reyes sat in Col Adams's working office drinking his coffee. Col Adams sat behind his desk watching him. LCDR Reyes had one of those looks that said he didn't like things that he had seen but not a whole lot he could do about it.

"The space station is a slave market. Oh, you can buy a variety of things to include upgrading one's ship. The station administrators are willing to upgrade the ship. They have a space dock that they can do this with. They even have crystal technology and the know how to incorporate it. But I wonder if it is a smart thing to use them."

"Alright, John, I will send a tight beam message to the flagship with your report. We will see what else in addition to the star maps we may desire to acquire. Meanwhile draw the proper payment for the maps. You and your team will go back and acquire them."

"Yes, Sir." LCDR Reyes excused himself and left the office.

Col Adams shook his head. *Great slave traders even out here. Well, no doubt they wouldn't do anything about it; after all they didn't have any information about this sector or these people.* He turned to his computer and keyed up LCDR Reyes' report and added his assessment. He then keyed up the Communications Officer and entered in his code. Once the system was accessed, he sent the message on a tight secure beam to the *Intrepid*.

The Admiral sat in the conference room with his Chief of Staff, CAPT Lindsey, Dr. Vance and Michael O'Shea his diplomat. They each had a copy of the *Defiant's* report and were finishing reading it.

The Admiral said, "Opinions."

Dr. Vance said, "This station has items that we need. It would help us to have this information about the crystals and maybe even to use their station to upgrade. But using their facilities very well could compromise our security."

"I agree, our security would be compromised." MajGen Connington seconded.

CAPT Lindsey looked up from the hand device, "I think we should acquire as much of the technology and maps as possible but not utilize their station. Our scientists and engineers can figure out the technology and information that we acquire." She looked at Dr. Vance who nodded in agreement.

Mike O'Shea responded, "Anything we purchase aids the slave trade in this sector. Don't we have a responsibility to stop these transactions or at least not to add to them?"

Dr. Vance responded, "We wouldn't be adding too much capital into this system but we would be gaining a whole lot more. It is worth the price."

MajGen Connington went further, "We need to know about space and what is out here not to immediately affect a change or create enemies that could prevent us from achieving our mission. We are explorers not a bunch of do-gooders."

"Yes, that is true," continued O'Shea, "but we shouldn't add to the misery of others. I would advocate that we attack and stop this evil practice but... well that would create enemies for us out here and jeopardize our mission. Instead, I say that we travel on and not add to their misery by providing them any capital."

The Admiral sat back in his chair, "Well great. I wasn't expecting a slave market all the way out here but we have run into pirates so we should expect things like this. We have an ethical question in front of us. If we answer it by our values, it could cost us our mission and lives. If we ignore it then we may be safe but others suffer. If we purchase the things that could aid us, we may very well aid in the suffering of others."

He continued his thoughts in silence. The others waited. After several moments he let out a deep breath.

"I want star maps, databases, and weapons for our study along with other technologies. My interest is not in technologies or toys. Rather my desire is to gain all the intelligence on these species and the area of space that we are involved with and likely to be involved with. My reasoning is for the safety of Earth herself. If we don't know anything about this area and those that dwell in it then our planet and people are in danger. When we travel out here, as we will, we need to prepare to fight off pirates and slavers. I am not ready to start a war out here though. We will prepare for the future by acquiring knowledge. Mr. O'Shea you are right to point out the moral issues and the policies from our own nation but we are not positioned correctly to affect a change at this time and I don't know if we ever will be. CAPT Lindsey send to *Defiant* the items that we will purchase."

"Yes, Sir."

"Meanwhile has *Nautilus* figured out anything about that signal that they tracked?"

MajGen Connington answered, "They have figured out the direction that it was sent to but nothing else. They are still monitoring the frequency for anymore transmissions."

The Admiral nodded and dismissed them.

After everyone left, Kevin shook his head and put it down on the table. His thoughts went back to Earth and all the evil that human trafficking had produced over the millennia. Of course, slavery was out here, why wouldn't it be? But now an even greater threat existed towards Earth. His fellow humans could end up as slaves to some alien. He wondered about all those stories of alien abductions. How many actually occurred or were they just stories? If so, how many of them were slavers visiting his planet? His anger started to rise as he thought more about this. He got up and paced around the table. He knew he made the right decision about not interfering with the station's practices and to acquire the technology. But it still made him angry at the thought of such a practice and that humans may have already been kidnapped by aliens or could possibly be turned into slaves.

He was out of range to contact Earth with this warning and he hoped that they could return before anyone could leave her and travel out into deep space.

•   •   •

LCDR Reyes purchased several items to include energy weapons, generators, crystals, various spices, and other technologies from the mall. He purchased a few databases that Capt Jackson and Mr. Peterson indicated had information that related to their mission. He was able to get schematics on shields, drives and generator technology. His purchase of the star maps was the most difficult. He had to buy what he knew would be totally worthless maps in order to avoid giving away any information of where they came from or where they might be heading. LCDR Reyes and his team were back aboard the *Defiant* waiting to go. He was going over the scans of the slaves in the slave market. Medical had given them a scanner to take bio scans and he was able to go into the market and make the scans. All of this data would be sent to the *Intrepid* once they had jumped from this sector. He was sitting in the ship's conference room with Capt Jackson and Mr. Peterson categorizing the items with a couple of scientists in order to send the items over.

Col Adams watched the station on the ship's main view screen as they departed. His Helmsman maintained a straight track away from the station. This suited him fine since they would achieve greater distance between his ship and the station. The station was very specific about the heading they were to take and was so emphatic about it that Col Adams was starting to wonder about it.

"Comm, send a tight beam message to the flagship with our heading. Also, let them know that the station was very specific about it and that we are going to yellow alert." He turned to his Ops, "Sound yellow alert and get me a status on all systems."

"Aye aye, Sir."

The Admiral sat in his chair reading the communiqué from the *Defiant* on one of his view screens. CAPT Lindsey had alerted him to the message. He was thinking about the implications of this action. He looked up at the main view screen which had the station on it and looked at the screen to its left that showed the tactical picture. The

Defiant continued slowly along the track provided by the station. The *Nautilus* maintained a parallel course shadowing the ship. The rest of the fleet was on a course that placed the station between them and the other two ships. He suddenly did not like this picture. The *Defiant* was outside of the protective envelope of the Strike Group. It further weakened the overall capability of his fleet. He was thankful for the fact that the *Nautilus* had a stealth capability which rendered her almost invisible.

He looked at CAPT Lindsey, "Have the *Excalibur* head at full speed to join up with *Defiant*. Have *Nautilus* go to General Quarters. Bring the fleet in tighter and let's plot a circular course around the station. I want to keep an eye on it. Monitor the frequency that *Nautilus* picked up on. Have we broken the code on it yet?"

"No Sir, we have not."

He grimaced, "Okay, keep working on it. Even if nothing happens and we jump away I want this broken. Alright, put the fleet at yellow alert."

"Yes, Sir." She turned and started issuing orders for the transmissions to the fleet. The Admiral watched his bridge crew and was pleased with their actions. He watched his viewers along with the main viewers on the bulkhead. The *Defiant* was already at yellow alert, *Nautilus* was always silent. *Excalibur* signaled they were at yellow alert and were moving off to join up with *Defiant*; her fighters were being loaded into the tubes to be launched. Meanwhile the fleet was indicating that they were achieving the alert status and were closing up ranks. Not too bad on how quickly the ships were achieving the status. The *Intrepid*, *Icarus*, and *Chesty* reported their fighters were in the launch tubes, armed and ready. The fleet started moving off on their new heading.

Col Adams noted that he received word from the station that they could not jump yet since they were still in the station's traffic circle and it would be unsafe for the station. He looked at his Astrogator for his confirmation of this. He shook his head no and indicated that they were a safe distance from it. He leaned forward looking at a couple of screens.

The bridge crew were starting to tense up at the anticipation of trouble. Col Adams rubbed his chin with his hand, "Bring the shields online."

"Yes, Sir," responded the Tactical Watch Officer and he flipped the switch and watched as the shields energized. "Shields online, Sir."

"Very good. Anything on the sensors?"

"No, Sir." The Watch Officer responded.

The Col sat back and was deep in thought. They were now approximately thirty kilometers from the station when the lights flickered; klaxons began to sound and then stopped. The drives suddenly went offline and the ship started to turn.

"Helm is not responding, Sir." The Helmsman reported.

The Col immediately switched his comms for the engine room. Nothing occurred. He reached forward for the sound activated phone, "Engine Room status."

The Chief Engineer responded, "Sir, everything is offline. I can't explain it."

"Do we have anything?"

"No sir, we are trying to get the drives online."

"I want the shields first then the drives and sensors."

"Yes, Sir."

"Damn!" He looked over at the Helmsman, "Can you tell about..."

Suddenly the shipped jerked to a halt, the entire bridge crew grabbed for something to keep from falling out of their seats. Col Adams grabbed his chair. That was an awful jolt.

"Sir," the Helmsman was speaking, "forward motion has stopped but I can't get helm control."

The *Excalibur* was halfway between the station and the *Defiant* when *Defiant* suddenly seemed to lose control and stopped dead in space.

CAPT Murphy called for General Quarters, klaxons sounded throughout the ship.

"Helm, slow us and turn port by five degrees. Sensors, what happened to *Defiant*? Prepare to launch fighters." The Captain said.

The ship began to turn onto the new course.

The Tactical Watch Officer reported, "Sir, sensors are picking up an energy field around the *Defiant*. It appears to be coming from sources that are in the area surrounding her. I think it is some kind of energy net designed to drain power and stop a ship."

"Can you target the sources?"

"I believe so, Sir."

"Anything else on sensors?" As he finished asking the question the main viewer showed a hyperspace well opening.

"Send the coordinates of the energy field sources to the fighters. I want them to knock out those items. Once the fighters are away, bring the shields and weapons online. Keep us away from the energy field and let's engage whatever is coming out of the well."

Ten fighters received the coordinates of the projected devices and received launch orders. All ten fighters launched, five from one arm and five from the other. They formed up two wings and headed towards the coordinates; weapons charged. The *Excalibur* fired up her shields and began moving towards the ships that were coming into normal space.

There were three ships of approximate size to the *Excalibur*, they had the appearance of a solid block with the nose of the ship sloping down to a snubbed nose. The *Excalibur's* sensors picked up several weapon systems that were charged. CAPT Murphy was angling *Excalibur* towards the ship to his left.

VADM Brannigan ordered General Quarters when it was reported that *Defiant* had come to a full stop. His first thought was the station and how it was responding. It was reported that ten ships, slightly smaller than the *Defiant*, were launching from the station. A quick scan indicated that their weapon systems were inferior to the fleets. He ordered all but the *Chesty's* fighters away to attack the ships from the station.

MajGen Connington approached the flag chair, "Well, it appears that the station uses energy fields to capture ships. They probably use them to capture them for slaves and steal technology."

VADM Brannigan responded, "Yes, that is a safe assumption especially with these ten ships being launched. Apparently though this group isn't used to having a fleet around them. If you notice those ten ships are heading for *Defiant* just like those three are. They are ignoring us and *Excalibur*."

MajGen Connington thought about this, "Then I recommend we send a strike team against the station and destroy it."

"Destroy it? What about the innocents onboard?"

"How do we know who is an innocent?"

"Doesn't matter, we will determine the fate of the station later, first let's win this battle. CAPT Lindsey keep the *Intrepid, Chesty,* and *Icarus* here to keep any other ships from departing the station. Send *Scimitar* to aid *Excalibur*."

"Yes, Sir."

Col Adams hated this portion of any operation, just sitting waiting for something to happen. He already had the XO get with the Rangers and ensure they could repel boarders. They were ready for any attack on the ship itself, now he just needed power and maneuverability.

"They have left us," complained the Comm Officer.

Col Adams responded, "No Ensign, no one has left us. They are either working on how to free us from the energy field or they are in a fight. I just wished that we could get out of this thing and engage."

CAPT Murphy wasn't too happy. His shields were taking a beating; he had already lost his starboard shields. He had his ship roll away from his two opponents and was trying to break through their shields with his energy weapons. He really wanted to send in his missiles but his sensors indicated that the shields could stop those. He was happy to see that the *Scimitar* was on its way which caused the third ship that had come through the hyperspace well to engage her vice stay on his ship. At least he was holding off these two ships. He just wished his fighters would get through with that energy field and was considering calling them back.

Admiral Brannigan watched the tactical view screen. Soon after the *Scimitar* went off to aid *Excalibur* one of the three ships had turned and engaged her. The *Excalibur's* fighters were trying to break the energy field but were having difficulty. Meanwhile the other thirty fighters were engaged with more ships from the station. They were holding their own. The surprise was the station itself. Soon after they deployed the station had opened up on the remaining three ships. The *Intrepid*, *Icarus*, and *Chesty* were holding off the fire and attempting to break the station's shields.

"Captain, do you have a fix on the station's generators?" He asked CAPT Lindsey.

"Sir, it appears that the main generator is at the bottom below the third disk."

Admiral Brannigan keyed up the Commanding Officers of the *Chesty*, *Icarus,* and *Intrepid*, "COs, here is what I want. *Intrepid* will drop on the z axis and take out the generators below the third disk. *Icarus* and *Chesty* go up and gain entry into the station. *Icarus* provide cover for *Chesty*. Marines gain entry and take over this station. Caution to you, don't assume that those that are to be sold into slavery are friends, they probably are not. Get in there and take that station!" He switched off the comm just as the COs were acknowledging the order. Within moments the *Icarus* and *Chesty* moved up the z axis to attack the shielding at the top of the station while his ship moved down to attack the shield.

"CAPT Smith," he had keyed in the *Intrepid's* Commanding Officer, "we will enjoy a rough ride through the station's shields if that is required." She acknowledged and prepared the ship for the attack.

The *Intrepid* began exploratory fire against the station's shields attempting to find a weakness. CAPT Smith looked at her Tactical Watch Officer who seemed perplexed by the lack of impact on its shields. Meanwhile the Marines were suiting up in their EVAs/body armor and boarding their transports. The *Chesty* launched her ten fighters that would provide close support for the transports as the *Icarus* was laying on the fire at the shields protecting the top of the utmost disk. Meanwhile one of the fighters flew at an angle and began to penetrate the shield.

CAPT Murphy was shocked at the sudden light up on one of the screens where one of his opponents was on. The enemy ship suddenly lisped onto its port side and started to roll out of control venting its atmosphere out into space. It was no longer a player in this fight. All fire from this ship had stopped and it was starting to roll into the other enemy ship.

"CONCENTRATE ALL FIRE ON THE OTHER SHIP. Move us onto the other side and let's try and get them to collide." CAPT Murphy ordered his crew. Excitement was in his voice as he yelled his initial order and the crew was energized.

The *Excalibur* began moving onto the port side of the remaining ship employing constant energy fire onto its shields. She was not letting up on the fire trying to overload the enemy's shielding and attempting to make it maneuver into the out-of-control ship. The sensors indicated that the shielding was beginning to weaken on the enemy ship. CAPT Murphy had missiles launched at the ship and one did get through and impacted the port side of the ship. It had the effect of cracking its hull. At this time both enemy ships collided. The explosion lit up the view screens and all fire ceased from the ships. The shields collapsed and the energy weapons of the *Excalibur* started punching gaping holes into the side of the ship and the explosions continued.

"What is the status of the *Scimitar*?" CAPT Murphy requested.

After a few moments, "Sir, she is holding off the other ship but doesn't seem to be making any impact on its shields."

"Tactical, are these two ships anymore of a threat?" He asked his Tactical Watch Officer. The Watch Officer checked his scanners and responded, "No, Sir. They are currently dead in space."

"Great and congratulations. Now let's get over and assist *Scimitar*."

The *Excalibur* moved up and to its starboard and moved into position directly behind the third enemy ship. Once she was in position, she opened fire from her main energy cannons and maintained a constant fire. As the enemy ship attempted to maneuver the *Excalibur* matched its movement in order to keep directly behind her with constant fire.

The *Scimitar* immediately dropped below the alien ship and then quickly maneuvered to the top side and fired four missiles into the top shields. Her sensors indicated that the shields dropped and she fired six missiles directly into the exposed hull. The explosions lit up their view screens as the enemy ship began igniting.

The lone fighter from the *Chesty* got through the shields and shot an emitter that appeared to be for the shields. Meanwhile *Icarus* had a constant barrage of fire upon the shields. She smashed the shields after the emitter was destroyed by the fighter. The Marines began their assault upon the disk. The fighters swooped in upon the emitters destroying the fire systems and knocking out dampening fields. The Marines' transports landed on the disk and they exited in orderly fashion heading for the airlock. They quickly blew it open and entered. The station was ready for them. The internal defenders of the station fired into the airlock when it was blown. The Marines backed out at this first fire and tossed in grenades. The resulting detonation blew the defenders back killing several of them. The Marines charged into the lock and forced the remaining defenders back. After the initial area was secured, they moved into the remaining areas of the top three decks securing them killing any who resisted. Those that surrendered were rounded up and locked into the same slave cages as the captured creatures.

The fighters from *Excalibur* finally blew apart two of the devices that held the *Defiant*. The energy field began to weaken. They went to work on a third one.

Intrepid was able to ride through the shielding and disable the power system of the station.

Scimitar returned to the *Intrepid* in order to protect her while *Excalibur* traveled back to the location that *Defiant* was held to aid in freeing her. *Chesty* and *Icarus* maintained their position. With the Marines having captured the top portion of the disk and the other ships in place no one else was departing the station.

The Admiral along with his Aide, Dr. Vance, Mr. Peterson, Mr.

O'Shea, CAPT Lindsey, and the Fleet Anti-Terrorism Security Team (FAST) walked along the station's command deck. MajGen Connington remained onboard the *Intrepid* to command the fleet and keep it at alert status. *Defiant* was finally freed from the energy field and her power was slowly being restored with life support as the primary system to be repaired. The Admiral stepped into the Station Commander's office. The commander was dead; the Marines had killed it in order to keep it from setting the self-destruct of the station. The Admiral looked at the creature that was the Station's Commander. It was a bipedal creature with fur along its body. It would have stood over six feet tall. The Marines went center of mass for the kill and was successful which indicated a similar internal organ structure to humans. The head was intact showing three eyes, slits for nostrils and a mouth. The Admiral had found this to be interesting and more to his mind wishing that this wasn't necessary for his fleet's survival but it was. He lost two fighters in the space battle and a squad of Marines in the take down of the station. Several crew members on the ships were in medical and fortunately none of them were critical and would be returned to duty in a matter of days. He wasn't too pleased about the situation. Two encounters with aliens that resulted in battles.

Mr. O'Shea looked sad, "I wish we could have spoken to him and maybe had a peaceful resolution."

"Yes, that would have been nice," The Admiral responded, "but remember he or it, maybe it is a male, was a slaver and desired to capture our ship probably for that purpose and piracy. We had no choice but to eliminate him." He sighed, "Now I have to decide what to do about this station and those on it."

O'Shea looked shocked, "What do you mean? We leave it right?"

"Maybe," said the Admiral, "I don't want to leave an enemy on our track. When we come back this way what will we have? A station that will fight us or not?"

"What do you intend to do then?" asked the Diplomat.

The Admiral shrugged, "Maybe destroy it after we get all the data we can from it." He looked to Dr. Vance, "Get your scientists started on raiding the databases. I now own this station by right of conquest and I want all the data and technology possible."

Dr. Vance looked both excited and concerned, "Yes Admiral, but is that the right thinking."

"Not necessarily but these people attacked us for our technology and persons for slaves, in my thinking and therefore deserve no less. The evidence suggests such a thing." He then looked to Mr. Peterson and CAPT Lindsey, "Find me someone who would be in charge of this station with this one dead and who could speak for the captives. Maybe we can find a solution to this situation without the station's destruction. Dr. Vance in addition to the raiding I want to know who or what put this station here. That signal that brought those three ships here is an indicator that someone does own this thing and will be interested in what happens. I want to know if I am dealing with more pirates or an actual government."

"Yes, sir." The party split up to carry out the Admiral's orders.

Colonel Roberts entered the room while the Admiral was staring at the Commander's remains.

"Sir, we have total control of this station. My Marines are stationed throughout all three disks augmented by some of the ship's Master-at-arms. The populace is subdued but I can tell they are slightly concerned about their well-being."

"Good, let's keep them slightly concerned it may just help keep them under control until we depart. I am; however, hoping to find someone that we can make comfortable and trust. Any thoughts?"

"Not on whom that can be. We have been busy securing the station."

"Thank you." The Admiral turned to him, "contact *Intrepid*, see what is on the scanners and tell my CAG that I want a CAP on this place."

"Yes, Sir." The Colonel turned and left to carry out the order. The Admiral considered if he could carry out his desires while they were here and what danger there would be. He looked to his Aide, "contact Dr. Vance, I want to know how quickly with this station's facilities we could upgrade the generators, shields and weapons."

"Yes, Sir."

He then turned to the FAST, "Let's go for a walk."

CHAPTER 5

Twenty days later the fleet was on the move. *Defiant* was fully repaired and all ships were upgraded. Their shields, weapons, drive system, and other systems had greater power and consistency. The Admiral was happy with these results and the fact that he didn't have to destroy the station.

His victory over the alien fleet and the station was due to the *Nautilus* and the lone fighter from the *Chesty*. The *Nautilus* had come into the battle by concentrating her fire upon one spot of an alien ship while *Excalibur* was battling two of them. Once *Nautilus* had punched a hole in the ship's shields, she launched one of her hypersonic missiles into the ship rendering a floating hunk of metal that collided with the other alien warship. The other key factor was the fighter that went through the shield and destroyed the shield emitter of the station. Admiral Brannigan had no problem awarding the fighter pilot and providing to *Nautilus* a replacement hypersonic missile.

Now they had used the station's garage to upgrade all of their ships. They had better shields to withstand any attack. With the station's technical schematics and guidelines their ships should be on par with any other ship in these regions. All of the ships were about to lose their shields in the space battle but now they had a fighting chance. In addition, their weapon systems were far more improved. They could deliver as much as they receive. The lasers output was at least equal to that of the alien ships that came against them. In addition, all other systems had a more consistent and stable power source. Even the *Nautilus* was improved but this one was a little trickier. They had to clear all of the inhabitants off the third disk so they couldn't see the ship. This was accomplished and now he had a much-improved fleet.

The other gratifying factor was the station and its inhabitants. He was able to set the captives free. Michael O'Shea had provided letters of introduction to some of these species. They were careful not to let anyone know anything about whom or what they are or where Earth is; they didn't even mention the planet. They looked to the species that seemed the most civilized or friendly people to give these letters to that had a government. The other species they allowed them to depart from the station. The new Station Administrator seemed friendly. It didn't know where the transmission was sent to or where the ships came from and didn't seem to care. They hadn't found any information in the databases about the station's controllers or the ships. This fact still bothered the Strike Group's leadership. But they went ahead and put the creature in charge with a type of warning that they would be back this way.

Now the fleet was forming up. They were able to retrieve information about the energy field and the devices that created it in order to avoid any more of the traps. There were two other such fields. They had deactivated them, captured a few of the devices for study and destroyed the rest. Now they had the freedom to maneuver and began heading towards their jump point.

The *Nautilus* had already made the jump to the next point to check out the area and to perform the final test to the hyperspace drive upgrade. VADM Brannigan sat in his command chair waiting for the jump back while the fleet moved into position. Part of him wanted to jump along the heading of that strange transmission but his mission to the Kammorrigan home world took precedence. It would have to fall to another commander to follow that track. *Oh well,* he thought. He was waiting patiently while the Strike Group made their final adjustments to get into position. They were outside the scanning range of the station so the Administrator could not follow their route. Now they just had to wait for the *Nautilus* to return.

It didn't take long for the *Nautilus* to return giving a green signal to the jump drive and thumbs up for the area they would be jumping to. The signal went out from the *Intrepid* and the hyperspace well opened up and the fleet moved through. The engineering departments showed successful hyperspace engines and astrogation showed they were on their designated course. This jump was only for a day's travel to test the new upgrades.

After a day the jump was completed. These new upgrades showed that they could travel further and faster than the engines with the old power systems. The crystals and the schematics for their use in generators and reactors proved to be a success to the fleet. The reports were positive across the board. Now the Admiral was anxious to get to their destination. They had been traveling for seven months. The station was a blessing in not only the technological advance but they were able to replenish stores from it. Now came the experimentation with the food items. Medical and the biologists had cleared the food items fit for human consumption, now they had to figure out how to cook the stuff. Everyone was looking forward to the new food.

CAPT Lindsey began her work with the Astrogators from all the ships in plotting the new course for the fleet to get to the Kammorrigans. The test showed they could travel farther in the same amount of time and everything had to be recalculated. Fortunately, the star maps that they were able to acquire would aid them. The scientists and astrogators had scoured the maps to ensure they had correct maps that would aid in the travel to and from Kammorriga. They discovered that none of the maps indicated that Earth was charted. Ensuring they had the right maps they bounced them off of the maps that they had created during their travel to this point. They were moving along at normal space at the jump site waiting for the astrogators to recalculate the course.

The space that they were in was empty in regards to traffic, stars or other heavenly body. The sensors didn't pick up anything. The Admiral authorized for a CAP to be launched while they were making their calculations and flight training. The Marines performed sustainment training along with the pilots while at the station but this was open space which gave another form of sustainment training for the pilots.

VADM Brannigan, MajGen Connington and Michael O'Shea sat in the Admiral's office having dinner together.

"Alright Mr. O'Shea what is it that you are concerned about?" Asked MajGen Connington.

"Well Sir, it is the ease with which we raided the station for the information and technology. It doesn't seem right to me. We should have negotiated a settlement with the administrator that we put in charge."

"I see," VADM Brannigan said then he took a sip of his wine thinking about his response. After all one could argue that Mr. O'Shea had a valid point and he should not have made the raid on the system.

MajGen Connington apparently thought differently, "What are you talking about? Of course, we had the right and we did what was appropriate, we violated nothing!"

"Wait a minute, Paul. Mr. O'Shea has a point. Mr. O'Shea, this station doesn't appear to belong to any legitimate government. It is probably a raider or a pirate station and thus doesn't have any rights under a legitimate government like on our planet. Being a raider or pirate, they are criminals. So, are we looking at a criminal? I don't believe we did anything wrong because this station doesn't claim a legitimate government in which case, we may be required to live by our government's rules in dealing with a government that we have beaten. But since this is more of a criminal station, we may say do they have any rights? I judge that since they are of a criminal organization or outpost, they don't have these rights. Since they attacked us and we defeated them then what is on the station is ours by conquest. Do we have a responsibility of arresting them? If we do, what government do we turn them over to for judgment and then the information becomes evidence which would have to be preserved. Since there doesn't appear to be a government to govern that area of space, and we did look for one in the station's records, it is fair game to anyone who can take the station. In this sense yes, we took it by force because it attacked us and we claimed what was in their station. We don't have to worry about legitimate governments or law enforcers since this is unclaimed space."

Mr. O'Shea chewed that answer over along with his food. "Well, that makes this like the wild west."

"Yes, in a lot of ways this is the wild west. We have unexplored space and until it is all claimed by legitimate governments there is a free reign. Now our own ethics and code of conduct has to be our guidelines. A question is do we have the right to claim space? Yes, we do but do we have the capability to control the space? That is yet to be seen and like we have already seen we are taking space and planets."

Mr. O'Shea nodded "I guess then we haven't violated any laws then but I would advise caution in our future dealings."

"I agree and your advice is noted." Answered VADM Brannigan. He meant what he said about taking the advice. It is important that they follow the rules of engagement and guidelines of their government. With the Kammorrigans and any other government it could mean the difference between a peaceful and profitable relationship or war.

The door's buzzer sounded and VADM Brannigan touched the button that opened the door. CAPT Lindsey came in and sat down because the Admiral had gestured her to. She looked tired and excited.

"We have plotted our new course Sir. We can shave two months off our time with these new drives."

"Excellent, have the engineers improved our communication among the ships while in hyperspace?" asked MajGen Connington.

CAPT Lindsey looked a little annoyed by the question; there already was a communications officer on the staff that was working that issue.

"No Sir, we will be having the comm guys working their experiments while underway. Meanwhile we can jump anytime and should be there in ten more jumps."

"No way for one jump then?" asked VADM Brannigan.

"We don't feel comfortable with that. This is our first long distance travel and we still want to check our heading every so often. If we did one long jump we could end up off course."

"You don't trust the astrogators and your ability?" asked the VADM.

She smiled knowing that he was kidding since he was fully aware of their limitations.

"Alright, we will follow your course headings. How long will it take us to get there?"

"Approximately two more months if we don't encounter any other obstacles."

"Good."

CAPT Lindsey smiled and started to leave.

"Anything to eat, CAPT?"

"Thank you, Sir, but no."

The Admiral nodded and CAPT Lindsey departed. He sat back thinking two more months and that was cutting their travel in half. Not bad in the long haul.

They finished their meal. O'Shea and Paul continued various small talks while Kevin ate in silence thinking about his wife. It was times like this that he found himself missing her. She was a great lady in his mind. He regretted all the years that they had been apart but his desire to serve continued to keep him away. He was definitely looking forward to the day of retirement but this this was awesome. He finally got to space. A childhood dream come true and now he was leading a fleet of explorers and warriors to meet a potentially civilized, advanced, and peaceful alien intelligence. No while he missed her this was definitely the adventure of a lifetime and so far, he had a great crew to lead. All of them were and maintained their professionalism. What more could a commander ask for.

The jumps were going well. They traveled for a period of six days in hyperspace and would come out right where the astrogators said they would. Their calculations were on the mark. They would spend a day comparing the space to the star maps and updating them. Then back into hyperspace. The communications officers onboard the ships and on the flag staff were attempting to figure out how to improve communications in hyperspace with each other. All they had at this time was failure. After the third jump from the station, they requested a couple of days in normal space to attempt to figure out how to resolve the issue. VADM Brannigan gave them three days. There wasn't anything on sensors to indicate a threat and he felt this was important for them to resolve. The fleet launched a CAP to provide their protection. Meanwhile they executed various maneuvers while the commos were trying to solve their problem.

While the engineers were working the problem, Dr. Vance and CAPT Lindsey informed the Admiral they had news about the star maps and requested a time to brief them. Kevin agreed but desired all his ships' Captains to be present along with key members of the staff. During this lay over, the flag bridge summoned all the ships' Captains to the *Intrepid*, save the *Nautilus*, she had jumped that day to the next location along the route to Kammorriga.

As usual, the Commanders were seated at the table in the main conference room. Dr. Vance, his Chief Astronomer was there along with CAPT Lindsey and her Chief Astrogator. MajGen Connington was in his chair while Maj Clark stood by the door looking out waiting for the Admiral. They were waiting for the Admiral to arrive and chatting among themselves. When Maj Clark spotted LT Shapiro coming down the passage way with the Admiral behind him, he called stand by to the room. Everyone stood up. As the Aide entered the room, the Major called attention on deck. The Admiral approached his chair and told everyone to be seated. Major Clark closed the door and secured them and then seated himself behind the Admiral and Chief of Staff next to LT Shapiro.

"Hullo everyone, Kevin said. He then looked everyone over. "I'm glad to see all Commanders here. It's good to see you in person for a change." He nodded to everyone in the room.

"Okay, so, Ops you have the information from the star maps, yes?" CAPT Lindsey nodded in response. "Yes Sir, we do. Dr. Vance with his team and the astrogators have torn into them and have some interesting facts." She then turned and indicated for theDoctor to take over.

A knock at the door brought them short. Major Clark got up and answered the door only to find Mr. O'Shea at the door. He looked at the Admiral who motioned for the Diplomat to enter.

"Welcome Mr. O'Shea, glad you could make it." The Admiral gestured to a seat at the table. Mr. O'Shea took the seat while the Major secured the door and took his seat.

Kevin looked over at Dr. Vance. "Alright Jack, what do you have?"

Dr. Vance nodded and touched his hand-held pad, the lights in the room dimmed slightly and the screen at the far end of the room brought up the first of several images of the galaxy. Dr. Vance then zoomed the screen in to their current position.

"As you may recall Sir, the Kammorrigans sent us coordinates to send a message back to them. While we know the message was a general message sent out and not specifically to us, they asked that a return call be sent. We didn't. We have been suspicious of the Kammorrigans since they sent incomplete information about the technology that was provided in the message. So, our route of travel used Earth's position and the coordinates that we were to send the message to." As he spoke, Dr. Vance adjusted the view screen to show the two points and then brought up a route. "We used all of our telescopes on Earth and those in orbit to plot this route and try to determine what we could. But our information was lacking and thus incomplete. However, we plotted this route to the best of our abilities. As you know, we purchased and then later just took every star map out of the station's database plus from the merchants. We didn't take any from those who were visiting the station nor from the slaves that we had set free. Just the ones from the station and kiosks." He looked around the room and saw everyone was attentive. "We have analyzed all of them. We found the ones in the kiosks to be either real basic maps, which we had limited use for or just junk data." He looked around the room and saw some of the reactions from the Commanders. "But the station had good maps, albeit, some holes in the data. For instance, the signal that was sent from the station to whomever just before attacking us, that information was not in the system. We also have seen other holes in the data, perhaps deliberately deleted but we don't know that either. Could just be gaps in their knowledge."

Kevin and the Chief of Staff just nodded.

"Alright, the good news is, we have been able to plot a better route to the coordinates provided using the data from the station." Dr. Vance used his device and turned the current route on the screen to a red color and brought in a new line using the color green. "As you can see, this new route is slightly different. Partially it's different from the maps we have now acquired and partially from the upgrades we have made. We can make it to Kammorriga faster now. That is the good news."

After reviewing the screen, Kevin then looked at Dr. Vance. "What is the bad news?"

Dr. Vance let out a soft sigh and glanced at CAPT Lindsey, who just shrugged her shoulders.

"Well Sir, there is incomplete information on the map."

Kevin frowned. "Okay..., what does that mean?"

Dr. Vance continued, "Well it means there is incomplete information of the locations that it makes sense for us to make jumps to. We still not dare make a single jump to Kammorriga. We need to come out of hyperspace at certain locations to ensure we are on track. But there is missing information about those locations. Nothing about planets, asteroids, comets, nothing. It appears that the data is deliberately missing. We won't know what is there until we jump there."

The Admiral looked at MajGen Connington and frowned a bit. Paul just shrugged his shoulders and looked at Dr. Vance. "Is that really an issue, Doctor? After all we send the *Nautilus* out before us to make sure the space is relatively safe or give us a warning."

Dr. Vance nodded his head and glanced over to CAPT Lindsey.

She spoke up, "It is an odd thing to delete or deliberately not record information in a map. The fact the information is missing alone doesn't mean a thing but deliberately it is concerning. Further, there is nothing. That is to say no warnings about this space or that and no amplifying information. If we go along the new route, yes, we get to the objective faster. However, we could jump into the middle of a pirate system or owned space by someone who may find our intrusion to be trespassing and start shooting at us."

Paul nodded and looked back at Kevin.

"Mph, okay, got it, Doctor and Captain." Kevin looked around the room. All the Commanders were looking at him. "Any assessment on the risk of these systems? Are you recommending we stick with the old route?"

Dr. Vance looked to CAPT Lindsey who just glanced back at him.

"Sir, we don't have a clue about any risk. The risk is really the same as we jump to the next set of coordinates. And, as the Chief of Staff just pointed out, we do have the *Nautilus*. The recommendation is to use the new route. We desired for you to know that information is deliberately missing on these points along the route."

Kevin nodded. "Okay, I have that." He steepled his hands together and touched his nose with the fingertips.

"What do we know about the regions we are passing through? Are there any governments out here?

Dr. Vance looked over to Mr. O'Shea who just grinned back at him. Kevin could see this made the Doctor a tad uneasy. Then Mr. O'Shea spoke up, "Admiral, the team has been scouring the information. There are indicators that there may be some smaller governments in the area. After all, we did send letters of introduction to those who we set free and who took their ships to their homes. But that is all we know at this time."

Dr. Vance continued, "We do think there was something out here at some time. We are still analyzing the star maps along with other relevant parts of the database to determine the civilizations that are or were out here."

Kevin nodded, glanced at MajGen Connington and the other Commanders. "Any questions or concerns from the Commanders?" They thought for a moment and shook their heads no. Kevin then looked at CAPT Lindsey, "Send the new route to all the ships, follow our procedures for the jumps. Everyone, ensure you run drills on your ships for general quarters as we come out of jump. Josephine, ensure the procedures are reviewed by everyone while we wait for the communications team. This lends a greater need to sort out the hyperspace well. While we can read the presence of all our ships and have limited communications between us, we need to be able to fully scan the well and improve those communications. But we will not stay here longer than approved. I want to jump to the next point on the new route on time. We will follow the new route." He looked at everyone ensuring they understood.

Just as he was about to dismiss everyone, the comm system in the room came on. "Admiral, this is flag bridge. The *Nautilus* has made the return jump and is signaling us about the following position. May I pipe CAPT Strickland through Sir?"

Kevin looked around the room. "Yes, please do so now."

The viewscreen darkened and then lightened with CAPT Strickland, the Commander of the *Nautilus* came into view.

"Yes Allen, what is it?"

"Admiral, greetings and to staff and my fellow Commanders. Sir, we just returned from the other position. The jump point is only a short distance. We found another station there. We didn't approach too close. There was absolutely zero traffic coming to or from the station, no real energy readings and zero communication traffic."

Kevin looked around the room. Everyone was watching the screen but seemed to grow a bit excited.

Mmm, Kevin thought, *another station and this one seems dead.* He looked at Dr. Vance, "Doctor, is this jump point one of the areas with missing data?"

Dr. Vance looked at him, "Yes, Sir."

Kevin rubbed his chin for a few moments while everyone sat in silence.

"Alright Allen, send the information to *Intrepid* for dissemination. Everyone return to your ships, go to yellow alert and prepare for jump. We will check this out. Dismissed, except for Dr. Vance, CAPT Lindsey, and Mr. O'Shea, you too, Paul."

After everyone departed to return to their respective ships or stations, Kevin looked at Dr. Vance and CAPT Lindsey.

"How many more of these surprises do you think we will encounter and do we check out each one or can we just bypass them?"

They all shrugged their shoulders and glanced at the view screen. CAPT Lindsey spoke up, "I think we best check out this station but to check out everything will delay us. We need to provide *Nautilus* with guidance on the scans they take and the information they return with so in the future we can make an informed decisions about how to proceed."

"Agreed Captain. Paul, you and Josephine get together and figure out those protocols and get them over to *Nautilus*."

"Yes, Sir" with that Paul motioned for the others to return to their stations and left the room himself.

Kevin sat there in thought with Major Clark and LT Shapiro sitting quietly behind him. Finally, the Admiral stood up and they did also and followed him out of the conference room as he headed to the flag bridge.

CAPT Lindsey finished studying her board and turned in her chair. As she made the turn she glanced at the Chief of Staff in his chair and then looked at the Admiral. "Sir, the readings indicate the station is dead. It appears to be very similar in size and shape to the last station but with extremely low energy output and indeterminate life signs. *Nautilus* is moving away after her scans." She thought for a moment then, "It appears it may be safe to board her but assume a vacuum or at least a very minimum environment."

Kevin thought about the information for a bit. He then keyed up the *Chesty* from his chair controls. Col Roberts appeared on the monitor.

"Colonel."

"Yes, Sir."

"Send a platoon of your Marines over to *Defiant* and have CDR Ramirez send a platoon of Rangers also. I want them to board the station on the top disk. I want them in EVA suits and fully armed. Prepare a QRF just in case."

"Acknowledged, Sir. I'll have it done at once. *Chesty* out."

"Out here."

Kevin then looked at CAPT Lindsey.

"Have the *Chesty* and *Scimitar* move to a location they can affect a rescue and give cover fire. Then have the rest of the fleet move in a supporting position to them. Inform *Defiant* I want her to dock and send in the Marines and Rangers." Kevin thought for a moment. "Send Capt Jackson over to the *Defiant* and have him go in with the team. Might as well have LCDR Reyes lead the team."

She acknowledged the orders and turned back to her board to execute the orders.

LCDR Reyes thought, *wow aren't we the lucky ones.* Col Adams looked at him, "Well John, we drew the lucky straw and will be hosting a boarding party. You get to lead them in. After the team from the *Chesty* arrives and Capt Jackson get with them and determine how to board. With these readings I believe this is going to be a completely different situation. Obviously, the Admiral does too." LCDR Reyes acknowledged the order and left the bridge to meet with the team leaders after they arrived.

The *Defiant* held her position as the team members where being shuttled over. Once Col Adams had a plan for boarding, he would send it over to *Intrepid* for the Admiral to approve. Once he had the approval, then they would go to the station and board her.

The *Defiant* was pulling up to a docking section. She had run every scan she could on the station and confirmed it appeared to be a dead station in space. LCDR Reyes was at the airlock and suited up. He would enter with a squad of Marines with him. After the initial entry another squad would take up a defensive position to protect the airlock. The Rangers were preparing to be the quick reaction force or QRF should a problem arise followed by the rest of the Marine platoon with them.

The entry would be different this time. Without power and no communications from the Control Center, LCDR Reyes and his team would have to force an entry. The tube would be from *Defiant* and maintain a soft seal only, that alone would be dangerous. The other aspect would be the attempt to open the station airlock without blowing them into space. So, they had tethers attached to their suits just in case.

Defiant pulled up and came to a halt. The Airlock Technician extended the ship's own tube. The Marines placed a four-man team called a fire team into the airlock along with a crewmember to attempt entry. The system showed the tube made a soft seal; the Technician closed the *Defiant's* inner hatch. Once it cycled through, he opened the outer hatch. He and the Marines went along the tube. Two of the Marines went to a kneeling position aiming their carbines at the station hatch while one Marine held a flashlight that sent a bright beam to the hatch. The other Marine was on his comm set back to LCDR Reyes while the Technician approached the hatch. He was glad to see a control panel. He easily pried it open and place the leads from his own device onto the alien system. The machinery started clicking and within a few minutes the hatch began to cycle. The Technician made a few adjustments. He could tell this hatch had not been opened for quite some time, it was having difficulty cycling open.

"Should we blow it?" asked one of the Marines. "No, it will open in a bit. Just kinda stuck but it will get there." Responded the Technician.

After a few minutes of the Technician tinkering with his device and the hatch external controls, the hatch began cycling open. Out of the small opening came a puff of atmosphere. The Technician quickly unhooked his device and stepped quickly through the fire team back to *Defiant's* open external hatch. Once inside, he cycled it closed and opened the inner hatch. Two other Marine fire teams entered the airlock and the Technician quickly sealed the inner hatch, cycled the atmosphere and opened the outer hatch. The first fire team had remained in place and they could see the alien hatch open. It was completely dark inside except for the light beam from the device one of the Marines was holding. The Gunnery Sergeant had the first fire team move into the station and the second move quickly up and into the station. Both fire teams moved along the alien tube while the third team moved inside the structure. When the first fire team came to the hatch at the other end of the tube they stopped. They called for the Technician to come in and open this hatch. By this time LCDR Reyes and the rest of the Squad had made the transfer from *Defiant* to the station. The Technician came up and in a similar fashion closed the outer hatch, and opened this hatch. As it began to cycle open, he moved behind the Marines.

When the inner hatch had cycled opened and nothing appeared the two fire teams moved through and formed a semi-circle perimeter at the inner hatch. They were facing out in all directions into the terminal area. LCDR Reyes along with the Platoon Commander and Technician entered into the semi-circle of Marines. The third fire team came in behind them.

LCDR Reyes looked at the 1st Lieutenant "Okay, nothing here thankfully. Bring over the rest of your Platoon and have the 2nd and 3rd squads take up a defensive position here. Also, have Capt Jackson join us. Once we have assembled, I want to move quickly to the command center and download everything we need, we will bring the 1st squad with us. LCDR Reyes scanned the area since the Marines turned on their own lights. The furniture was damaged and scattered about the area. The equipment was smashed or covered in dust. He sighed heavily. He wanted to move quickly and quietly and get it over with.

Col Adams listened to LCDR Reyes' initial report and his plan to move quickly to the Command Center with a squad of Marines. The entire area was dark and unorganized. No creatures to be seen but John seemed apprehensive about the whole affair. After John made his report and informed the Colonel he was moving out, the Colonel keyed the comms for the Ranger Lt onboard his ship ensuring he had communications with the Marine squads at the hatch and the one that John was leading. The Lt assured him he had and the Marines and Rangers were ready if needed. That made Col Adams feel better.

LCDR Reyes, 1st Lt Peters and the 1st Squad with Capt Johnson arrived at the mall area. So far, there were no instances. Unlike the first station, this one had a smaller mall area, only a ground floor and one upper balcony area. The same mall light in the ceiling was present but was a lot dimmer than in the other station. The entire mall area was in disarray. John just shook his head. He couldn't rub his face due to his helmet being on. The Corpsman that was with them had taken readings of the atmosphere and it showed they would not be able to breathe it, so they remained in their EVA suits. At least the Squad's EVA had battle armor incorporated in them, John was a bit envious of them for that fact.

The 1st Lt touched John's arm and pointed to his left at a ramp with an upward approach to another deck. LCDR Reyes motioned for them to proceed up the ramp. The Lt had a fire team take the lead followed by himself, the LCDR, radio man and the Corpsman. The remaining two fire teams brought up the rest of the squad. The ramp continued but instead of the open space of the mall it became a tunnel. John knew this would lead first to an administration level and continue to the command level. They continued to climb passing hatches or open areas. The entire group kept moving forward at a quick but cautious pace.

The whole team was starting to relax and loosen up and they picked up some speed. They kept scanning the whole area as they moved rapidly up the ramp.

The Gunnery Sergeant in charge of the Marine squads at the hatch was constantly scanning the room and ensuring the Marines kept their positions. The Marines had a movement sensor with each fire team and one of them went off softly. The Gunny moved to the Marine and checked the sensor. It showed movement. He keyed his communications and inquired from the 1st Lt if they were in the area. When he received the response, he alerted the Marines to be on the ready and radioed the Ranger Lt that they had movement.

Col Adams had the *Chesty* alerted to movement and inquired from the Ranger if he was ready to move into the tube. They were ready. He then keyed up LCDR Reyes and informed him there was movement at the entrance tube and asked for a status.

"Sir, we are moving along rapidly and I suspect we will be at the command level shortly?

"Good, I will....."

Suddenly a scream burst through the entire system.

John turned to see 1st Lt Peters disappear down a tunnel.

"What happened?" He yelled as the second fire team moved to the entrance of the tunnel and shined their lights down it. They saw nothing.

"What happened and where the hell is the Lieutenant?" Screamed LCDR Reyes.

"Sir, he was grabbed by something and pulled into this tunnel." Answered the Sergeant.

"Well, what do you see?"

"Nothing, Sir. The thing has disappeared with the Lieutenant."

"Damn. Check for his signal. *Defiant*, the Lieutenant has been grabbed by something. No idea what. Do you have the Lieutenant on the scanners?"

After a few moments, "*Defiant* here. Sorry, no."

The Corpsman answered, "Nothing Sir, sorry."

LCDR Reyes stood there thinking of the options. Does he try and find the Lt? As a Squad or break them up. Damn, he hated the thought of leaving the Lieutenant down that tunnel. He approached it himself and looked down it. Absolutely no sign of the creature or the Lieutenant. He looked the entire tunnel up and down. There were a few openings.

"*Defiant* to LCDR Reyes, John, appraisal please." Col Adams was asking.

"Sir, there is no sign of the Lieutenant. There are several openings in the tunnel that a creature could have escaped through. We don't have a signal from the Lieutenant."

"Would the internal scanners be able to help find him if you reached the Control Room?" asked the Colonel.

"No idea, Sir. We don't know what the room looks like yet. If it were operational, maybe." He noticed the Sergeant was scanning with a different device.

"Sergeant, is your device looking for human signs and if so, can you find the Lieutenant?"

"I am tuning it for the Lieutenant base signs that we have on record, but its range is limited considering the materials of the station." He shook his head, "Nothing sir."

"Col Adams, Sir, we could go looking for him but this thing seemed to move fast. No idea where he could be."

"Okay, John, standby. We have *Intrepid* online and will confer with the Admiral and Col Roberts."

Kevin just sat in his chair. Everyone was a bit stunned by this. "Recommendations, Colonel."

Col Roberts had his team around a planning table and scanners looking for the Lieutenant.

"I hate to leave a Marine behind, Sir. But we can't locate his signal. He could be anywhere in that disk by now and we don't have a communication from him either." Col Roberts turned to his staff who was obviously attempting to give the Colonel options.

Kevin keyed his mic, "John, we are out of time. We have a squad just sitting in a tunnel exposed. To try and find one man in that entire station would take most likely all the Marines. We still don't know what else is on there."

Col Roberts turned back to the view screen. "Sir, have the team move on. We will continue to scan the disk. Besides, *Defiant* has reported some sort of movement at the main hatch. They may need to pull out of there. I'll prepare a rescue team should we get something. But at this time, we have nothing to go on to find the Lieutenant."

Kevin responded, "Very well." He turned to CAPT Lindsey, "inform the *Defiant*."

LCDR Reyes looked at the Marines. "Alright, we have a job to do. We will get the Lieutenant should we get anything that tells us where he might be. Okay, move out and let's be extra aware now."

The team started moving forward. John saw that several of the Marines took their weapons' safeties off. He knew they were now ready to shoot anything despite the risk to themselves. He was fine with that.

The Gunny was looking in the direction of the movement but couldn't see anything. The Marines had the area lit up pretty good but there were several shadows. Suddenly every motion sensor they had went off at the same time as several strange creatures of multiple sizes and shapes came bounding towards them.

The Gunny didn't hesitate and ordered all Marines to open fire. He then keyed his communications. "*Defiant*, we are under attack at the tunnel hatch."

Col Adams keyed in. "How many and situation?"

"Too many to count, Sir. We are killing several and more are coming."

"Are you able to hold and secure the place? Ops, prepare to send the Rangers over."

"Sir, don't send them. We need to fall back to the ship. There are too many of them to hold this position."

Damn, thought the Colonel. He ordered up the *Intrepid* and *Chesty* to be keyed in.

"Grenades," ordered the Gunny and four grenades were sent into the mass of creatures. The resulting explosions rocked the area. For a brief moment the mass was slowed but only for a moment. More started to pour into the area from a variety of openings.

"*Defiant*, we just fired four grenades but more are still coming. Request both hatches to the *Defiant* to be open so we can get through the tunnel."

Col Adams didn't hesitate and ordered Engineering to cycle open both internal and external hatches, override the system if they had to. Meanwhile, the Rangers took up positions to provide cover fire at both hatches.

"Okay, Gunny, we are ready. Bring your Marines home."

"Yes Sir, alright Marines. We will fall back by fire teams. Number Three first then the Second. The First will come with me. We will begin after grenades are both fired and thrown. Ready. Grenades"

The Marines either fired grenades from their weapons or threw them. The resulting explosions tore into creatures and metal alike. The flow of creatures stopped and the Marines started filing through the tunnel at a run. The Gunny along with fire team one guarded the tunnel as the rest of the Marines made it into the *Defiant*. The creatures started their assault again. The Gunny ordered his remaining Marines into the tunnel as he fired a grenade into the assaulting group.

The Gunny turned into the tunnel and made it to the outer station hatch and turned in time to shoot a creature that was almost on him. He continued firing into them as they came. His Marines made it to the ship, turned and aimed their weapons back into the tunnel. However, they couldn't fire without hitting their Gunny.

The Gunny started to turn into the tunnel when one of the creatures grabbed him. He spun around and blew its mid-section apart. Three more were nearly upon him as he fired. He changed magazines and started firing. They kept coming. He stepped into the *Defiant's* tube firing at the assaulting things the entire time. Still his Marines nor the Rangers could acquire any targets to shoot. By this time the Gunny had to change out magazines again to keep up his fire. The damn things were nearly at the station hatch. He shook his head and grimaced. Suddenly he charged forward and as he entered the station's hatch, he keyed it shut. The hatch cycled closed as the Marines at the *Defiant's* hatch were screaming at the Gunny. Two of them started forward as the other two Marines and the Rangers grabbed them pulling them back in. There was the sound of an explosion inside the station just as the station hatch was nearly closed rocking the *Defiant's* tube. A Ranger quickly keyed the *Defiant's* outer hatch closed as the tube broke seal and the *Defiant* began venting atmosphere. Everyone in the airlock grabbed something as the Rangers and Marines at the inner hatch started cycling the inner hatch closed to try and save the ship.

"Sergeant, status." Yelled LCDR Reyes into his communication to be heard over the gunfire. "Projectiles at 50% and energy weapons at 65%, Sir." The Sergeant replied.

The Squad had made it to the Control Room without any further incidence. They were able to open the hatch and acquire the system. The Marines set up a defensive position at the hatch with a fire team inside for defense against anything that might appear from a vent or another entry they did not know about.

As Capt Jackson and the Technician began accessing the systems is when the attack came. The Sergeant and his Marines were in a fire fight. They were holding the location.

"*Defiant*, this is Boarding Team, come in" John had keyed up.

"*Defiant* here, John, what is your status?" Col Adams had answered while he ensured the *Intrepid* and *Chesty* were listening.

"Sir, we are at the Control Room and accessing the systems. We are attacked though from an indeterminate number of aggressors. We are holding our own at this time. Captain, pull up the schematics of this station. Will we be able to get back to the ship?" As the Captain was accessing them.

"John, you're not going to be able to get back to us. The entry way is under assault and it looks like we are going to have to abandon this hatch."

"Well, this onslaught here is tough but seems manageable. Let me review the schematics and get back to you. Boarding party out." LCDR Reyes turned to Capt Jackson but kept his communications open to the ship.

"Well, Captain."

"Internal sensors are down for the most part but we can tell there is a lot of life forms and they seem to be coming into this section from other places." He looked over at the Technician's screens. "Great. The databases have either been scrubbed or destroyed. We are not getting anything from them."

John nodded and started to say something when the Captain continued.

"Sir, there was a warning signal on a general broadcast. For some reason it has been shut off. Nothing wrong with it. The message is continuing on a repeat cycle warning ships to stay away. The transmitter has just been shut down."

LCDR Reyes asked, "Can it be turned back on?"

"Yes, sir."

"Then do so and make it where it can't be switched off again."

"Done, easy day." John just looked at the Captain.

"Sergeant, status."

"Projectile weapons down to 25% ammo and energy weapons down to 33%. Sir, we need to get out of here and fast."

"Roger. Captain, those schematics."

Capt Jackson had them up and reviewing already. "Sir, through the hatch to our left is a tunnel to an external airlock. We can escape through it if there isn't anything in between." He turned to the Technician who gave him a thumbs up. "It appears to be empty. Don't know if we can open it or have to blow it."

"Okay. *Defiant*, did you catch that?"

"*Defiant* here. Yes, we did. The *Chesty* is already angling to the upper portion of the disk. Send the coordinates. I think Col Roberts is readying transport for you"

"*Chesty* here, yes, transports are in the tubes. Get out of there."

"Thank you. Sergeant. Toss the grenades, get in here, and seal that hatch. We are departing through another hatch."

The Marines moved into the Control Center, tossed two grenades, and quickly closed the hatch. With an energy weapon they sealed it.

Meanwhile, Capt Jackson turned the warning message on and coded the system requiring a counter code to turn it off. As they got up from the boards, John motioned for a Marine to destroy them.

They quickly opened the other hatch and two Marines had their weapons positioned to fire into it. Nothing came out. They shined their lights into the tunnel and saw nothing but the tunnel.

The entire team moved into it quickly as they heard something hit the other hatch hard. They turned and saw it had buckled under the blow. They moved even faster into the tunnel and closed the hatch. With the same weapons, they sealed the hatch. As the team moved forward, the Sergeant planted a claymore type explosive aimed at the hatch with a contact wire for detonation. He ran to catch up with the team as they moved along the tunnel.

They reached the outer hatch and the Technician hooked up his device and started the cycle. The hatch moaned and did not open. He keyed it up again and the hatch made sounds but failed a second time. The Sergeant moved next to him and looked over his shoulder. The hatch seemed stuck.

"Boarding Team here." The Sergeant keyed a Marine link from his radio man's system. "We can't get the hatch open. We need to blow it. Are the transports here yet? Also, the aggressors may already be in the Control Room. It is only a matter of time before they come up this tunnel."

"This is Rescue One, we are nearly to the hatch. We are five minutes out. Blow it if you have to."

"Roger, we are setting to blow it now."

With that everyone moved down the tunnel a bit as two Marines set charges. Suddenly, an explosion from down the tunnel happened.

"Fire team One, take positions and be ready to open up." The Sergeant ordered. "Blow that hatch!"

As Fire team One opened fire on creatures moving up the tunnel, the other hatch was blown open by the Marines. Everyone was being sucked out of the hatch as they grabbed ahold of various items to keep from being blown into space. Meanwhile a couple of creatures went flying past them out of the hatch.

Rescue One landed on the disk and began disembarking Marines as two creatures flew out of the airlock. They quickly moved up to the hatch to see their comrades hanging on while the tunnel equalized to the vacuum. Meanwhile they could see a few of the creatures moving up the tunnel. One Marine started to aim when the Boarding Party started to scramble out of the hatch. Rescue One Marines grabbed them and started moving them toward the transports. When they were clear of the hatch, two Marines fired grenades into the tunnel killing several creatures. They then retreated to the transports. The transports began lifting off as they filled with the Boarding Party and Rescue Marines.

Kevin sat in his chair watching the *Defiant* drift away from the station hatch. The explosion had torn her transfer tube. Her outer hatch was still cycling close when the tube was ripped away from the station hatch and caused her to drift.

The team was able to close her hatches and Col Adams and his crew got control of her drift rather quickly. She moved away from the station smartly and smoothly. Soon a damage report would come in.

Meanwhile on another screen he saw the transports depart from the *Chesty* to rescue the Boarding Party. Two Marines dead. He rubbed his chin. They didn't get any information, materials or equipment and definitely didn't find out what happened on the station. The only positive was turning the warning back on for other ships to avoid the station.

Kevin sat in his office along with his Chief of Staff, CAPT Lindsey, and Mr. O'Shea. Paul watched Kevin closely. He knew the Admiral was not happy with this event.

"How is the *Defiant*?" Kevin asked.

"All crew members are good; ship is intact and fully operational. The hatch tube will be repaired shortly." Kevin nodded.

The Boarding Party?"

Paul answered, "All of them made it back with no injuries. Just the Lt and the Gunnery Sergeant didn't make it. Col Roberts is putting the Gunny in for decorations for his sacrifice to save the *Defiant*." Kevin nodded again.

"Well, this answered our question. Should we check out all these map gaps on our way to Kammorriga? The answer is a definite no. Unless *Nautilus* picks up something of significance to us, we skip them. I don't want to lose anyone else on a useless side trip. Clear?"

Everyone acknowledged.

"Sir, Josephine and I have those protocols for *Nautilus* that you asked for and ready for your review." Paul continued. Kevin nodded again and motioned to his computer for them to be sent to him. "Yes sir, you will have them shortly."

"Okay, well, let's see the decoration recommendation from Col Roberts. Have a fleet wide stand down for the two Marines like we have had for our other losses. I'm sure Col Roberts has new leadership for the platoon." Kevin said. "Then let's get on to Kammorriga.

CHAPTER 6

VADM Brannigan called for a meeting among his intelligence, operations, and science sections. He ensured that Mr. O'Shea was present at this meeting in the conference room.

"Ladies and Gentlemen, we are six jumps away from entering the home space of the Kammorrigans. I of course studied the reports that we had on them back on Earth but that was several months ago." The Admiral was saying. "Now we are getting closer to their space and I want updates. We will need to know what we are going to encounter when we get there. So, unless you have updates now." He paused and watched the table. No one indicated they had anything. "Alright, MajGen Connington I want you to head up an update brief to me. We have six more jumps that is approximately forty days. I want after we complete five jumps, or in thirty days, an update. Let's look again. Let's looks again at their language and the science that they sent us. In regards to the science, and no I don't think they are hostile, but let's ensure they cannot shut down any of our systems. I want any cultural items that they sent us to be analyzed by both the diplomatic corps that we have and our scientist to include anthropology, xenobiology, and geophysics. I want the astrogators and astronomers to look at the information that they gave us on their space. I am looking for tactical along with scientific and diplomatic avenues in this matter. What moons, planets, and asteroids arc in the space? Do they have a fleet of home guard ships and if so, did they provide us with any information? I want to know how they have instructed us to approach and any hidden code in the information. Further, I want the database information we gathered from the station we took. Include that information in your analysis. Again, I want this in thirty days, which should be plenty of time for you to glean the information. CAPT Lindsey, I want you to take this information and with Mr. O'Shea give me options at the meeting as well. While this is a scientific and diplomatic mission, which we all need to remember, we also are the military representatives. I want solutions along all three fronts and integrated to make sure we don't make a diplomatic mistake that could lead to a fight but I want a solution if there is one. Mr. O'Shea and I will be the lead with the Kammorrigans when we arrive. The military options are not to be the first option but a support option. Our science department will be in support and at times will be the primary, I am sure. Military will not be a forefront player. We are not out here to engage militarily but we have the might to back up diplomacy or to affect an escape. Let's hope we don't need it. Questions?"

Everyone indicated no questions and MajGen Connington dismissed them.

"Paul, stay behind." VADM Brannigan said when everyone was departing. Once everyone had left the room, he looked at him, "Paul, I want a first strike option from the ships. I am not so hopeful to think that we may not need to run out of there fast and keep them from pursuing. It is a last-ditch plan if all else fails." Paul scratched his head, "We have no intel to make such a plan, Sir."

Kevin smiled, "We will. I have already decided on a course of action. I want you to have a method to receive the intel and be able to take advantage of what is discovered."

Paul looked a little puzzled but said, "Yes, Sir." He could tell the Admiral was done and got up to head out.

"Oh yes Paul, don't tell anyone except Lindsey and maybe CDR Ramirez. I don't want any of the other departments to know."

"Yes, Sir." Paul left the conference room.

Kevin looked to the far end of the conference room. He didn't like the fact they have only run into hostile species to date and was really hoping for a friendly outcome with the Kammorrigans. He expected Mr. O'Shea and Dr. Vance to give him the best method of approaching and speaking with them in order to have a peaceful relationship that would result in a trade treaty or even a neighborly relation. He didn't expect to achieve an alliance. That would be too much to hope for and as he had already seen they lacked information on the space to make an alliance with anyone; but a trade treaty would be the goal. He was counting on these two departments to do that.

LT Shapiro was in the Admiral's closet. He was inspecting each of the Admiral's uniforms, container of ribbons, medals, and pins. He was giving them each a very close inspection. He knew the Admiral had to look his best with the upcoming meeting with the Kammorrigans. He selected the service dress blues the Admiral would wear. He began inspecting the shoes. Yes, he thought this pair would do perfectly.

"Gmm." He heard a noise behind him and turned to see the Admiral.

"Hello, Sir."

"Mmm, so going through my stuff, are you?" Asked Kevin, who knew very well his Aide was doing his job.

"No Sir, just picking out the clothes you will wear and ensuring all is in order."

Kevin smiled at him. "Yes, good job. I think I will stick with the blues the entire time there. No need for any tactical items. So, let's make sure I have plenty of them."

"Yes Sir." Answered the LT, then he hesitated and turned to the Admiral, "Sir."

Kevin was departing but stopped and turned back to the LT. He could see he was a bit nervous. He nodded at him.

"Sir, the Marines desire you to have a weapon on you."

Kevin just started to laugh and then stopped. "No. I will have at least one or two of the FAST with me at all times. Besides, I will have you around at all meetings, etc. You will be acting as my secretary on this trip. Plus, I already know you have been trained as a personal bodyguard by the FAST and you will be carrying." With that Kevin just smiled at him and left the area.

LT Shapiro was surprised. He could have sworn he had done everything to keep his training a secret like Major Clark made him promise to.

Five jumps later they had travelled several light years. Now they were one jump away from their destination. The area of space had a star in the distance. It's light barely reaching the Strike Group. The sensors didn't show any nearby planets or ships in the vicinity. They still hadn't been able to improve their communications while in hyperspace but they had figured out how to improve scanning each other and have tactical displays while in the well. This in itself was a major accomplishment. Dr. Vance had assigned a team of engineers that understood sound and light waves to assist the military communications officers in improving the communication problem. They had assisted with the scanners and he hoped they could help in this manner. The Admiral really desired the ability to scan any ship outside of his own fleet in hyperspace but that was proving to be difficult. The fleet was moving slowly towards the sun. It was on the star maps and the fleet was updating their records. The astronomers and astrophysicists were interested in the star and the long-range scanners were already giving them data on it and the surrounding space. The plan would have them jumping long before they reached the star but the next several hours may determine something else.

The conference room onboard the *Intrepid* was full. All the ships' Commanding Officers were present along with CAPT Lindsey and her Chief Astrogator, the MEU Commander, Wing Commander, Special Operations Commander (CDR Ramirez), and the Intelligence Department were present, Dr. Vance along with his linguist and cultural experts not to mention the three scientists that had worked the Kammorrigan data, Dr. Mulligan was present and in a place of prominence sat Mr. O'Shea the Fleet's Chief Diplomat. They were waiting on the Strike Group Commander and Chief of Staff to arrive. This would be the last meeting prior to their jump to Kammorriga. It would be the last chance to deal with any issues or contingency planning prior to meeting with the sentient beings that they had received a welcoming call from.

The Commander and his Chief of Staff who was also the Deputy Commander of the Strike Group were down the passageway in VADM Brannigan's office. Part of him did not want this meeting. He was anxious to make the last jump as he was sure the rest of them were. But he didn't want to make the last jump. It meant the travel phase would be over. They hadn't explored enough of space. In essence they just took a lot of pictures, yes, they made four very important discoveries, a space station that was a slave market, another space station that was dead except for the multitude of deadly creatures, crystals as a source of energy, a mining planet of those crystals relatively close to Earth. But they were at the end of that phase and was about to jump to meet their mission. Would they be successful?

He looked at Paul, who was sipping at his coffee looking out the space port at the stars. He was obviously in his own thoughts as well. Kevin looked at his wife's picture and then at the reports on the screen. He sorted through them and had them filed by the system. Nothing had jumped out at him so he wasn't going to waste his time. He thought about the trip so far. It proved to be either boring or met with hostiles. He just shook his head. He was trying to personally get ready for the various meetings he and Mr. O'Shea would be a part of. He knew his Aide had everything ready for him to meet with the Kammorrigans. Now, the rest of the team had to prepare him and Mike O'Shea to be successful. Finally, it would be up to him to succeed. He let out a sigh; it was nearly time to go to the conference room. He had been looking through the various reports and study on the Kammorrigan message that had been sent to Earth. From what they said it was a random directional signal. If so, then it was a fishing expedition to see who they could contact. Hopefully the team had more relevant information. He stood up and Paul got up at the same time. He sorted the few papers on his desk and closed his computer logs. "Well, I guess we shouldn't keep them too much longer." Paul just smiled and finished his coffee. They exited the office and walked down the short passageway to the conference room.

"Attention on deck" All hands in the conference room came to attention when MajGen Connington entered the room and Major Clark called for it. VADM Brannigan entered the room and told them to take their seats as he took his. He looked around the room and was satisfied by whom he saw there.

"Okay, we are here to receive our final briefings on the Kammorrigans and this mission. I will want to hear from Ops and Diplomacy before we decide to make our final jump. We are one jump away and I want this to go off without a hitch." VAMD Brannigan told the group.

Major Troy, representative from the Intelligence Department stood ready waiting for the go ahead. MajGen Connington looked around the room from his chair, he was attempting to read their faces to make sure they understood what the Admiral wanted.

"This mission is first and foremost a diplomatic one," VADM Brannigan continued, "everything we do must be in this light." He looked at MajGen Connington who motioned for Major Troy to begin his briefing.

"Admiral, Chief of Staff, Commanding Officers, and staff, the Intelligence Department has gone over the taped message from the Kammorrigans and databanks that we retrieved from the Space Station. Bottom line there isn't much more information than what we already know. The records from the station indicates that the Kammorrigans govern a large area of space. It doesn't appear that they allow too much information concerning themselves to be known. The station didn't have too much information on them. They do have a space fleet which we lack any information on the number, disposition or type of ships. The records did not provide us any insights as to their intention towards their neighbors or anyone else. That is, we don't know today just like we didn't know when we first received the message that these people are hostile or not. The station had more information on the different species or governments that are relatively near the station but not this far out. Bottom line is we don't know that much about the Kammorrigans.

What we have learned from the station's databases is more historical but might be relevant.

This entire space was governed by, what appears, to be empires that collapsed. The Station's information didn't give a reason as to why they faded away or much of who they were. But, the entire area in which Earth is a part of is generally ungoverned. Yes, there are smaller governments that have emerged since they fell. The Kammorrigans did exists during their later years but wasn't much more than a mention in the cosmic records. Only after the three empires fell did they begin to emerge as a power. They grew in the systems they now govern. That is all the information we could gather from the station."

The Admiral looked around the table for questions. He wasn't pleased about this lack of information. MajGen Connington spoke up, "You surveyed the entire databases and message?"

"Yes, Sir," responded Major Troy.

"And you didn't find out any more than this?"

"Yes, Sir," Major Troy answered a little hesitantly since he could see that MajGen Connington didn't like the answer.

"Sir, we scanned the databases three times and was going through them in detail. We are still working on this process. So far, we haven't found any more information."

MajGen Connington sat back with a look of disgust and looked at VADM Brannigan then back at Major Troy, "This is totally unacceptable." He then looked around the table. "Do you have anything else?"

"No, Sir." Responded Major Troy and moved to his seat.

MajGen Connington looked over to Dr. Vance while VADM Brannigan looked at his hand device pretending to be reading something of interest while maintaining a calm appearance. He too was upset that nothing else was found out by the Intelligence Department.

Dr. Vance pressed a button and brought up his brief. He felt bad for the Major knowing the way the military were on their officers, especially intelligence and operations. They were to find the issues and present solutions.

"Sir, on a cultural front with the Kammorrigans, we don't know anything outside of their apparent desire for smooth, rounded tunnels. We don't have any information on what they look like or their planet. Linguists did not find any errors in their translation nor did we find Anything in the mathematics that we were not aware of already. Sir, we reviewed the message and the databanks." Continued Dr. Vance as VADM Brannigan brought up the message on his hand-held device. "We really didn't find anything different than the Intelligence Department except for one thing..." He paused momentarily and the two Commanders looked at him, "the message that we received from the Kammorrigans do not seem to be directed at us. Rather it was a general message sent out into space that we intercepted. The message did not truly include the final details of a hyperspace drive. It gave the blueprints that we worked off of but not the final equations that were necessary to actually operate it. Instead, the message told us to send a message back to the coordinates that we are traveling to now. We assumed that if we sent the message that the final equations would be provided. It is obvious that we did not send a message back in order to ensure our planet's safety. But we do find it curious that they did not provide the final section."

MajGen Connington looked at him slightly confused, "So how are we out here?"

"Oh that, well our own engineers and scientists already had their own theories on space travel. The information in the Kammorrigan message was enough for us to figure out which path to go down and we figured out the last bit of information."

"Good for our guys." MajGen Connington responded.

"One important thing to consider in this." Continued Dr. Vance, "The Kammorrigans don't know that we are coming. They did provide us information to transmit back to them, a greeting. We have modified the greeting to send once we do jump into their space, hopefully their home world. The coordinates indicate that this will be true."

The two Commanders looked at each other and then at each Commanding Officer. MajGen Connington spoke, "That is interesting. I didn't quite realize that they did not expect us to come. This could cause difficulties to jump right into their space, or their home world space without any announcement."

"CAPT Lindsey," asked VADM Brannigan, "have you had a chance to contemplate this?"

"Yes, Sir, Dr. Vance and I have spoken about this and what it could mean."

"And what do you have, Provided Dr. Vance doesn't have anything else at this time."

Dr. Vance indicated that he was done.

"We have surmised that we will definitely be raising an alarm when we jump into their space and could initiate a fire fight if we are not careful and in lieu of what we have encountered so far on this mission, we think our assessment is correct. With that assumption we have come up with three different courses of actions." She paused to bring up the slide on the viewer.

"The first is to send in the *Nautilus* to perform a reconnaissance of the space and then come back with more information. We then would have a decision point on whether to jump in one ship or the entire fleet. Number two is to send in one ship to make initial contact, alert them to the rest of the fleet and the diplomatic charge. We would send in the *Nautilus* to monitor the situation. The third is to jump the entire fleet into their space in a non-threatening formation and send the greeting."

"What is non-threatening?" asked MajGen Connington.

"Good question." Answered Dr. Vance, "without knowing anymore about their culture, one ship could elicit a hostile response or the entire fleet either tightly compacted or spread out could be misinterpreted by them as hostile. The only thing we have going for us is the greeting message."

"No matter what, we have a gamble." Said VADM Brannigan who was thumbing through the presentation on his hand device. "We really don't know what their reaction will be if we even send in one ship since we have not received or gleaned any intelligence about them from a military, political or cultural aspect. In short, we just don't know. We have no clue about what we don't know in addition to this so we are going in blind no matter what."

Everyone around the table nodded at him. He shrugged his shoulders and frowned at this, and then he looked at MajGen Connington. Paul Connington was used to plans being developed around knowns vice no data and a pure assumption which his planners were not even making assumptions. He thought about this and sat up in his chair looking at the Admiral.

"Sir, our mission is to make contact with the Kammorrigans and attempt a friendly dialogue. Our staff cannot provide an estimate of hostility or what may or may not be hostile. We will have to gamble and I would prefer having the firepower of the entire fleet with us."

VADM Brannigan suddenly remembered that he had not heard from his Diplomat. He turned to Mr. O'Shea who was sitting in his chair thinking about the situation.

"Well Admiral, I would rather negotiate from a position of strength. I am not too concerned about offering an offense by just appearing in their space. They did send out an invitation so they shouldn't be too surprised when we jump in. Of course, I would send out the greeting that we have put together and have the fleet in a non-hostile formation. But I would rather have the entire fleet there. We could proceed with only one or two ships to the planet and have the other ones hang back.

This shows a non-hostile intent but a willingness to attack if one has to. We bring power as a backup. It will give them pause wondering what else is out there. My team and I have looked at the tapes ourselves and I think this is the best way of handling the situation."

VADM Brannigan nodded slowly at this, glanced at his hand device and around the table.

"Ladies and Gentlemen, I agree with Mr. O'Shea and choose the course of action that the entire fleet goes in. CAPT Lindsey ensure that the fleet comes into their space in a non-hostile manner. The *Nautilus* will come with us but not as the first ship, I want her to jump in last under the cover of the other ships. The *Intrepid* and either the *Scimitar* or *Defiant* will proceed slowly towards the planet sending the greeting. MajGen Connington, I want you to transfer over to the *Chesty* and take command of the ships that will be standing by while the other two head towards the planet. I and Mr. O'Shea will head the diplomacy effort. Paul, I want you to ensure that the fleet is ready to take any action that is necessary to protect the fleet. CAPT Lindsey, I want an emergency jump location provided to each ship in case we have to get out of there in a hurry. Commanding Officers ensure you keep the coordinates properly updated with the star drift. A Commanding Officer will not leave his or her ship. Only the Executive Officer if required. Captain Jackson and Mr. Peterson will accompany the Diplomatic Team." He sighed, "I guess I will have to take part of the FAST Platoon." The MEU Colonel and MajGen Connington both nodded.

"Alright, fine. Paul, ensure that you keep the deflectors online to block out any scanning. If you need to raise shields but keep weapons offline unless you have to." MajGen Connington nodded. VADM Brannigan gave a look to MajGen Connington and then said, "Alright dismissed and get ready for the last jump." He stayed seated as everyone else got up. As the group was leaving MajGen Connington touched the arm of Colonel Roberts, the MEU Commander and motioned for CAPT Strickland, the Commanding Officer of the *Nautilus* and CDR Ramirez to stay behind. After everyone left the room, MajGen Connington gestured for them to sit. VADM Brannigan was reviewing his hand device while they looked at each other and waited.

Finally, VADM Brannigan looked up.

"Gentlemen, I don't trust the Kammorrigans. Dr. Vance hit it on the head. They didn't give us the final details to make the hyperspace drive. They wanted us to send them a message first. This could indicate that they were being cautious to avoid what we are doing or a confrontation by a hostile species or it could mean that they wanted to know about a species that could match them or add to their governance. We don't know at this time. So, I not only want all the SEALs onboard the *Nautilus* but I want the Recon unit onboard as well." Colonel Roberts started to object and MajGen Connington held up his hand to silence him while VADM Brannigan continued. "CAPT Strickland, I want you to proceed to the planet after you jump. I want you to perform a cursory survey of the planet and determine where to drop off the units. I want you to set up a secure communication system to receive intelligence from these units. Transfer the data on a tight beam to both the *Intrepid* and *Chesty*. Be ready to retrieve them in a hurry. I want to know about the planet, the type of people we are dealing with, their vulnerabilities, if I have to attack them the best targets, etc. Colonel Roberts this means that you will need a quick reaction force to go in and rescue them while we keep the Kammorrigans off of you and then we all jump away."

"Sir," responded Colonel Roberts, "this could elicit a very strong military response by them."

"Yes, if our teams are caught it could. These teams and our communications cannot be detected by them. I want to know about these people and the SEALs and Recon teams are able to do this. A no go criteria is the atmosphere of the planet. If they cannot operate effectively outside of EVAs then we have to go with the sole diplomatic method and normal scans. MajGen Connington is the sole point of contact in this matter. I will brief CAPT Lindsey prior to the start of the diplomatic mission. We are the only ones that know this plan. We won't jump for another day so you have one day to get the teams and the ship ready."

"Yes Sir." Colonel Roberts, CDR Ramirez and CAPT Strickland said and left for their ships. MajGen Connington sat for a moment and then left to get ready to transfer over to the *Chesty*.

VADM Brannigan was looking over the message from the Kammorrigans while sitting in the conference room. He took a deep breath and slowly let it out and looked up. He was about to put several men's lives into harm's way but they were trained for this type of mission. He needed the information. He knew the crew would be biting at the bit to get onto the planet and meet the Kammorrigans but he couldn't let that happen if they were not friendly. Even if they were not accepting of them, he and Mr. O'Shea had to get them to accept them and make a trade arrangement. That was the primary mission. Meet the Kammorrigans and arrange for free trade. How do you do that without any information? Commodore Perry was credited for the opening of Japan. However, a single ambassador who came after the Commodore, was the one who arranged the trade agreements. Now he was the modern Commodore Perry and after seeing what is out here, he had to succeed.

As Paul approached the door to his office, he noticed CDR Ramirez standing next to it.

"Hello CDR, please come on in."

"Thank you, Sir."

Paul opened the door and went to his chair. He poured himself a glass of water before sitting down and motioned for the CDR to get a glass. The CDR politely turned him down and the General offered him a seat. As CDR Ramirez was sitting down Paul said.

"You have questions about the away teams, yes?"

"Yes Sir. The *Nautilus* already has two four-man teams with her. She is already at capacity. How many more teams are you desiring aboard?"

Paul rubbed his chin, "Well how many more can she hold? We want as many as possible plus a Recon squad. We need to blanket key areas of Kammorriga with teams to collect intelligence and beam back to the ship the information."

The CDR shook his head. "Okay Sir, but that is a lot of men for *Nautilus* to carry besides how would she get them all planet side?"

Paul reached over to his computer and pulled a thumb drive from it. He toyed with it briefly then handed it to CDR Ramirez.

"Take this with you over to *Nautilus* and share with CAPT Strickland. We have modified some transports to become well I guess we could call them drop ships. They need to be moved to *Nautilus*. The ride down will be risky and we are not sure they could make it off the surface. It will be a rough ride down we believe. Funny thing is, no one knows why we destroyed five transports to make them. Also, you need to plan for a quick reaction force most likely the Rangers to be able to secure as many of them as you can. We don't want to leave anyone behind. Which means you have to have trackers on all members."

CDR Ramirez had taken the thumb drive and put it into his utility pocket.

"How long to make all the preparations? Only a day?" He shook his head.

MajGen Connington looked at him for a moment then keyed up a timeline on his computer. He looked it over.

"I'll request from the Admiral to give you three days total to make the arrangements. But I know he won't budge on more than three days. That will be the most I can get out of him. So, tomorrow will be day one. Best utilize the rest of today. Go ahead and head over to the *Nautilus*. We will inform both ships of your itinerary."

"Yes Sir" with that CDR Ramirez got up and left the office heading to the hanger decks.

Paul took a drink of water and then keyed the Admiral.

CAPT Allen Strickland, Commander of the *Nautilus* listened to his Officers and Chiefs complain bitterly at the orders. They kept asking what the *Chesty* was for and why they had to do this. Finally, CAPT Strickland grew tired of the endless complaining and shut down their griping. As he informed them, this was the order and they best figure out the problem. It would be the riskiest mission she had received so far. CAPT Strickland would have to bring his ship into a low orbit around the planet to launch the teams to various locations and remain undetected. That would be the fun part and most risky. The part everyone hated was the extra personnel on a very tight ship. The jump to Kammorriga was a full seven days and so she had to accommodate all the extra persons and equipment during the jump. Finally, the Officers and Chiefs began working the problem. They went to every space to figure out where to put equipment and personnel. Part of the problem was solved once they figured out how to house the drop ships, the equipment would be organized and placed inside the drop ships themselves. The people, that was tougher but they were working it

The next few days were busy for the fleet. The first day, *Nautilus* repositioned everything in the hanger and requested the drop ships be brought over. It took the entire first day to place the drop ships aboard the *Nautilus*. Meanwhile, CDR Ramirez was back aboard the *Chesty* and was preparing the teams. The Recon squad was made up of twelve men, for three teams. He had two SEAL teams already with *Nautilus*, for five teams. He then prepared five more SEAL teams. A total of ten teams of forty men would be dropped onto the planet.

The equipment would be data recorders and communication equipment. The signals were being preprogrammed into the communication equipment along with the ability to self-destruct them if they were captured by the Kammorrigans. They would have small arms plus explosives just in case. They were given the capability to mark targets for either the space fighters or the ships to unload nuclear devices on. The food would be small packets. There would be no re supply of food so they were given scanners to determine if the planetary food would be edible. If it was then they were to augment their stores with the planet food. Each person was given rare materials for purchase since they didn't know what the currency would be. If that didn't work, then they were to steal what they would be required to survive and carry out their surveillance mission.

Meanwhile, Col Roberts and his planners were assisting CDR Ramirez with the drop zones based off the thumb drive that MajGen Connington had provided to CDR Ramirez. These would be provided to *Nautilus* before they made the jump to Kammorriga. Plus, Col Roberts required the information for his rescue teams to get the forty personnel off the planet. Not to mention to program his own ship's fires with the data if required.

The evening of the second day, the teams were transported over to *Nautilus*. CDR Ramirez went over to ensure they were berthed correctly, the equipment staged in the drop ships. He worked with CAPT Strickland's crew ensuring they had all the information and communication signals worked out. At the end of the third day, both CAPT Strickland and CDR Ramirez were satisfied with the details. As CDR Ramirez took his shuttle back over to the *Chesty*, CAPT Strickland signaled to the flag bridge on the *Intrepid* that all was ready. *Intrepid* signaled the fleet that at 0800 the next day they would make the jump.

·   ·   ·

The hyperspace well opened and out of it came six ships along with a seventh that no one could see. The formation of the ships was spread out with the largest being in the middle. The next largest was behind and above it. The next in size were two ships and they were in front and slightly below the large ship. The next two were the smallest in size. One of them was directly in front of the largest ship and the other was below the next in size. The stealth ship was behind the second largest and immediately moved off on a heading that was different from the rest of the fleet.

The fleet had entered normal space in close proximity to a planet that was in a solar system with a yellow sun. There were five planets in orbit around the sun. The planet that they jumped around was the fourth one from the sun. It had two moons. The first moon was in an orbit that resembled Earth's moon. The second was half of its size and was farther out.

The fleet slowed to a halt. The lead ship, the *Intrepid*, sent out a greeting to the planet. After five minutes they sent the message again. After fifteen minutes, they sent the message again and then the lead ship along with the ship in front of her, the *Scimitar*, headed towards the fourth planet at a slow speed. The *Chesty* took her place and the *Defiant* closed up the rear. Each ship had their sensors active.

They noticed that there were ships in orbit of the planet along with several satellites and a space station orbiting the planet. There were ships going to and from the planet on a routine route.

The *Intrepid* and *Scimitar* moved into a high orbit above the planet. The *Scimitar* took up a position just aft and slightly below the *Intrepid*. They had their deflectors up but their shields and weapons were offline. Three ships headed towards them from the station. Two of the ships took up a position above and to the aft of the *Intrepid* and one in front of her. The *Intrepid* waited but began scanning in an obvious manner the planet. They avoided scanning the ships.

The planet was heavily populated. It also was industrial by the pollution content in the air. The atmosphere was breathable by human standards but not necessarily healthy. There were centers of manufacturing and what appeared to be agricultural areas. They were able to identify the space ports and ship production facilities. The planet had an ocean. It took up a third of the planet and had several islands. After two orbits they located what may be the government center of the planet. After a third orbit they located what they presumed to be planetary defense systems. They continued to perform scans and to log what they were finding.

Meanwhile the *Nautilus* went onto the dark side of the planet and conducted scans of the planet. After consulting with their Medical Officer on the effect of the air on the Marines and Sailors they determined they could continue with the mission. They scanned the atmosphere and the space hoping for meteorites that would be striking the atmosphere. As luck would have it there would be some coming towards the planet in a couple of orbits. The *Nautilus* ensured they would remain on the dark side. Meanwhile her crew prepped drop ships that would drop the reconnaissance teams onto the planet. Their scans indicated that the drop ships could be hid on the planet's surface without too much difficulty. The prepped for launch.

CHAPTER 7

For three days there was no response to the greeting call neither did the *Intrepid* send another greeting. Instead for the three days they scanned the planet, its moons, the solar system and ships that were coming and going. They were gathering a lot of data. When they were in direct line with the *Nautilus*, they received on the secure channel a tight beam of data that the *Nautilus* was collecting. The Reconnaissance teams were gathering data on the population and environment. They would send the information to the *Nautilus* once a day on a tight short beam.

Dr. Vance, his team and the Intelligence Department were analyzing the data as it came in. The results were interesting. The planet had a variety of power sources that fed off the Geo thermal energy of the planet. The energy possibilities were enormous but it seemed dangerous with the pollutants from the various plants on the planet.

VADM Brannigan sat in his chair waiting. The images on the viewscreens were amazing. He watched them fascinated by their escort ships. They had begun to scan them along with the other bodies in orbit. The information would be helpful if it could give them any hint as to how to deal with this civilization. They waited for the Kammorrigans to figure out what they were going to do now that his fleet was in orbit. His crew continued their work. They were excited about being here. Nine months of travel to get to this point and meet those that sent the original message that brought them here. They were eager to go down to the planet but they understood they had to wait to make sure the planet was safe for them.

Kevin sat in his chair drinking his coffee waiting. This was the fourth day of orbiting the planet waiting for a response. They had received several pictures from the ground crew and all of them were still alright and apparently undiscovered. The pictures of the Kammorrigans were interesting. They were three legged like a stool with a torso. They had four arms, two of which resembled tentacles and two that had hand like appendages. They had one head which extended out of their torso in a manner that suggested they lacked necks. They had two ears that tapered to points along the side of their head and they were relatively small. They had two eyes but the pictures were not clear on the facial features but they could tell there was a mouth and some form of a nose.

The planet and ships around them had scanned them. They could tell that the deflectors kept the Kammorrigan scans from gathering details of the ships. However, they could tell that these scans told the Kammorrigans that the ships had their weapons and shields offline. They waited.

VADM Brannigan had nearly finished his coffee when the Communications Officer sounded excited.

"Sir, we have a communiqué from the planet."

"Put it on the speakers", he said.

The speaker sounded with the translated voice, "Welcome visitors to Kammorriga. We are pleased that you received our invitation and traveled over a great distance to meet us. Please send your official party down to our governing center to meet with us. The landing coordinates are provided in the beam. Again, we welcome you to our home world and are looking forward to meeting you in person." The transmission ended.

VADM Brannigan looked around his bridge to see excited faces. Mr. O'Shea was allowed a station on the bridge slightly behind and to the left of the admiral. He too was at his station and seemed excited looking at the Admiral.

Communications, please send the following, the Admiral said, "We are pleased to accept the invitation and will prepare two shuttles for our official party to arrive in the morning your time at the provided landing coordinates, SESG EXPLORER out."

He turned and looked at Mr. O'Shea, "Ok, we are a go," then he turned to CAPT Lindsey, "Let's make sure we are ready to launch in the morning. You will stay onboard and command the two ships here while MajGen Connington commands the overall Strike Group in my absence."

"Yes, Sir." She replied and turned to her station board to alert the Admiral's Aide and the FAST along with Capt Jackson, Mr. Peterson and the diplomatic stations.

Dr. Vance happened to be on the bridge at the time and looked pleased. He picked up his hand held device to see who he had chosen to go along with the team, he smiled at the name of the very competent engineer, Lucy Venrose. She would be a good addition to the team to provide the Admiral with any technical insights into the technology. He nodded at the Admiral as he left the bridge to alert her of the go status.

The USS Intrepid beamed a message to the Chesty to alert them of the go word from Kammorriga. This would bring the rest of the Strike Group closer to the planet, not quite an orbit but close enough to present a picture of readiness.

The next morning the Official Party stood in the hanger deck. During the rest of the previous day there had been more communication with the Kammorrigans. It was arranged for the two shuttles to carry the Official Party and their FAST Platoon down with an honor escort provided by Kammorrigan Space Authority. The party would be placed in quarters in the government center. The agenda for the first day would be a simple meeting with presentations of who was who and an official letter from the President of the United States wishing for a prosperous relationship between the two worlds.

The FAST Platoon would place a squad on each shuttle and keep the third squad on the Intrepid with the Platoon's Executive Officer as a quick reaction force. The *Chesty* had the Rangers on standby as an additional quick reaction force with a company of Marines as back up.

The rest of the Official Party included VADM Brannigan, Mr. O'Shea, Dr. Lucy Venrose, Capt Jackson, Mr. Peterson, the Admiral's Aide, LT John Shapiro, an assistant to Mr. O'Shea, Fred Evans, and the FAST Platoon Commander, Major Clark. The Admiral desired more officers and a couple more scientists but Mr. O'Shea recommended with a first contact with a total alien nation (human or otherwise) this was a very large party and anymore would be too cumbersome. He had advised the Admiral that it showed a military pomp and power and yet it was balanced with reason in the form of diplomacy and science. When the Admiral inquired about seeming to be paranoid or overly militaristic, he had replied that it was balanced. They were showing science and diplomacy, the message and weapons status showed they were interested in peace and trade, the military was a protective force. It also demonstrated that they were willing to back up their presence and word with force. The Admiral took stock of this along with his experience and accepted this as his Official Party. Five fighters were already launched to provide a CAP with five others waiting to receive the shuttles out of the launch bay as an escort to the planet's honor escort. CAPT Lindsey had insisted on this and the coordination with the planet's honor escort was arranged very carefully to avoid any mistakes. In this manner she demonstrated they were capable of providing their own protection and yet respect the air space of Kammorriga. The escort issues seemed to be taken rather well by both sides. They boarded the two shuttles.

Intrepid received authorization to launch the shuttles and they launched the shuttles. They left the launch bay and took their position behind the v shape escort of the fighters with the Admiral's shuttle in lead and the other one slightly to the left and behind. They flew along the route towards the planet that the planet Orbital Authority had provided them. All was smooth. The Admiral watched out the window gazing at the planet as Major Clark monitored the pilots and the situation. When they reached the upper atmosphere, the escort fighters peeled away and flew over the area as the two shuttles entered the atmosphere enduring the ionizing effects. The Kammorrigan's escorts ships waited to receive them after they left the effects. They came out of it without incident and angled in behind the escorts as briefed and proceeded towards the Government Center with its official landing pad. The *Intrepid's* escort fighters returned to their mother ship and the CAP followed. The *Intrepid* ensured they had a ready alert of fighters and the *Chesty* had the Rangers with a five-ship close air support at the ready five alert. They would launch within five minutes once alerted.

The shuttle pilots acknowledged the radio communication with their escort and continued their descent. There was a total of fifteen escort craft around them. They had three in front of them guiding them down with three on either side and three behind them. Three other escorts flew in circular and a random pattern to ensure no other craft were approaching the shuttles.

At first, they had to fly solely on instruments until they came through some high-level clouds and emerged into a clear but what appeared to their eyes to be a murky atmosphere. The atmosphere indicators on the shuttle showed a breathable atmosphere but confirmed heavy pollutants in it.

They came onto an approach vector to the landing zone. It was in a rather large clearing between several large buildings. Two of the buildings on opposite sides of the landing zone were tall skyscrapers. There was a large orb building off to one side of the zone and several smaller and varied in size and shape buildings around the zone and spread out from the area. As they came down the escort ships left except for the three in front and they fired flares in a ceremony of diplomatic visitors. The shuttles landed and the escorts flew a CAP over the area in a ceremonial flight.

On the landing site that the Admiral's shuttle landed on was a blue stripe with yellow borders from the shuttle to the steps going down from the landing zone. They did not exit the shuttles right away. The pilots contacted both the Zone Authority and the *Intrepid* and gave a status report. Major Clark waited for confirmation from the pilots that the Zone Authority authorized the departure from the shuttles. When he received it, he opened the shuttle hatch and deployed his squad and stepped out onto the stripe last. The second shuttle opened its hatch and the squad deployed around the landing zone while Major Clark's took up a position along the stripe while two stood beside the shuttle hatch. The Major then proceeded halfway along the blue stripe and stopped. The personnel on the second shuttle stepped out and stood over by the blue stripe leading to the stairs.

A Kammorrigan Officer came up the stairs and headed towards Major Clark. For three legs he seemed to move quite smoothly. He wore a blue uniform indicating his rank. Something that they would have to learn. The Kammorrigan moved up to Major Clark, saluted by placing his left hand, the one with digits, over his torso. He then indicated that the Kammorrigan welcoming party was ready to receive the *Intrepid's* official party. Major Clark turned slightly and made a hand motion indicating all was ready.

VADM Brannigan was in his dress blues and placed his combination cover on and stepped out of the shuttle with Mr. O'Shea following him, who was wearing a business suit. They moved down the blue stripe on the landing zone with the two FAST Marines that were stationed by the hatch coming in behind them. Dr. Venrose, Capt Jackson, Mr. Evans and LT Shapiro moved in behind them followed by three more FAST members. When the Admiral was approaching Major Clark, the Major made a hand motion and two of the FAST Marines moved in behind him and he moved towards the stairs. Major Clark descended the steps; these were wide low circular steps, a total of six. After he and the two FAST Marines followed behind the Kammorrigan officer as they headed for the door to the welcoming center followed by the rest of the party. The rest of the FAST moved back towards the shuttle. The Squad Sergeant looked at his roster for the two teams and made a couple adjustments to the guard rotation. The landing zone pad was theirs for the moment and they were taking up a defensive position along it to keep the shuttles protected. The Marines that were not on the guard duty would rest inside the shuttles along with the pilots but would be prepared to move to the Admiral's side if he needed them.

Major Clark entered the hatch first and noticed that the hallway was a tube. It was a tunnel that ran from the doorway to another open door at the far end; its sides were smooth and metallic in appearance. He found that his head nearly scraped the top of the tunnel. Major Clark stood at five eleven and was a foot taller than the Kammorrigan officer that met him. He moved down the tunnel towards the opening. When he stepped out, he scanned the room that he was in. It was a rather large circular and wide room with three openings, the ceiling was approximately twelve feet high, the walls were smooth and curved from the floor to the ceiling.

At one end stood several Kammorrigans. About a third of them wore what appeared to be uniforms while the rest wore an assortment of robes, all of the clothing were quite colorful which appeared to indicate their positions of rank and office. Major Clark's two FAST Marines spread out from behind him as he walked forward. He stopped at approximately halfway and stepped to the left to let the Admiral and Mr. O'Shea proceed with their two FAST Members. Of the three that came in last, two stood at the entrance of the tunnel into the room and the last one followed the other members of the party.

The Admiral and Mr. O'Shea stepped forward and halved the distance to the waiting Kammorrigans. Their host looked at each other and spoke among themselves, and then two of them separated themselves and strode forward to the Admiral. One was dressed in blue with gold and the other one had a form of a robe that was a rich crimson, blue and silver. They came within three feet of the two and stopped.

The one in the robes said, which was picked up and translated from the translating device, "Welcome to Kammorriga Admiral Brannigan and Mr. O'Shea. We are pleased to make your acquaintance. As the Chancellor of the Kammorriga Space Regime we thank you for answering our invitation and have come all this way to our planet. We hope we can have a prosperous relationship."

"Thank you," began the Vice Admiral, "We are very glad to make your acquaintance. We also welcome the opportunity for a prosperous relationship that we both can profit from."

The chancellor nodded, "We have our greeting ceremony if you would follow me."

The Chancellor led the entire party to an upper floor of the building and out onto a curved balcony. As they approached the railing, which curved from the floor upwards, they peered out over an elongated circular courtyard. As the party filtered around, the Humans on the left side and the Kammorrigans on the right, a loud blast of horns and yells were heard from the entrance in front of them. Several Kammorrigans appeared moving in a fluid and indistinguishable fashion to the Humans. They flowed like water into the courtyard. They wore a variety of colors. Their tentacles waved and their hands flourished as they shuffled along on their three legs. The Humans were baffled and awestruck.

Next came a more orderly group bearing several banners, mainly with blue or deep crimson fields and a gold sixteen-point star with silver tips on each banner. They swayed and flowed in column form till they reached the center at which time they broke into several groups flowing all over the enclosure with the previous group intermingling with them. This performance lasted for an hour. After which most of the performers left the enclosure leaving behind two groups. The remaining performers formed up on either side of the courtyard with the blue banners on the left and the crimson banners on the right.

A single Kammorrigan entered the enclosure and strode to the center. In a loud voice it began speaking and at times chanting in a sing song method. The translator only picked up part of it. This performance by the lone Kammorrigan lasted nearly two hours.

Afterwards came several other groups with a variety of colors and instruments flowing into the enclosure. Their motions were quite indistinguishable to the Humans. These groups moved into and out of the enclosure waving banners and flags of various colors but always with the same gold sixteen-point star with silver tips.

At long last the Chancellor turned to the Admiral and all went quiet. He held out his right hand which had eight digits. Two digits appeared to be thumbs while the other six varied in both size and number of knuckles. The Admiral held out his hand. The Chancellor briefly touched the Admiral's palm with the center four fingers. To the Admiral the digits felt both cold and hot and a bit clammy. He echoed the motion with his index and middle fingers. The Chancellor bowed and motioned them back inside where escorts would take them to their rooms.

VADM Brannigan sighed heavily after the door to his room was shut. LT Shapiro scanned the room for listening devices. He nodded to the Admiral indicating nothing found, which doesn't mean that there weren't any listening devices just that their technology didn't detect any. Meanwhile the Admiral went over to the window and looked out while LT Shapiro scanned the refreshments to ensure they could be consumed by them. The Admiral was taking note of the weather and the green gray of the sky. The buildings appeared similar yet slightly different from his own planet's. LT Shapiro poured a drink and handed it to the Admiral who took it with thanks and sat down in a recliner. It was comfortable and the drink was smooth and strangely refreshing. The bell rung and the Lieutenant went to answer it. The Admiral was glad for the Lieutenant, he didn't like the job of an Aide and he was happy he never had to do the job but was thankful for the Lieutenant. Mr. O'Shea came in and was offered a drink and a seat.

The Chancellor led the entire party to a upper floor of the building and out onto a curved balcony. As they approached the railing, which curved from the floor upwards, they peered out over an elongated circular courtyard. As the party filtered around, the Humans on the left side and the Kammorrigans on the right, a loud blast of horns and yells were heard from the entrance in front of them. Several Kammorrigans appeared moving in a fluid and indistinguishable fashion to the Humans. They flowed like water into the courtyard. They wore a variety of colors. Their tentacles waved and their hands flourished as they shuffled along on their three legs. The Humans were baffled and awestruck.

Next came a more orderly group bearing several banners, mainly with blue or deep crimson fields and a gold sixteen-point star with silver tips on each banner. They swayed and flowed in column form till they reached the center at which time they broke into several groups flowing all over the enclosure with the previous group intermingling with them. This performance lasted for an hour. After which most of the performers left the enclosure leaving behind two groups. The remaining performers formed up on either side of the courtyard with the blue banners on the left and the crimson banners on the right.

A single Kammorrigan entered the enclosure and strode to the center. In a loud voice it began speaking and at times chanting in a sing song method. The translator only picked up part of it. This performance by the lone Kammorrigan lasted nearly two hours.

Afterwards came several other groups with a variety of colors and instruments flowing into the enclosure. Their motions were quite indistinguishable to the Humans. These groups moved into and out of the enclosure waiving banners and flags of various colors but always with the same gold sixteen-point star with silver tips.

At long last the Chancellor turned to the Admiral and all went quiet. He held out his right hand which had eight digits. Two digits appeared to be thumbs while the other six varied in both size and number of knuckles. The Admiral held out his hand. The Chancellor briefly touched the Admiral's palm with the center four fingers. To the Admiral the digits felt both cold and hot and a bit clammy. He echoed the motion with his index and middle fingers. The Chancellor bowed and motioned them back inside where escorts would take them to their rooms.

"Man, that was long," he started, "I think we did well with the ceremonies." Mr. O'Shea took a drink, "Umm, this isn't bad."

The bell rang again and the Lieutenant went to get it.

VADM Brannigan said, "Yes long and noisy but necessary I suppose. Was this ceremony put on just for us or do they do this for all dignitaries?"

Major Clark entered the room and the Lieutenant came up with him. The Admiral indicated for them both to get something to drink and be comfortable. Mr. O'Shea took another drink.

"I asked that and it was definitely a ceremony that they do for all dignitaries. It was a normal greeting for them. It gave us the same status that they provide everyone else that comes here. It sits well that we were given this ceremony. Now of course starts the hard part. We have been working on a strategy; in fact, Fred is putting on some final touches. We will adjust as we go."

The Admiral nodded his head and looked at Major Clark.

"Sir, the shuttles are good to go. The Landing Zone Authority has requested that we move them to one of their VIP hangers. I have three Marines checking it out at this time. My intent is twofold, we can secure the hanger and we can make a quick escape if required."

The Admiral nodded, "If it meets your criteria then make the move. We will be here for a few days and we have flexibility since we arrived earlier than planned. We shouldn't be hogs with their LZ."

"Yes, Sir. We also made contact with the fleet to give them a status. All is well with them and their analysis."

The Admiral smiled his thanks with the understanding that his intel gathering teams were still operational and undetected.

"What time do we have to meet them?"

Mr. O'Shea said, "0900 by the adjusted time. The first hour will be a small greeting party then we move into an exploratory meeting with some of their ministers."

The Admiral nodded, "I want to see your strategy then at 0700 unless you can give me information tonight. I would actually prefer tonight with a follow up in the morning." He looked at his Aide who nodded his understanding.

The first days of negotiations were exploratory only. Both sides were attempting to find out what they could use from each other in terms of trade. The Kammorrigans kept trying to figure out where the home planet was located for the Strike Group. They proved to be deft at trying to pry it out of the team but the team kept on their toes and did not let the info out. They did tell them that they are humans and appreciated the invite. The team was able to find out some more about the technological capability of the planet. Their weather controls were in place. It seems the Kammorrigans actually liked the condition of their planet so their entire planet maintained the atmosphere. This made the team happier that their quarters had scrubbers for the ventilation. At the end of the day, they had agreed to provide a list of items available for trade, primarily finished goods.

The team transmitted the data to the *Intrepid* and was analyzing them in their quarters. Dr. Venrose and Capt Jackson were able to secure a tour of a couple of their technical labs and manufacturing plants. Mr. O'Shea and the Admiral would get a tour of some of their schools and the following day would be able to see one of their military installations. Meanwhile both negotiating teams would be reviewing the lists.

The tours at the military stations only showed the standard military inspections that would be performed on Earth. It demonstrated that the Kammorrigans had a military might but no specifics, which would only be expected. The schools were definitely different from Earth's but it demonstrated the social thinking of the society. This society had a nurturing yet militaristic mentality. The younglings or children had one of their parents (it was not identified how they had their children) and some other individual that were teaching various skills.

Dr. Venrose and her team came back with better information but limited from their tour. They saw technologies and production methods that were more efficient than those on Earth. They were able to gather information freely given by the Kammorrigans. They were excited by their find. This bothered Kevin. He stood at the window to his room drinking from a glass of the liquid that was provided. He looked out the window thinking about the last couple of days and the way things were progressing. He had learned over the years that sometimes you showed expressions and at times you did your best to show nothing. It was a ploy with diplomats that one used to communicate. Did these Kammorrigans show them various sites along with their greeting ceremonies to learn their non-verbal communications? Yes, they must be learning our communications and how to read them. Makes sense from a negotiating standpoint to gain trade leverage but did they desire more than this?

He turned to his Aide to summon Mr. Peterson.

•   •   •

Petty Officer First Class Seymour was quite adept at moving stealthily. The other three men of his four-man Special Ops Team were equally proficient. They had to move through various urban and rural areas back on Earth without being discovered and they took great pride in their abilities. But this world made the other missions seem like training exercises.

This world of the Kammorrigans was perpetually gray; the air was thick and difficult to breathe in without a respirator. At times the night sky would glow with strange colors that the SEALs could not explain. The nights were also cold while the days were hot and humid and at times unbearably so. The two extremes made it difficult to keep their cover while moving through the cities and what appeared to be farms.

The people were totally strange. The way they moved with their three legs like a stool still made his skin crawl and those two tentacles whipping around. But the strangest parts of them were their freakish eyes and the two arms with digits. The way those parts moved together just sent shivers through him.

Everything about their cities was tunnel like or circular. It proved very difficult when they first landed to adjust to the landscape not having anything but smooth circles. It was a little better now they had been there for a couple of days. At first it was difficult to hide but as they started learning how the circles were laid out within the buildings, streets and malls they could cover themselves and observe the Kammorrigans.

They were an odd lot. Their interaction with each other at times seemed violent and yet submissive. They obviously had some sort of rank structure. The clothing they wore identified them by some rank. The blue and red seemed to be military. The blue and black colors were somewhat difficult at first to figure out. The white and black seemed to be workers. The gold and silver seemed to be a priest type which implied a religion but they had not discovered any form of temples or churches. The yellow colors seemed to be some sort of law enforcement. It was difficult to truly identify them since their translating device had quit working only a few hours after they had landed.

On the third day of their scouting, they came across a very disturbing area. In this area there were several different types of creatures with various locking devices. The Kammorrigans wearing blue and black colors were the ones operating the area. They were using a whip like device and stun guns to move the creatures around. The team decided to hide out on one of the roofs to observe this area. They were taping the abusive behavior of the Kammorrigans when one of the team members saw one of the creatures escape. It was a short four-legged furry creature. Petty Officer Seymour and another member took off on an intercept line to observe what they could.

The creature was able to slip into a small circular tube that the two SEALs knew where it would come out at and headed to intercept the creature. They got there just in time to see the creature poke its head out and look around. They quickly moved into position just slightly to the left of the creature and when he moved out from the tunnel, they grabbed him and pulled him into a vent. The little creature looked scared at first and after he looked them over its look changed to one of curiosity.

Petty Officer Dickens pulled out the translator and attempted to turn it on.

"Come on Jack, get that thing working. I want to talk to this guy."

"I am trying to get the damn thing to work but it is a piece of shit."

"Yeah, yeah. Come on get it working. We need to know what this guy knows."

Petty Officer Dickens kept playing with the translator trying to get it to work when the furry little creature reached out and grabbed the device. Petty Officer Dickens started for it but Seymour stopped him. The creature turned the translator over and over and then opened it and worked on a few things. It then closed it and pressed some of the keys. Suddenly the thing activated, the creature held the translator up to its mouth and slowly spoke into it. After repeating what it said slowly and carefully into the translator it then it handed it back to them.

"You are not Kammorrigan and I hope you don't help them." The creature said.

"No, we are not with them. Who and what are you?" Petty Officer Seymour asked.

"I am from Alia. I hope you don't turn me into them."

"No, we won't."

"What are you and what are you doing here?"

"We are humans and we are trying to learn about the Kammorrigans."

"Why are you here?"

The two Petty Officers looked at each other thinking about how much they should tell this creature.

"We received a message from the Kammorrigans and came here to learn about them."

The creature looked at them very closely. They could tell that it was thinking about them. Finally, it shrugged and continued.

"I am a slave here trying to figure out how to escape from this horrible place."

The two Petty Officers looked at each other and looked back at him.

"Our planet is a peaceful one and we had just started to explore space when we received a message from deep space. It was the Kammorrigans inviting us to space travel but they desired to know where our planet was. They didn't ask that of you?"

"We didn't tell them instead we figured out where they were and traveled here."

"That was smart of you." The little creature sighed, "I only wish we were so clever. Instead, we told them where we were and they came to our world and decimated the planet and took us into servitude. My world is now a polluted poor planet and my people now must serve them." They could tell the creature was both sad and angry. It looked up at them. "Leave this place and never make contact with them, ever. They are foul creatures that just want your planet for resources and take you into servitude. I ask you to take me with you. You must have some way to get off of this ugly world."

Petty Officer Seymour looked rather solemn and was thinking about what the creature asked when Petty Officer Dickens said.

"How do we know he hasn't been outfitted with a tracking device?"

The little creature suddenly looked very saddened and without hope.

"Come to think of it no one has ever escaped from here. I don't remember all the time I have been here. They could have implanted some sort of tracking device in me." He looked at them with eyes that appeared to lack any form of hope.

"It is best if you continue without me. If I am with you, they will discover you and then you will be trapped like me. I only hope that if you can help out Alia you will. We would be very grateful."

And with that the creature scurried away from them before they could react and was gone. The two Petty Officers looked down at the floor with grief in their hearts. The Alian seemed like a kind creature and they couldn't afford to help it since they would endanger their mission. They carefully looked out from the vent and headed towards the rest of their team. They knew they had to head for the Government Center to join up with the Admiral's team.

The drop ships proved they could take off from the planet. It was tricky but they were able to launch into orbit without being tracked. The *Nautilus* had picked up all but one team. They were still in a high orbit waiting for the remaining SEAL team to come back. It had been a whole day since the teams had returned. The information they had gathered did not make the Kammorrigans look friendly. But it would prove useful information. Still they had one team left on the planet and the CAPT was getting nervous since he had not been able to establish communications with them.

•   •   •

Capt Jackson, Mr. Peterson and Dr. Venrose came back in a bit of a hurry but trying to seem nonchalant. They were very disturbed over what they had discovered. They were able to gain access to one of the more secure buildings, as a guest of course, but were able to get access to some areas that told them more about the Kammorrigan society. Now they had to report out to the Admiral.

Kevin was disturbed by what was discovered but walked quite calmly with Mr. O'Shea to his meeting with the Kammorrigan leadership. He still wasn't quite sure how to approach the subject and now was concerned about acquiring a trade agreement with them. Further he wondered if they would use a trade agreement to go after Earth. They would find that out soon enough. They were walking through a tunnel system slowly spiraling upwards. They were following one of the government employees of the center whose job it appeared to be an escort for VIPs. He was glad that this meeting only required his Aide; unfortunately, one of the FAST was with him at the insistence of Major Clark. He was going to refuse but Mr. O'Shea felt it was imperative to have him along. He thought this was strange that a diplomat would insist on a bodyguard, especially at a trade negotiation meeting.

They approached a set of double doors made in a circle and waited while the escort touched a pad off to one side of the doors. The two metal doors swung inwards revealing a circular room with a semi-circle table in the middle with seating devices on one side of the table and two chairs within the semi-circle. It had the feel of an interviewing room vice a negotiating room. They entered and waited. After a little while six Kammorrigans entered the room and proceeded to take the seating devices. They indicated the chairs for the Admiral and Diplomat. LT Shapiro stood to the Admiral's right and a little behind while the FAST Marine stood near the door.

"Gentlemen we have enjoyed your company and we hope you have enjoyed our hospitality." The Lead Kammorrigan negotiator, Slavuu Makuuu, said.

Mr. O'Shea spoke for the group, "Yes, we have. We do appreciate the hospitality and we appreciate the tours."

"You still have not told us where your home world is."

The Admiral spoke at this point, "We are shy and prefer not to say."

Slavuu Makuuu nodded his head. "Well anyway, have you seen enough to be able to discuss trade?"

"Yes, we have," responded Mr. O'Shea. "We can offer several items from raw materials to manufactured goods, from technological to clothing items."

"Those items can be useful or pleasing. We obviously have items that we can offer as well. Those too can be along the same lines."

Mr. O'Shea nodded his head in return. VADM Brannigan sat listening feeling like this really was not a trade negotiation as much as an interview. The mannerism of the Kammorrigans didn't seem like negotiation but exploring what they could find out from them. He took a look at the other five Kammorrigans at the table. It definitely wasn't a situation where equals would be sitting at. It took a little time but one could figure out the features and the expressions of the Kammorrigans. It wasn't too difficult to see that several around the table were being more of an inquisition type of personality rather than a trade group looking for the best deal for their people. He made a slight hand motion to Mr. O'Shea for his awareness.

Mr. O'Shea had been listening very closely to Slavuu Makuuu ensuring that he wouldn't miss any hidden meanings to the words when he noticed the caution motion from the Admiral. He sat back taking a breath and looked around the table before refocusing on Slavuu Makuuu. It struck him as an odd thing the way how four of the Kammorrigans were studying them while the fifth one was looking over some sort of document on his screen at the table. Slavuu Makuuu was still talking about various manufactured items along technological lines when he got again a question about the coordinates of Earth being a part of the negotiation. He just shrugged like these items may or may not be important.

"We would definitely like to explore more about the galactic currency in this part of space", responded Mr. O'Shea. "I think we ought to be part of this system to maximize our profit and ability to conduct trade. Is this something that you can assist with?"

"Well," Slavuu Makuuu began, "I think we may be able to but of course the collective civilizations will of course need to know where you come from."

Mr. O'Shea slightly nodded his head to the left with a little downward smile, not quite a frown.

"That will depend on them."

Slavuu Makuuu tried not to make a grimace type of look but they could tell that he really wanted to know where they had come from and didn't like the answers he was getting. He looked over to the Kammorrigan that was studying the screen. Both the Admiral and Mr. O'Shea caught the signal that he gave to Slavuu Makuuu. The Kammorrigan made a sound that may have resembled a sigh and looked at his own screen and tapped in a few items. He looked up and one of the other Kammorrigans stood up and brought over a pad and gave it to Mr. O'Shea and returned to his chair.

"Are you able to provide items like these?"

Mr. O'Shea looked at the list of items seeing that they were already translated into English. He took his time reviewing the list. He noticed that the device had various grooves along the sides and back of it. He carefully placed it on his notebook cover and looked up at the Admiral and then to Slavuu Makuuu.

"I will have to take this list back but from my cursory scan I think we can come to an arrangement." He spoke with his hands at this point and made a slight signal to the Admiral who noticed the concern. VADM Brannigan glanced at the device and back at Slavuu Makuuu who was watching the device and his screen. Slavuu Makuuu looked at his companion who was watching the screen who made a non-committal shrug. The Admiral knew for sure the device could communicate with the device in the table about them. Neither he nor Mr. O'Shea was sure what the device was but apparently the Kammorrigans had expected him to hold it and read something about him. All six of the Kammorrigans started reviewing their screens and keying in items. VADM Brannigan thought they must be communicating with themselves and maybe others trying to figure out how to continue with them. Several times over the past five days the Kammorrigans had shown them various items but always working in some way to attempt to locate Earth and even what the name of the planet was. They had inquired in several different ways about the path that they had journeyed along or how long it took them, how many jumps they made. They were successful in evading answering any of these questions but Kevin felt that this was about to come to an end. They were going to be asked directly again and he would tell them that they wouldn't say at least not until they had a very good trade relationship going. He intended that they would never find out after learning what his intel team had discovered about the Kammorrigans.

Slavuu Makuuu made a sound of disgust and looked right at the Admiral.

"Admiral, how can we have any form of trade or trust if you will not share with us the location of your world? We want to know this information."

Admiral Brannigan looked him in the eye and thought briefly of the response he was about to make.

"Trade is not truly based on such knowledge. Trade is a benefit that can assist us both and a way for both of us to earn each other's trust. Yes, we have found this world in your governance but it does not mean that it is equal knowledge. This planet may be your home world or it may be an outlier in your space. But we desire an equitable trade relationship and learn more about each other. It is a form of information sharing. Trade is not based on trust but economic development and trust can come from it. We will not tell you the location of our home world nor the area of space that we came from."

The Kammorrigan sat in silence looking shocked at this last statement. He looked over at the other members of the team sitting at the table. It was clear that he didn't really expect to be turned down over such a blunt demand.

"I see. In order to have fair trade we demand this information."

"You will not get it. The information is nonnegotiable. Trade items are negotiable and we are willing to work to this end."

"That is not good enough, Admiral."

"Too bad." Kevin felt that this was about to go bad real soon. "I think that we probably ought to take a few minutes before we start down a path neither of us desire."

"Neither of us desire Admiral." Slavuu Makuuu's eyes suddenly took a slight change in color. "Admiral, we have been more than ready to take you and make you tell us where your world is. We have scanned your ships and have brought more of ours in to defeat them. We will take you as our prisoners, your ships will now surrender at once to us and you will give us your planet."

Mr. O'Shea felt the device on his leg heat up and knocked it off as an electric charge came out of it. VADM Brannigan stood up before an electric charge with through the chair. LT Shapiro moved into position while the FAST Marine immediately leveled his rifle at Slavuu Makuuu and shot him between the eyes. Slavuu Makuuu fell back onto the floor and died. The other five Kammorrigans broke for the door. VADM Brannigan looked at Mr. O'Shea who appeared shocked.

"We must move." He looked at his Aide. "Contact the others and let them know we are on the move and let's get out of here."

"Yes, sir."

The four of them moved out of the room back the way they had come with the LT making the call to the others.

They moved quickly but not running in order to avoid suspicion and running into any security teams unwittingly. The FAST Marine was in front with the Aide coming up from the rear.

Major Clark was pissed when his Sergeant informed him of the page. Here he was sitting pretty in his quarters with the Admiral and O'Shea in trouble.

"Get the ships fired up and the rest of the team mobilized." He barked as he got up and quickly strapped on his body armor. The Sergeant nodded and plucked his comm system off his own body armor to call the rest of the team and pilots. When the Major had his systems on, they headed out the door.

"What is their location?"

"Not sure Sir but they are on the move."

"Damn, then let's head towards the hanger, the Admiral probably is heading in that direction."

"Yes, Sir."

MajGen Connington emerged from the elevator shaft onboard the *Chesty.*

"Why the alarm?"

"Sir," The Senior Watch Officer stood up from his chair, "There are Kammorrigan ships moving in on the *Intrepid.*"

"What is the status of their systems?"

"It appears that they have shields up and may have weapons online."

"What is our status?"

"We have not energized any systems."

MajGen Connington looked at the tactical display and stood there thinking. The display showed four Kammorrigan ships closing on the other two.

"Bring our shields and weapons online. Close up formation, prepare to launch fighters. And bring us in to support the *Intrepid.*"

Everyone started moving and sending orders and MajGen Connington took a command seat as the MEU Commander came onto the bridge.

The Admiral and his companions reached a four-way intersection. They stopped just before entering the intersection. The way ahead was clear but they had heard movement down one of the other tunnels. The Marine had held up his hand motioning them to stop. He moved along one of the walls to the intersection as quietly as possible. He took a small device out of one of his pockets on his body armor. It looked to be a dental mirror. He held it in one hand and slowly extended it where he could look in the mirror of the device. He briefly held it there and brought it back and put it away. He looked up at the Admiral and motioned that there was a force of six Kammorrigans down the passageway and they were making their way along the corridor. The Admiral grimaced and shook his head. He then looked at the Marine and indicated that he should take them out. The Marine nodded and pulled a grenade from a pouch, pulled the key and tossed it down the corridor. A few seconds later it went off and they quickly moved through the intersection at a jog. No time to lose they had to get to the hangers and off of the planet. The Admiral ran through his head what he had brought down to the planet. Fortunately, it was only a few changes of clothing and a hygiene kit but he knew his Aide had brought more. He stopped.

"We have to get to the quarters and either destroy what we brought or retrieve it."

The Marine started to object but the Admiral held up his hand.

"No choice in the matter."

" Sir, we can't."

"Back to the quarters."

The Marine just sighed and motioned for them to follow him.

Major Clark was moving towards the hanger while checking the skyline. He had his Sergeant and two of the other Marines with him. He didn't like this. He knew the other Marines were already with the two shuttles and the pilots were prepping to take off. They would have to exit the hangers and move more into the open of the landing platform to get off of the planet. He was concerned of any guns that could destroy the ships before they could launch besides the fighters that the planet had. He could only hope to get a message back to the *Intrepid* to send escorts. He stopped suddenly. Looked around at all the Marines.

"Where are the others?"

The Sergeant immediately went pale.

"Oh shit, they must still be in their quarters."

Major Clark grew red in the face, angry at himself.

"Okay, Sergeant, take six men and go get them."

"Yes, Sir." The Sergeant barked some orders and six Marines peeled off and all seven of them ran towards the building where they were being housed in.

Major Clark moved into the shuttle and opened a communication link with the *Intrepid* and gave a status report.

The Admiral and his party made it without any more instances to the passageway where their rooms were located only to find four Marines in a standoff with some Kammorrigans. They entered their room with the Admiral telling the Marine to keep the door open to keep from being shut in. They quickly gathered up their computers and any information that was in the rooms. The Admiral noted how his Aide had already gathered his personal effects to his annoyance but there was no time to reprimand him for his diligence. He approached the Marine.

"It should be ok to go back the way we came."

The Marine glanced at him and back down the passageway's curve where his comrades were holding off the Kammorrigans.

"Perhaps Sir, but we definitely have to take out that group."

The Admiral thought for a moment then breathed, "Do it but do it quickly."

"Roger." The Marine moved off and took out a grenade from a pouch. "Fire in the hold," he yelled. The other Marines ducked into the room as he tossed the grenade down the passageway. They heard it bounce once, twice then the explosion. It seemed to rock everyone in their place. The other Marines brought out the rest of the party and they headed off down the passageway back the way they came hoping that the Kammorrigans would think they went the other way.

Major Clark had the ships out of the hanger and they were firing up. His remaining Marines had a perimeter around the ships. They all were watching the roofs and entry ways towards the hangers. He was getting nervous. He had not received any word from either the Admiral or his other Marines. The pilots were in the ships going through their launch procedures waiting for the Official Party. Major Clark glanced back at the ships when the first shot was fired. He ducked just in time to see one of his Marines rolling to a kneeling position and aiming down one of the entry points that he surmised the shot came from. The Marine took careful aim and fired. The Major moved over to get a better view when he noticed that a Kammorrigan went down from his Marine's shot. The creature was wearing a blue and black uniform with some strange devices but it wasn't the only one. Other Kammorrigans wearing blue and black uniforms with some sort of energy weapons were moving in a formation down the street way. Major Clark called for two more Marines who took up positions in a kneeling position and they began firing down the way picking their targets carefully, taking them out. Some of the Kammorrigans fired back but their weapons which definitely were some form of energy weapons were missing. They were in a hurry trying to get off shots while the Marines were being steady and taking their time to place well aimed shots into this group.

The Admiral with his party was moving through the corridors without any hindrance. He wondered about this since surely the Kammorrigans wanted to capture them. The Marine in front of him was obviously nervous about them and seemed to be growing more agitated by the lack of response from the Kammorrigans.

"Stop," said the Admiral. The whole group stopped and the lead Marine motioned them to spread out. The Admiral approached the lead Marine.

"I know, it is nerve racking that we have not encountered anyone."

"Yes, sir. It really is starting to bug me that no other alarm has arisen and we are moving so freely. This must be some sort of trap."

"Yes, I feel the same. But what would you recommend we do if not keep moving towards the ships?"

The Marine thought for a moment. "Sir that is what bothers me. We have to get to the ships but it is like they are letting us move to them. Should we keep going? Have they captured the ships? What will we encounter in the open? They may have figured out that in these close quarters we have the advantage or they don't truly realize that the Marines are hampered with having to provide protection. I am sure that you and the other officers aren't carrying any weapons."

"No, only LT Shapiro is carrying a side arm." The Admiral looked at the floor in thought then he shook his head. "The ships may have been taken or there may be a trap waiting to spring on all of us. For sure they desire to capture us but they must have a plan that we don't know about. Either way we have to get to the ships and the Marines must stay sharp and calm about this."

"I agree. I just wish I knew where they were at."

The Admiral smiled at him and said, "They are all around us."

The Marine just looked at him and then smiled. As one the group began moving off.

Capt Jackson, Mr. Peterson, Dr. Lucy Venrose, and Mr. Fred Evans sat in the room. It had been some time since they reported to the Admiral about their findings. They had discovered that the Kammorrigans captured whole planets and enslaved their populations. But worse, they were experimenting on the various creatures. Torture it was. Not only used them to practice new weapons on but also various drugs and techniques. They seemed to enjoy the pain they were inflicting upon their captives.

Now, they sat in the room waiting and wondering what was happening. Only Capt Jackson had a weapon. They only had one FAST Marine with them and he was in the other room. They had just finished packing up their various computers and clothing. Capt Jackson told them he thought they would be departing today after what they found.

Suddenly the door opened and the FAST Marine entered the room with all of his equipment.

"We have to leave now. Seems the Kammorrigans have decided to capture everyone."

Dr. Venrose looked scared as Fred Evans turned pale.

"Damn" breathed Capt Jackson. "Where to?"

"The ships. We have to get to the shuttles and fast. My Sergeant is headed our way with six Marines. We need to move towards them."

"Wait. If they are coming here, shouldn't we wait for them?" Asked Capt Jackson. "After all, they are on the move and know where we are. We don't know where they are."

The Marine grimaced and picked up his comm system.

"Private Murphy to Sergeant Carlos, come in please."

The system crackled, "Send it."

"Sergeant, should we wait or try and meet you?"

"Wait there. You could miss us. We will be there momentarily, have everyone and everything ready to move out."

"Yes Sergeant, ETA?"

"Fifteen minutes, out."

"Out here."

The Private moved to the outer door and began listening.

Capt Jackson had checked his watch for the fifteen minutes. He pulled out his weapon and ensured it was loaded and a round in the chamber. He then went to his bag and pulled out two more magazines and placed them into a pocket he could reach.

After ten minutes a knock came at the door.

Everyone froze and the Private checked his carbine and flipped the safety off.

He then keyed the intercom to the door and asked who it was.

"Escort for next tour at another manufacturing site." Came the answer.

The Marine keyed the pad again and stated, "this is everyone's rest period. Thank you but we can't attend. Maybe tomorrow."

There was silence after that.

The next thing Lucy knew was her ears were ringing as she was trying to pick herself up off the floor. She opened her eyes to see the room in total disarray and Kammorrigans coming into the room. The door and door frame seemed strange and there was some sort of smoke in the air. Capt Jackson picked himself up off the floor and drew his pistol and started shooting Kammorrigans. She thought why is he making noise? A Kammorrigan leveled something at the Captain and he fell down. She looked at him and saw his eyes were cold.

Then she heard the Marine's carbine and knew the Kammorrigans had blown open the door and they were in a fight. Fred grabbed at her and started pulling her off the floor.

"Come on Lucy, we have to get out of here."

The Marine's head suddenly vaporized and Lucy screamed.

The Kammorrigans came for them both. Fred attacked the lead as two others grabbed him and one came after Lucy.

She found something and picked it up and hit the Kammorrigan in the head.

She screamed again as an electric shock hit her in the stomach and she fell down.

The Kammorrigan started dragging her by the feet out of the door as she noticed Fred had a huge gash in his head. He was unconscious.

She tried to struggle but the tentacle had her in a vice grip that she couldn't break. She yelled for help.

At that moment Sergeant Carlos and his six Marines appeared and began firing at the Kammorrigans. They returned fire and the Marines spread out.

The Kammorrigans at first held their own but the Marines' fire was rapid and they began taking casualties.

Almost all were down when the one who had Dr. Venrose by the legs turned and placed its stun rod on her throat and turned it on to full. She felt extreme pain as the rod sent electric currents through her throat and her blood vessels burst. She couldn't even scream since the Kammorrigan pressed hard on her throat and held the switch to full.

Sergeant Carlos quickly stepped up behind the Kammorrigan and at point blank range shot him in the head. After the Kammorrigan fell dead the Sergeant looked with anguish at Dr. Venrose's dead body.

"Major Clark, Sergeant Carlos."

"Send it."

"Sir, we were too late. Capt Jackson, Mr. Peterson, Mr. Evans, Dr. Venrose and Private Murphy are dead. We can try and bring their bodies with us."

There was a moment of silence. "Bring them along but if you can't make it with them then ensure you use incendiary devices. We don't want the Kammorrigans to have them."

"Yes, Sir. ETA will be twenty-five minutes. Out." With that Sergeant Carlos motioned for the bodies to be picked up. He reached down and picked up Dr. Venrose and threw her over his left shoulder and took his carbine in his right hand. After the Marines destroyed the computers, they picked up the rest of the dead and began moving back to the shuttles.

The blue and black uniformed Kammorrigans kept coming firing wildly. This surprised the Major but he figured they must not be used to a well-organized resistance. Suddenly one Marine fell. The shot that got him came from the roof. The Major turned and fired a three-round burst in the direction and then steadied. The Kammorrigan stuck his head up swinging his weapon around when a shot took him out but not from the Major. Major Clark looked around and saw a hand come up from another roof top waiving at him. A rifle with a scope came online to take out one and then two Kammorrigans. The Major smiled to himself; a SEAL team had taken up position. He moved to check out his Marine who appeared to still be alive but out of it. He had some form of goo on him. So, the weapons were a stunning device. He looked up about to give a warning when out of a door from a nearby tower came the Admiral and his party. His five Marines were providing him cover and direction to the whole party on how to move quickly to the ships. This operation became a lot easier with the SEALs but he had to ensure he picked them up after he got the party onboard the shuttles. Major Clark looked up into the sky, damn where are those fighters.

The *Intrepid* took the hit hard on her port shields. It rocked her but the shield held as she returned fire with all batteries on her port side at the lead ship. CAPT Smith was maneuvering her ship into a synchronized orbit above the Government Center. She wanted to get her ship directly above the location to provide ships fire and give her fighters the shortest possible ride down the gravity well to support the Admiral on his ride up. Meanwhile they had four Kammorrigan warships engaging her while three were engaging the *Scimitar*. The rest of the fleet was trying to get to them but they were having their own difficulties.

As the Admiral and his party with the Marines started moving out of the opening towards the shuttles, they were spotted by the Kammorrigans. Several of them started rushing towards them. The Marines maintained a steady fire on the advancing Kammorrigans as Major Clark had five Marines give cover fire to them.

The Admiral was moving at a quick pace as his Marines told him but not to run, they needed to ensure they had him covered. The whole team was moving when a Kammorrigan appeared and leveled a weapon right onto the Admiral. Before he knew it, LT Shapiro moved in front of him. He fell down and the Admiral looked at him and saw his chest had a charred hole in it. Private Smith who had been with them since they left the conference chamber fired several rounds into the Kammorrigan then tried to grab the Admiral.

Kevin kept looking at his Aide, LT John Shapiro. When the Marine grabbed him, he shook him off. Kevin then bent down and picked up John's body and said, "It is okay, John, you're going home." With that the group moved off to the shuttles as five Marines raced to reach them from the shuttles.

The Admiral and his party reached the ships as the SEALs provided cover fire from the roof tops. The Major was relieved and motioned for everyone to get onboard. He had already told the pilots to lift off when everyone was onboard.

"How do we get them?" The Admiral asked the Major.

The Major motioned to one of the shuttles and said, "The SEALs are on one building we will lift to its roof and they will come onboard."

"Good." Suddenly the Admiral went pale. He noticed Sergeant Carlos with his Marines appear and they were carrying four bodies with them.

Major Clark yelled at the Admiral, "Sir, get in the shuttle now! I'll get them here."

The Admiral handed the Lieutenant's body to a Marine then turned around.

The SEALs fired at a rapid pace from their position as the Marines gathered up their fallen and moved onboard. The first shuttle had already started lifting off. Major Clark approached the Admiral and stopped. He noticed the fire in the Admiral's blue eyes. Those eyes looked old when he last looked into them after LT Shapiro was killed and he saw Dr. Venrose's dead body being carried by the Marines. Now; however, there was a fire of pure disgust and rage in them. Major Clark felt deep within his bones that all hell was about to break loose as he watched the Admiral glare at the Kammorrigans and the buildings. The Kammorrigans that saw him seem to freeze. Then with a swift motion the Admiral turned and boarded the shuttle with the Major clamoring behind him. The shuttle's hatch sealed and they lifted off.

• • •

The shuttle pilots watched as laser fire from orbit zipped past them as they climbed. They felt some relief when ten of their fighters flew past them shooting at something that was apparently behind them. They continued to climb in an attempt to reach the *Intrepid*. Apparently, they were being jammed. They had not been able to reach her since before they had launched. The fighters appeared around them and formed up in an escort pattern. They continued upwards and cleared the pollution clouds to find the darkness of space but with flashes of fire between their ships and the Kammorrigans.

One of the fighters took up a lead position and they flew behind it. As long as they followed the lead fighter, they would be safe from the *Intrepid's* fire. The fighter pilots would know the safe route through the defense pattern to avoid being shot down by the *Intrepid* but should they stray from this path the *Intrepid's* guns would destroy them.

The *Intrepid* remained between them and the Kammorrigan ships while her other fighters kept any Kammorrigan fighter ships from coming around her to attack the escorted shuttles. The Admiral appeared between the two pilots peering through the window. He watched as they flew into the pattern designated by the *Intrepid* and approached the docking arms to be brought onboard. He looked down at the board and noticed that the communication system was still out. He placed a hand on their shoulders and returned to his seat.

The flag bridge was a buzz of activity when VADM Brannigan came onboard it. CAPT Lindsey noticed his arrival and stood up out of the command chair.

"Admiral on deck." She called alerting the flag bridge to his presence and took her own seat. He strode over and took his chair turning its screens to the views that he desired.

"We are under attack from seven Kammorrigan warships. Four on us and three on the *Scimitar*. The *Scimitar* is moving off to engage them, away from us allowing us to bring our fighters back. The rest of the fleet is being engaged by another six ships."

The Admiral nodded and looked over his screens.

"Have you figured out the planet's ship manufacturing sites and industrial bases?"

She looked at him briefly and moved to his far-left screen and punched up a display of the planet with the areas indicated in yellow. "Yes, sir."

He viewed them. "Ready my nukes."

She turned a stunned look at him. "But, Admiral."

He held up a hand silencing her. "Prepare my nukes for launch."

"Yes, Sir." She moved off to prepare the order.

"Tactical Watch Officer, I want these ship manufacturing facilities and industrial sites to be targeted."

"Aye aye, Sir." The Tactical Watch Officer plotted the displayed information into his keyboard. CAPT Lindsey meanwhile notified CAPT Smith of the order to use the nukes and keyed in her codes. When the Admiral's board flashed the ready signal, he keyed in his codes for the launch.

"Ensure you only launch the required number to take out these targets and no more." He advised the Tactical Watch Officer.

"Aye aye, Sir." He yelled back with the excitement of an officer that was about to unleash devastation in a manner that no one had seen for several decades. His heart burned at the thought of such power that was about to be launched on a race. But these weapons were placed onboard for such an act should the Admiral call for it.

Mr. O'Shea had entered the flag bridge at the Admiral's last order. He looked nervously at the Watch Officer and CAPT Lindsey. She just glanced at him and turned back to her board. He approached the Admiral and said in a voice that only the Admiral could hear.

"Admiral, I know that the reports were bad but this. Isn't it a bit much for the Lieutenant and Dr. Venrose."

The Admiral turned his gaze upon him and he gasped at the look.

"This may be in response to their deaths but the evidence that our teams gathered indicate they desire the destruction of our way of life and enslave our planet. Too many species have been enslaved by this group among others that we have encountered. I will not let these dogs take our world. No, it isn't. Now take your seat or leave my bridge." He turned back to his board and reviewed it one last time. Mr. O'Shea stood straight up and just looked at him in shock. He moved off to his seat and sat down. He knew in some strange way the Admiral was right about the Kammorrigan's desire but this action would eliminate any form of diplomatic resolution in the future especially if they could survive it.

"Fire, fire at will." The Admiral gave the order.

Even on the flag bridge they could feel the missiles leaving their tubes and almost could be heard if you tried to listen.

It only took a few seconds for the missiles to enter the planet's atmosphere. The *Intrepid* had begun to move along an orbit launching the missiles as she went to ensure that each target would be hit. They all watched the viewscreens as the weapons mushroom blooms indicated detonation. All Hell was being unleashed on the Kammorrigans. Mr. O'Shea wondered what history would record of this moment.

The *Scimitar* had moved away from the *Intrepid* and more of the Kammorrigans seemed to be gathering around her. MajGen Connington was getting concerned. He already was torn about how to support the two ships and keep the fleet moving towards the *Intrepid*.

"Sir, the *Intrepid* is launching nukes onto the planet." His Senior Watch Officer informed him. He looked up in amazement at this news. Only the Admiral himself could order such action. It was already obvious that they had mission failure but it rated this type of action?

"Get us over there."

"Sir, more Kammorrigan ships are jumping into orbit. We are starting to get badly outnumbered." CAPT Lindsey informed him.

"Send the signal to make the jump to the rendezvous coordinates."

"Roger, Sir." She said.

Suddenly she looked up with a wild look in her eyes at the realization of why the Kammorrigans had not fired upon the *Intrepid* as expected. The *Scimitar* was between them and taking heavy fire. She checked her systems quickly getting a reading on the ship. VADM Brannigan watched his screens as the destruction of the various sites were occurring on the planet ensuring that the devastation he wrought upon them would take them years to recover from. He noticed the frantic way that CAPT Lindsey was working her board. He glanced at his own tactical and adjusted it to get a status of the fleet. The *Chesty* and others seemed to be handling the ships just fine that had engaged them and they were beginning to jump. He noticed that the *Intrepid* seemed to be free of any ships and had recovered all of her fighters without a loss. But the *Scimitar* was away from all of the ships and was taking heavy fire.

"Move towards the *Scimitar* and give her support." He barked in a voice that resonated around the bridge. He flipped several switches on his board opening a comm link to the *Scimitar*.

"CAPT Shura, what are you doing? Make the jump now."

The link crackled back at him and then CAPT Shura's voice came across brokenly.

"After you Sir, we will hold them for you."

"Captain, that is an order I want you out of there at once."

After several moments later of static.

"Sorry, Sir. Our jump drive is off line. Our shields are failing. It is now or never for you. We will hold them off of you."

The Admiral glared at his screen.

"Can you NOT get your drive online?"

"Too much damage. We had to get them off of you. Now go."

The Admiral sat back in his chair gripping the arms of it. He looked at CAPT Lindsey.

"Get us in there now."

The *Intrepid* moved off towards the *Scimitar* firing at the Kammorrigans with all she had. Missiles were launched, laser fire burning holes into their shields, the rail guns unleashing devastating fire upon their hulls.

CAPT Shura looked at his ship's status. The damage reports showed several decks ablaze. He was still able to maneuver but not well and could fire. He continued to fire his missiles and lasers. He had run out of rails for his rail guns. But his main drive was a slag of molten metal according to his Chief Engineer.

"Sir," he called to the Admiral, "It is no use, Sir. My drive is a heap of slag. We can't get out of here but you can. Please do it now."

The Admiral received the message and watched on the main screen as three Kammorrigan warheads followed by laser fire slammed into the bridge area of the *Scimitar* and four more missiles penetrated what little was left of the shield and shattered the engine area of the ship.

"Farewell, Captain." He said over the comm link. "Make the jump."

CAPT Shura looked around his bridge. Through the smoke of the electrical fires, he nodded his head in farewell to his brave crew. He smiled his defiance at the Kammorrigans and watched on his only screen that was left the missiles and fire coming at him. The *Scimitar* erupted into a ball of fire and burned out in the cold of space surrounded by Kammorrigan warships that had taken a beating. Many of them were damaged, four of them destroyed, and seven so badly damaged they were out of commission. But the ball burned a hot glow at them showing an unconquerable spirit.

CHAPTER 8

Three jumps after leaving Kammorriga, the Strike Group was preparing for a fourth. Each time after a jump the Kammorrigans kept showing up. They were somehow following them. They were jumping and traveling up to five days each jump and still after they went to normal space within an hour the Kammorrigan ships began showing up. The first time they destroyed the first ship and jumped. After the second jump; however, the Kammorrigans were coming in force. They thought that it would only be a matter of jumps or time and they would outrun them. They were following a course in the general direction back to Earth. The astrogators were plotting the next course. This one wouldn't be so much in a direct line to Earth but slightly off towards another quadrant of the galaxy. They hoped this would throw off the Kammorrigans. They jumped.

This fourth jump, after six days in hyperspace, surely would show them if they could go home or not. Immediately the astrogators began plotting the next jump. They would wait to see if any of the Kammorrigans would show up prior to making this jump.

One hour passed and no Kammorrigans. Two hours passed and no Kammorrigans. They began to breathe easier. Three hours passed and no one; the crews started to feel joy at the thought that they had lost them. At thirty minutes past the third hour; however, four Kammorrigan ships made the jump into normal space. This was followed by seven more ships and then ten ships. They made their fifth jump and the first four ships jumped right after them.

VADM Brannigan sat in his chair watching the main viewscreen. MajGen Connington was still on the *Chesty*. They had not had the time to transfer him back onto the *Intrepid* but this in a way made Kevin happier. At least both main ships had a Fleet Commander onboard to command the fleet should something happen to either ship. Fortunately, the engineers were able to make adjustments to the systems enabling him to watch what was happening in hyperspace as they moved through it. The systems at least registered the ships of the Strike Group and the four Kammorrigans that were following them. He found it strangely interesting watching this. He shifted in his chair and let his gaze wonder over the bridge. He finally settled it onto his operations officer.

"CAPT Lindsey, call Dr. Vance and have him meet us in my office." He got up and left the bridge as she made the call.

The door slid to a close behind Dr. Vance and he took one of the two seats across the desk from the Admiral. The porthole was open so they could see the tunnel that was hyperspace slipping past them as the ship traveled through the strange space. He noticed the Admiral was watching one of his computers viewscreens on his desk as it showed the Kammorrigans behind them following. The other computer had system reports on it. The Admiral would glance at them occasionally but kept watching the other ships. He flipped a switch on the status board that brought up an ordnance report of the *Intrepid*. It indicated that she still had four nuclear weapons, several different types of other missiles and her energy weapons and rail guns were online. She had not taken any damage during the battle over Kammorriga and her shields had held remarkably well under the direct fire. The data showed the *Scimitar*, while she was destroyed, was more than equal to any four or five of the Kammorrigan ships. She had taken devastating fire but both her shields and later her hull had absorbed the vast amount of fire until she was just simply overwhelmed by the number of adversaries. But the *Intrepid* and the other ships of the fleet were in shape and prepared for a fight. The Admiral switched back to the other system reports. Finally, he looked up at the Captain and Dr. Vance.

"Well, we have a tad bit of a situation here. For some reason we can't shake these guys by making jumps and now as you can tell we have four of them following us in hyperspace. Are they that much more superior to us, or at least in space travel?"

Dr. Vance answered, "Remember sir, they have had a much longer period of space travel than us. I would hope they could do something like this."

The Admiral smiled at him but his eyes showed he wasn't really amused.

"You are right. Since they have been traveling through space a lot longer, they should be able to do something like this. Okay, how do we stop them?"

"Stop them?" repeated the Dr.

"Yes, stop them. Our systems are online but can we fire our energy weapons at them, or our missiles or can we do something to destroy them or make them drop out of hyperspace?"

Dr. Vance crossed his chest with one arm supporting the other as he stroked his chin with his hand deep in thought.

"I don't know if we can really use the energy weapons in hyperspace and quite frankly, I would hate to try it since it could be disastrous for us. We could possibly melt the emitters or blow the generators. We could simply just miss due to the environment we are in. Firing a missile? Ummm, maybe but then we have the difficulty of locking onto a target again due to the hyperspace. We haven't done any testing nor have we analyzed the data to see how we could engage a target in hyperspace. What is interesting come to think of it is why haven't the Kammorrigans engaged us? Maybe they can't."

"Or maybe they are content to follow us to a final destination." The Admiral responded.

Dr. Vance grinned. "Yes, that could be the case. We could drop a mine. We can rig it with some sort of magnetic charge and plop it right in front of the lead ship and have it detonate when they hit it. They may not even pick it up on their sensors."

"That is a thought and probably the best one since it could be as simple as opening a hatch and letting it be sucked into space." CAPT Lindsey said.

"Well, I think we have a solution. CAPT Lindsey put your Ordnance Officer on it and Dr. Vance work with them to make it happen in the stealthiest manner but make sure it hits."

They both got up and nodded to the Admiral and left. He turned back in his chair and watched his viewscreen.

CAPT Lindsey came onto the flag bridge looking very tired. VADM Brannigan sat in his chair watching the screens. They were able to change position with the *Defiant* and placed them directly in line with the lead Kammorrigan ship. CAPT Lindsey went to her station and checked some readings before approaching the Admiral. The past five hours she and her ordnance people worked with a couple of engineers from Dr. Vance. They were able to change three high powered missiles into three very deadly mines.

"Admiral, we are ready. We have three mines at the ready in an aft airlock. We just wait the order to launch them." She looked up at the monitors.

The Admiral nodded his acknowledgement and looked at his screens. When he was sure the lead ship was in line, he nodded to CAPT Lindsey. She turned to the Tactical Watch Officer, "Launch the mines." He acknowledged the order and turned to his board.

They all watched the main view screen as the mines were launched one, two and three. They waited as the mines reached a halfway point between the two fleets and armed their magnetics and explosive charges. Within a minute the lead Kammorrigan ship impacted all three mines. The explosion was spectacular. The Kammorrigans did not have their shields up and the mines hit their hull and ripped into it. The ship slowed slightly due to the damage to her hull. The second and even a third Kammorrigan ship slammed into the lead ship causing an even larger explosion. The hyperspace tunnel reverberated with the shock-wave of the explosion.

The Admiral looked about the bridge. "Status."

The crew looked to their monitors and the Helmsman answered.

"Sir, the tunnel is experiencing the shockwave from the explosion. It appears to be settling down."

The last Kammorrigan ship dropped out of hyperspace. The Strike Group was able to remain in the tunnel and it stabled out.

"That was interesting," the Admiral said to CAPT Lindsey.

"Yes, sir. I am sure Dr. Vance will enjoy those readings."

"Make sure he gets them. We may be able to use those readings to develop weaponry for battle within the hyperspace."

"Roger, Sir."

The Admiral punched up some data on one of his viewscreens.

"Alright, one more day of traveling in hyperspace and then drop out of it."

She looked at him, "Yes, Sir."

"We need to change our course." The Admiral looked around the conference room table at the officers gathered.

"We can't lead the Kammorrigans to Earth which is what they desire. I want to head to the cloud that we found. When we get there, we will hide within it until we can figure out how they are able to follow us. We need time and they are not affording us this."

They arrived in the system and headed for the cloud upon arrival. They no sooner started to enter the phenomena when the Kammorrigan fleet began to appear. They flew into the phenomena and immediately upon entering their sensors started to read mainly static. They had already coordinated among themselves to head for the estimated center for their own safety. The Strike Group Captains were very concerned about crashing into each other but didn't want to separate too much in order not to lose each other in the cloud.

After checking his monitor, the Admiral instructed, "Bring the fleet to an all stop."

"Aye, aye, sir."

The fleet came to a halt.

"Now let us see what it is about our ships that keep them coming." The Admiral said.

"Sir, shouldn't we wait to see if they are going to follow us?" CAPT Lindsey asked.

"I don't think they will be following us in here. Send out crews onto our hull and troop carriers to scan our hulls for any devices that may not be normal."

She looked up with a little surprise in her eyes. "You think they planted something onto our hulls?"

"Yes, it is the only thing that makes sense to me as to how they can track us."

CAPT Lindsey turned to her station to send the signal by astrogation lights to the other ships to ensure they understood the order.

Ten hours after the searching began the crews had found five devices, one on each ship. The devices were brought inside the *Intrepid's* hanger for inspection. Meanwhile no sign of the Kammorrigans. The Admiral stepped onto the hanger with CAPT Lindsey and CAPT Smith to inspect the devices. Dr. Vance and a team of scientists and engineers were already on the deck inspecting the devices with various instruments. The Admiral approached and turned to CAPT Smith.

"You have not detected any signals leaving the cloud, have you?"

"No, sir," she responded, "the devices seem to be transmitting according to our electronic warfare section but it does not seem to be penetrating the cloud."

He nodded in satisfaction at the news. He waited for the team to finish their inspection. After several minutes Dr. Vance approached him and the two captains.

"Admiral, these are definitely Kammorrigan devices. From what we have been able to discern they are tracking devices. We have found the frequency that they are transmitting on. It is interesting that the signal can be carried through hyperspace. We need more time to study them."

"You won't have much longer, Doctor. so make your studies quick but don't stop them from transmitting." The Admiral turned to CAPT Smith as Dr. Vance looked at him slightly disappointed.

"Captain, launch a fighter to travel to the edge of the cloud and gather what information on the Kammorrigan fleet's disposition. The pilot is not to engage only to gather information and return to us. Ensure there is some method for him to get back to us."

"Yes sir." CAPT Smith turned to go over to a comm system to get a fighter underway.

"Admiral," asked Dr. Vance, "what do you intend to do?"

The Admiral turned back to him. "Get us out of here without getting us blown to pieces." With that he went over to one of the devices. It was circular, approximately three feet in diameter and metallic looking. It had a concentric circle that was one foot in diameter with the center slightly raised above the rest of the disk. The device was two feet tall. He looked it over and turned away to speak with CAPT Lindsey.

Capt John Hemming flew his fighter craft along the cloud veins. It was proving to be a bumpy ride. Since his launch from the *Intrepid* he had flown a straight line but the controls were choppy, the cloud was turbulent. He maintained the flight to the best of his ability keeping his craft on line with his destination. His orders were simple enough, proceed to the outer portion of the cloud and take readings, visual and electronic of the Kammorrigan fleet's disposition and then return to *Intrepid*. Under no circumstance was he to engage with the Kammorrigans. The fighter took a hard hit from the turbulence. His teeth shook down to their nerves trying to keep a hold of the controls while his fighter took the brunt of the force wave. He flew on. His instruments were static at best and outside of the tight beam from the *Intrepid* he would have been lost already. The beam was a communication signal to aid him in maneuvering through the cloud to and from the *Intrepid*. If he were to lose contact with this beam his only backup was the data of the flight path that was recorded by the *Intrepid* and downloaded to his fighter. He really hoped he would not have to rely on it with these eddies that he had to fly threw.

An hour after leaving the *Intrepid*, Capt Hemming made it to the outer perimeter of the cloud. He was still inside the cloud but could see the darkness of space and a few stars through the blue mist that made up the visible spectrum of the cloud. He slowed his fighter and the turbulence threatened to throw him off his course but he applied some power to bring himself to the outer edge where it seemed to be slightly calmer. He angled his craft to bring the nose and cockpit just up out of the cloud and immediately flipped and depressed two switches and buttons. His screens began to clear of the static and after a moment delay began to fill up with several blips. He looked down at the screen and saw over a hundred blips being counted by the systems.

Capt Hemming was shocked to see so many blips. He checked the other sensors. He was picking up their traffic and noticed something a little odd. He made an adjustment and focused in on a rather huge starship. The reading made him gasp it was approximately three times the size of the *Intrepid*. The sensors picked up three of them. He double checked and saw that he had the readings and turned his nose back into the cloud, made sure he had the carrier signal from the *Intrepid* and began the hour-long ride back to her. The fighter shook as violently as she had on the ride out but this time he applied more power, he wanted to get back to the *Intrepid* in less time than it took him to get out here.

The Admiral sat at the conference room table with MajGen Connington to his right, who had flown over from the *Chesty* once they had come to a full stop. Meanwhile CAPT Lindsey was working the data from Capt Hemming's flight with the Intelligence Department, Science Department and her operators. The Admiral sipped his coffee watching the viewer at the far end of the room contemplating the magnitude of this fleet that they were facing. He found it slightly odd that over a hundred craft had followed them this far, just for the remaining five ships of his Strike Group. The *Nautilus* had not checked in since they had left Kammorriga and he was wondering if she still sailed or was a casualty. But this fleet and the size of its capital ships were amazing. Perhaps this was the assault force to take Earth down. He wondered. Meanwhile his officers and staff were pouring over the readings from the fighter to gather what information they could. He took another sip of his coffee and put down his cup. Paul sat next to him in his own thoughts. Kevin wondered what he may be thinking about. They had talked briefly about what happened back at Kammorriga and how they were able to place the tracking devices on their ships. Apparently, they had desired to capture at least one of the ships but if they failed in that to track them to their home planet. Fortunately, the system they were hiding in, or rather waiting in was still several light years away from Earth. It would only be a matter of time before the bombardment of the cloud would occur. He figured that sooner or later the Kammorrigans would send in munitions to force them to leave the cloud and make another jump. He couldn't afford to do this. Here he would make his final stand or trick them into leaving the system before they could move on. He had already ordered another full sweep of the hulls of his Strike Group. VADM Brannigan wanted to ensure there were no other devices on his ships to track them. He even had ordered all their clothing, weapons, electronics and even hygiene items that were on the planet with him to include the two shuttles to be checked out. Not even by accident did he want to lead this fleet back to Earth.

CAPT Lindsey came over and sat down. She looked a little frazzled. The Operations Officer was a tough job. Everything always seemed to rest on their shoulders despite the fact that the Commander was the one that was responsible. She had spent several long hours trying to come up with a way to escape the Kammorrigans. She shook her head and in a low voice said to the Fleet Commanders.

"I don't really see a way to fight through them. We can't jump to hyperspace in this cloud. The electrostatic of the phenomena cancels out any form of astrogation and interferes with the drive system itself. If we could figure out the drive, we would be jumping blind and the fleet could be scattered. Should we proceed out to the clarity of open space we need several moments to get a proper fix and plot our next jump and that would bring us under their fire. With a concentrated blast they could potentially shatter our shields and knock out our drive. I am not sure how to get around them. Perhaps some form of jamming."

"Or maybe we make them jump away before us." Kevin responded. She looked at him.

"We have their transmitters onboard and they are still operational. We need to use them to trick them. You are correct, we cannot take them on in a fight so we have to make them go away and the best way is to send them on a goose hunt. And they have provided us with the best means possible for that."

He looked at her waiting for the thought to sink in. She took a moment and then it clicked.

"So, we have to somehow send those transmitters somewhere else and they should follow them."

"Yes," he said. "I figure that they are not really looking at the ships just the signals. They know we jumped here and flew into this cloud. Now they are waiting for us and I think it is safe to assume they have the cloud surrounded. But I am willing to bet they are looking for the signal to reappear figuring we haven't figured it out yet."

She shook her head, "still a risk though."

He shrugged and looked at MajGen Connington.

"It is a thought," Paul said. "Of course, if it fails then we lose them but if it fails then we are stuck just like we are now."

"Then let's make preparations." The Admiral looked over to where Dr. Vance was sitting with a couple of his engineers.

"Dr. Vance," when the Doctor looked up at him, "how long to prep five of our shuttles with jump capability and I really mean a jump capability? I don't want them to go a short distance but to make several days' worth of a jump."

The Doctor and his team seemed astonished. The Doctor started to object and then stopped and rubbed his chin with his hand. He picked up his hand device and keyed in something while looking at the screen. As he would look at it, he would make other keystrokes. At last, he got up and went over to the computer in the room and started keying in the items he was looking for. After ten minutes he sat back in thought and looked at the Admiral.

"You want five shuttles outfitted to be able to make long distant jumps?"

The Admiral nodded affirmative to him. Dr. Vance let out his breath.

"If we started working right now, we might be able to make them ready in a day if all goes well but more likely five days."

The Admiral grimaced.

"This won't be easy. We have components on the ship with power generation capability but it is miniaturizing a drive to fit on the shuttles. I am assuming that you want them to pilot themselves as well and that is another problem all together."

"Yes, I want them to pilot themselves since they will be empty. They only have to carry one item each." The Admiral responded.

"Well then I would say five days."

The Admiral pressed his lips tightly together in displeasure.

"Make it sooner, Doctor. I prefer one or two days at the most but we need them to be done right away."

The Doctor nodded and motioned the engineers to him and keyed in some codes into the computer which started bringing other science and engineering stations online. The Fleet Commanders got up and left the conference room. Now was the work of the engineers to redo the shuttles and he needed some sleep. Admiral Brannigan headed for his quarters and told CAPT Lindsey to head to hers to get some sleep. He needed her alert for the next move. MajGen Connington went to the flag bridge to check on their status and take his watch.

The first half day was busy going over the shuttle schematics and coming up with a new design for the engines. The next day and a half were busy building five engines to meet the requirement. The last day was outfitting the five shuttles. The guidance systems were proving to be the easy part. The plan involved taking the shuttles to the edge of the phenomena with the *Intrepid* and launch them. The *Intrepid* would have to provide cover fire while the engines spooled up and then launch. The *Intrepid* would have to duck back into the cloud to avoid detection while the shuttles enter hyperspace. Doctor Vance had his doubts about the success of this mission. His main concern was the same as the engineers in they were not able to test the drive or guidance systems prior to the launch.

The bridge crew was apprehensive. VADM Brannigan sat in his command chair. MajGen Connington stood next to him.

"Does the *Chesty* have all the data that the *Intrepid* has?"

"Yes, sir."

"Good ensure that you jump first followed by the *Icarus* and *Excalibur*."

"Alright but you will jump next."

"No, I want all ships away prior to my jump. We will have Capt Hemming give us the signal after the Kammorrigans follow our shuttles. You will follow them."

"I really think you should jump prior to the *Defiant*."

"No, we will be the last ship. I want to ensure we get the Captain back and we have the best firepower."

The Strike Group moved towards the edge of the cloud; the five shuttles were still onboard the *Intrepid*. The engineers kept running their system checks ensuring they would operate within the parameter set. The bridge crew watched their monitors and screens. CAPT Smith on her bridge monitored her crew. This would be a fight of their lives should the Kammorrigans close on them. They had been drilling for the past several days to be ready to meet the enemy and not fail. The fate of the fleet rested in her hands. She would take good care of them. Capt Hemming was in his fighter and CAPT Smith checked the system; he was ready but this time he wouldn't launch until they were close to the edge. She was proud of him; he had volunteered for this mission telling them how he was already familiar with the space distortions and could handle the flight. She checked to see that the ready alert was in the tubes as well. In fact, all the pilots aboard the *Intrepid* were in their fighters ready to launch. The wing was ready. The ships sailed on.

Capt Hemming took up a position similar to the last time he came up to the edge. The nose of his craft and cockpit were just outside of the cloud with most of his craft hidden by the electrostatic environment of the phenomena. He waited holding his fighter there. Soon the five shuttles appeared and were moving through the cloud out into normal space. They were in a v formation since it would be easier to control them. When they cleared the cloud, he punched in the codes for their drives to spool up and make the jump. Sure enough, when the ships cleared the cloud several of the Kammorrigan ships began moving in on them. The shuttles continued to move away from the cloud and he could tell by his systems that the guidance systems were taking their readings and applying the coordinates for Kammorriga into the astrogation system. The drives were spooling up. The Kammorrigans were accelerating into an attack vector. The shuttles jumped. He waited. The Kammorrigans continued to come. He stood by as they continued along their intercept vector.

Suddenly the Kammorrigan ships jumped and Capt Hemming could see several hyperspace wells opening and the Kammorrigan fleet proceeding into them.

VADM Brannigan was most pleased by the report that Capt Hemming was giving. The Kammorrigans were jumping away by the dozens apparently taking the bait. Now they just had to wait for the Kammorrigan fleet to jump away then they could leave the cloud and jump to their next point in space ensuring they would not be followed anymore. And then they would be homeward bound. It was taking several hours for the fleet to move out but it took them at least three days to arrive. The Admiral was wondering how large of a fleet this was and why would they all come here. He drank coffee from his coffee mug waiting for the enemy fleet to disperse to the point they could move out of the cloud. The turbulence of the cloud did influence his fleet but their size and helm controls were such they could maintain a stable platform despite the buffeting currents. They waited.

Five hours passed and the fleet was still dispersing into the hyperspace wells but now there were less than a dozen ships. Another hour and the screens should be clear. Capt Hemming was brought aboard several hours ago for rest and to refuel his fighter. Other pilots were taking up the watch as the Kammorrigans left the area. The bait was successful.

After three additional hours, the Admiral didn't see any indication that they couldn't move out. He gave the order and the Strike Group headed out of the cloud into the clear. Nothing showed on their screens as they cleared and began to move away from the area. The astrogators immediately began taking their bearings to plot their next jump. When they were about to make preparations for the jump the proximity klaxon sounded. Everyone looked at the tactical display and saw a Kammorrigan ship, one of the large ones, moving in on their position. The Admiral gave the order for the other ships to make the jump just as he saw fighters leaving the Kammorrigan mother ship. He gave the order for his own fighters from the *Intrepid* to launch on an intercept course and ordered CAPT Smith to engage the mother ship giving the rest of the Strike Group an opportunity to make the jump. The last thing he wanted was a call from this ship bringing the rest of the Kammorrigan fleet back so he ordered jamming operations to commence at the same time that his flagship moved to engage the Kammorrigan to keep her from jumping into the hyperspace well with his Strike Group.

The *Intrepid* launched all twenty of her fighters and fired her main missile batteries at the Kammorrigan mother ship while bringing her own shields online and main weapon systems. She moved out from the rest of the Strike Group and headed straight for the Kammorrigan.

The Kammorrigan ship was huge. It easily measured four times the size of the *Intrepid* and was a long cylinder shape platform with apparently several launch tubes out of which she launched forty fighters. They formed four circles of fighters of ten each and moved towards the *Intrepid*. The *Intrepid's* missiles struck the Kammorrigan's shields and exploded upon it. They moved into each other's main weapons range and began pounding each other with their energy beams. Both ships' shields conducted the fire around their shields lighting them up with various colors on the spectrum while they continued to pour fire upon each other. CAPT Smith's Tactical Watch Officer was attempting to find the precise frequency where a concentrated attack of lasers followed by a couple of missiles could shatter a portion of the shield so he could fire the rail guns and pour missiles directly onto the Kammorrigan ship's hull.

Meanwhile the *Intrepid's* fighter took up four five-man v formations and flew into the four circles of Kammorrigan fighters wreaking havoc among them.

The Admiral was checking to see if the rest of the Strike Group had made their jump yet. They hadn't. He ordered a direct comm link to the *Chesty* and ordered MajGen Connington to make the jump. The Admiral watched as the two ships closed with each other firing almost point blank into each other shields while the fighters fought their fight. At last, the *Excalibur* made a jump followed by the *Icarus* and *Defiant*. Only after those three ships made the jump did the *Chesty* follow.

Now they could make their jump once they recovered their fighters. The *Intrepid* suddenly shuddered, pitching up and backwards as if it lost its aft section. Next came the sound of the explosion. The Kammorrigan fire had penetrated the *Intrepid's* shields first. The blast knocked out the aft shield and part of a second burst of energy hit the engine room. The *Intrepid* careened madly but her Helmsman was able to right her quickly and bring the ship up in a way to protect the area. She still had power and power enough to fight. The Admiral was checking the damage control system along with CAPT Lindsey; the hyperspace drive had been knocked out. Now they needed to get people to Engineering to get the drive back online and he wanted to know how his flag staff could assist.

CAPT Smith swore under her breath. Her damage control board showed the one thing she did not want to see, her hyperspace drive out of commission. She was on the comm system to her Chief Engineer.

"How long to get it back online?" She shouted into the system. There was a lot of noise coming from engineering.

"I don't see how we can get it back online. The main drive is completely shattered and the backup system won't engage. We cannot even get in there due to a main space fire. It is amazing that we still have maneuvering engines for you. If we can keep the fire contained then you will still have those but if it somehow gets through those bulkheads then you will lose them. My priority has been to put the fire out and get the shields restored. I can't even get to the backups to see their damage."

Damn, she thought, "There is absolutely no way? We are in a fight for our lives and I need those engines."

"No way, Captain, the drive is lost and that fire is keeping us at bay."

"Do your best Commander." With that, she closed her mic. She checked her systems to see that she could still fire missiles, energy weapons, and rail guns but the fighters were canceling each other out. She had already lost fifty percent of her fighters and the Kammorrigans had launched twenty more. Her fighters were amazing since the enemy had lost thirty. Now it was a three to one fight and hers were doing an amazing amount of damage to the enemy's but they were still outnumbered. She looked at her XO.

"Have all the information uploaded at once to the Admiral's saucer. Inform the FAST Platoon that they must be ready to repel borders and to get to the saucer. In fact, whatever scientists, engineers and medical personnel along with wounded need to get there and ensure they have lots of rations. That is your priority now. I and the Ops will continue this fight."

He looked at her with anguish in his eyes but didn't argue with one look at the monitors he started carrying out her orders.

CAPT Smith told her Ops Officer the four remaining nukes were to be placed in the points of the two horns and armed to explode at contact. The Ops moved to make it happen. She was considering her options. She had to punch through the shields of this enemy to launch her main missiles but they were holding even against concentrated fire. That would only leave one option since they couldn't jump away and she hated it.

The scientists and engineers were confounded, why did they have to move? They thought they were in a secure place but the ship's Master-at-arms were forcing them to move and move into the Admiral's section of the ship. That was very crowded. They were seeing wounded personnel being moved in as well and a lot of stores. After several of them were crowded in with the FAST Platoon behind them the hatches were sealed shut. Then started some strange noises that made all of them concerned. Major Clark got a very curious look on his face.

CAPT Smith had backed her ship away from the Kammorrigan. So far, they were still holding their own against it despite the success of the one strike that melted her hyperspace drive. She was angling her ship to provide the most protection to the Admiral's section. The calls coming across the board that she and her bridge crew were ignoring indicated that the flag bridge knew something was happening. At the signal that everyone that could be squeezed into the flag section came through she opened up the internal communication system minus the flag section.

"All Hands," she relayed over the system. "As you may be aware our hyperspace drive is gone. The *Intrepid* is nearly dead in space. The upgrades are allowing us to fight on but we cannot sustain this fight. We will lose unless we sell our lives dearly for the Admiral, his staff and all the scientists and engineers. We will ram this enemy ship and trust that we will destroy it. It has been my pleasure and honor to serve alongside of you. Engineering and Damage Control, separate the flag section from the *Intrepid*! Helm, once the separation is completed bring us to full speed. Tactical, concentrate all fire and secondary missiles at a single point on the enemy's shields. Captain out."

She looked at her Helmsman.

"Angle the ship where our under weapons are used. Tactical, fire!"

The *Intrepid* shifted its orbit of the Kammorrigan where the underside was facing the enemy. At this time, she both fired her weapons systems and the separation sequence of the flag section.

"What the hell!" VADM Brannigan was at once beside himself. His chair's central view screen showed the separation sequence and the locking mechanisms as disengaging.

"What the hell is she doing?"

Everyone on the bridge was hurriedly punching in various codes into the systems to figure out what more information could be provided. The flag bridge Helmsman took his readings from the *Intrepid* as the ship sent its last helm information to his board. Soon he would be in control of the maneuvering jets of the flag section. He was working this information rapidly. He saw on his board the course he was to propel this section, now his ship, along in order to get the crew away from the conflict.

CAPT Lindsey yelled over her shoulder to the Admiral.

"Sir, CAPT Smith has already plugged in her codes and we are unable to override it. We will be separated from the *Intrepid* in ten seconds and our thrusters will fire automatically. We have no options. Helm, do you have the data required?"

"Yes Captain," he responded.

"Astrogation, do you have your bearings?"

"Yes, Captain," the Major at Astrogation responded.

"Very well," responded the Admiral. He sat back in his chair. *Dammit Karen, what the hell do you think you are doing? I know we could have gotten out of this mess.*

His section fired its engines and they were off.

At last, she thought the Admiral's section was away.

"Now, angle us back and bring main weapons to bear on the single point of impact on their shields and intensify." CAPT Smith ordered.

The *Intrepid* was sluggish in her helm but she responded. Within a few seconds of concentrated intense energy fire her Tactical Watch Officer cried out that an opening had appeared.

"Full speed ahead. Fire primary missiles and the rail guns." She yelled over the noise of the screaming ship's strain. The Kammorrigans continued to pour fire down upon the *Intrepid*, the shields were beginning to buckle along the hull and several relays were tripping across the ship.

The *Intrepid* lurched forward towards the opening they had punched through the enemy ship's shields. The missiles and rails were already through the opening and were impacting the hull of the ship. CAPT Smith could see the explosions and resulting vapor venting out of the ship following the debris that the missiles and rails had ripped open. She checked her board and confirmed the four nuclear missiles' warheads were all armed. She looked about the brave and determined faces of her crew. It was a shame to sacrifice them but the Admiral and scientist were more important for the defense of Earth.

The ship passed through the shields and was roughly buffeted by the edge of the energy, she barely fit. She continued a slow and ponderous approach as her own shields were failing and the Kammorrigan's energy weapons began striking more places along her hull. Explosions were occurring along many areas of the hull but it didn't matter now. The *Intrepid's* momentum would carry the ship into the Kammorrigans.

The intensity of the resulting explosion of the collision was enormous. The shockwave of the explosion struck the flag section violently. The Helmsman fought with the controls to keep the ship steady while the shockwave knocked it ten kilometers away from the ships. The section rocked violently while the Helmsman brought the engines online and turned the section into the shockwave and leveled it off to keep it from flying totally out of control. The section survived the shockwave without any damage.

The sensors of the flag section were momentarily blinded and the resulting shockwave bounced everyone aboard severely. The crew was overcoming their shock of the *Intrepid's* sacrifice when the sensors came back online and the view screens cleared. They looked with amazement at the wreckage of the Kammorrigan ship. It had a massive hole blown into one side of the ship with various gases still venting out of it. The Communications Officer reported that two of their fighters were still flying about but no sign of the Kammorrigans.

"Bring us into a docking pattern with the Kammorrigans," Ordered the Admiral.

"Sir, is that wise?" Began CAPT Lindsey.

"I will go aboard the ship along with a team to retrieve all data from her computer banks. The *Intrepid's* sacrifice will not be without gain. Meanwhile have Dr. Vance figure out how to get us a hyperspace drive. I want us to make a jump out of here at the earliest possible moment. See if there is some way to keep the fighters with us else bring the pilots onboard."

"Yes, sir."

The flag section headed towards the wreckage. CAPT Lindsey contacted Major Clark to provide a security detail and the computer scientists of the Science Directorate to be ready to go aboard the Kammorrigan ship to download its database. She contacted the engineering section to provide a couple of engineers to take a look at the engines.

Meanwhile most of the survivors were confused concerning what had happened. CAPT Lindsey contacted the few Master-at-arms to get control of the situation and get the added personnel berthed. She further made an overhead announcement that the section had separated and they were on their own, everyone needed to cooperate in order to survive and hopefully get home.

The flag section glided to a full stop near one of the hatches of the Kammorrigan ship.

"Sir, I insist that you remain here." Major Clark was very upset over the Admiral's desire to go onboard the Kammorrigan ship. They were both in EVAs with the Admiral about to put on his helmet. Major Clark had his helmet as well but was trying his best to convince the Admiral not to go.

"I am going aboard that ship, Major. Now you can either come along and protect me from any danger or stay on board here. Personally, I would rather have you and your Marines with me. Make your choice."

Major Clark looked away with a furious jerk of his head and put his helmet on. They both stepped into the airlock and it sealed.

The ship's interior had the same type of tunnels that they found on the planet. They moved along it, the entire FAST Platoon with the Admiral, two engineers and several computer scientists.

Major Clark looked at his XO, "Take the engineers and find the engine room. Make your inspection quickly. We will locate the computer banks and download what we can."

"Yes, Sir. Engineers with me, let's move." All ten of them moved off towards an elevator shaft that should take them to the engine room provided there was still enough power in the systems. The rest of the party approached what appeared to be a monitor to attempt to bring up a schematic of the ship. The computer scientists moved to it and began hacking it.

After several minutes they were able to bring up the system and found the schematics of the ship. They downloaded the schematic into a hand device. Once they had it the whole group moved off.

"Major Clark, I want to go to the bridge. Split us up."

"Yes, Sir."

Half of the party followed the schematics towards the computer banks while the Admiral, the Major and the rest of the FAST moved towards the bridge.

The bridge doors were sealed shut. The Marines took a C4 charge and placed it on the doors and set the timer. They moved off down the passageway. It blew. They moved into the bridge in formation ready to kill any more Kammorrigans that may still be alive. They found only the dead. The bridge itself was a disk in appearance. The height was twelve feet and the walls were all curved in a circle. There wasn't any elevation within the room. Various monitors and stations were around the room. There was no clear captain chair. They took pictures of the room and the Admiral moved around the bridge looking at his adversaries' bodies and stations. There was nothing left to figure out there. He motioned for them to proceed to the computer banks.

When they arrived, they found the computer scientists hard at work. This was an extremely tall room with a few Kammorrigan stations to monitor the system. There were some lights blinking on this level.

"How is it coming?" inquired Major Clark.

"Slowly, we could use more power but this system also has some passwords that we have to get through."

"Do you think the engineers in the engine room could help out?"

"Almost afraid for them to bring anything online, we don't know what effect that could have."

"What do you mean?"

One of them looked at him, "Well, it could bring a weapon system online and attack the ship or some internal defense system that could attack us."

"But if you need power then we need to have them do something." Major Clark clicked his communications device.

"Engineer team."

"Yes, sir."

"Do you think you can bring the systems online?"

After a moment delay, "No sir, the engineers are taking pictures but don't believe they have the time to bring anything online especially in any way that would be safe."

"Roger. Major out."

The Major looked about the space for anything that might appear to be a generator. He looked at his Marines.

"Alright Marines look around the area for a generator for this system. There must be backup systems. Find it."

"Roger, Sir." The Marines began looking.

Several moments later the engineering team arrived just as the Marines found a likely candidate to be a generator for the system. The engineers went over to it and got it working in a relatively short period of time. The computer banks began humming with more lights blinking. The monitors came to life as energy flowed into their circuits. The Computer Scientists started working even harder as the excitement filled them and soon, they got through the codes and the Kammorrigan ship's secrets were theirs.

They downloaded all the information and the team headed back to their ship.

"Alright, bring the two fighters alongside of us and let's set a course out of here. If and when we can get a hyperspace drive, we will make a jump. That is our priority." The Admiral looked around his bridge at his crew. It felt good to be onboard one of his ships, now his only one but he was concerned. The enemy could jump back at any time and there was no way he could fight them if they did. He had to figure out how to get his ship out of here and the sooner the better.

CHAPTER 9

CAPT Strickland and his crew ensured the *Nautilus* stayed in the shadow of Kammorriga. They had picked up all but one of the SEAL teams. They remained in orbit on the dark side waiting for the last crew to return in their drop ship. The Captain was slightly apprehensive about them. They had not checked in in over two days. The *Nautilus* dared not attempt to contact them since they were in deep cover and could not tell if they would be compromised. They waited.

The internal klaxon went off. It was a soft alarm since the ship was in silent mode. The Captain got up from his rack.

"What is it?" he asked after he acknowledged the alarm by switching on the comm system.

"The *Intrepid* is under attack, sir."

"I am on my way."

He went over to his wash basin and quickly washed and put his coveralls on. He grabbed the remainder of his evening meal, a half-eaten sandwich, and headed for the bridge. When he got there the Watch Officer reported Kammorrigan ships had attacked the *Intrepid* and *Scimitar*, the rest of the fleet was moving in on their position to provide cover. They have yet to be detected.

"Keep us that way."

The Watch Officer acknowledged the order and went back to his station as CAPT Strickland took his chair. He scanned the view screens and then the three in front of his chair that he controlled himself. He punched up the status of his ship and was glad to see all systems online and fully functional. He keyed for any orders that may have been communicated from either the *Intrepid* or *Chesty*. So far nothing had come through.

"Keep our shields down and our weapons offline," he ordered the Watch Officer.

"Aye aye Sir."

The last thing he wanted was to be detected by activating his systems. They were still in silent mode and had not been detected by the Kammorrigans. They were not moving towards them.

The crew monitored a small explosion on the planet in the location of the SEAL team's shuttle. The Captain lowered his head, *damn* he thought. They watched the results of the nuclear weapons exploding on the surface of the planet.

They watched the space battle and the destruction of the *Scimitar* after the rest of the ships had jumped. The crew just sat there. Never in their wildest imaginations did they ever think this mission would end in failure let alone one of their ships being destroyed. They finally looked at each other in silent horror.

CAPT Strickland looked down at his right monitor and saw that they were to jump to the emergency coordinates. He looked at his center screen and still saw several Kammorrigan ships in orbit.

"Alright everyone, alert. Stay alert. This is a tragedy and we will remember CAPT Shura and the brave crew of the *Scimitar*. But they gave their lives for the fleet to escape and we have a job to do. We must keep our heads and prepare to jump out of here. We must stay in silent mode and not be detected. We will monitor the situation. All hands will continue to monitor all of the electrical systems, communication nets and energy signatures. Remember our mission in all this. Monitor your systems."

The crew shook themselves out of their shock and began to monitor their systems. The Captain picked up the phone by his chair and punched in the code for the engine room.

"Cheng, status."

"All systems are online and waiting your command, Sir."

"Good, have the hyperspace drive ready to make a jump. We will probably be making several jumps and I want it primed."

"Not a problem Sir, we are ready and will give you all the power you require."

"Thank you, out here."

They were collecting large amounts of data from the planet and all the ships. They continued to collect even when the hyperspace wells started opening and the Kammorrigans entered the well.

"Alright move us away from the planet and put us on the far side of one those moons. Keep us in the dark."

"Aye, aye, Sir," responded the Helmsman.

"Astrogation, I want the coordinates fed into the system for the jump and begin making preparations for follow on jumps."

"Yes, Sir. Any idea about where the fleet may be heading?"

The Captain looked at her. Damn she had a good point. He opened the panel cover on the left arm of his chair and punched in his codes. The far-left screen shifted to the order section of the Captain's database. He scrolled through the orders looking for the contingency section. Upon finding it he scrolled down the various sections and stopped. He smiled.

"Forget the emergency coordinates; make our heading for the cloud system that we found."

She looked at him, "Aye aye, Sir."

She punched up the system on her screen and plotted a course.

"It will take eleven jumps to get there, Sir."

"So be it. Feed the jump coordinates to Helm. When we get to the other side of the moon, double check to ensure the Kammorrigans are not monitoring us. When we are sure open a well and make the jump."

He looked down not even waiting to hear the confirmation of the order knowing that his crew would make it happen. He was reading the orders and making his own plans just in case.

The *Nautilus* moved silently through the space between the planet and the moon. She was a sleek piece of machinery, all black with no lights. Her exhaust ports were designed where no light and very little if any energy would be noticed. There was no light emitting from any system of the *Nautilus* and hardly any energy signature.

She moved quickly and quietly around the moon and came up in her jump position. A few moments later a small, a very small hyper-space window opened up and she slipped into it and the well shut behind her. It happened so quickly that it didn't produce any readings.

. . .

The *Nautilus* jumped into normal space. The bridge crew waited for the systems to take a reading on their location. It didn't take but a moment for it to confirm that they were in the cloud system.

"Oh my god."

"What is it?" the Captain asked his Sensor Technician.

"The sensors are picking up a huge fleet. Already the count is over sixty."

"Passive sensors only and silent mode, to the max." The Captain ordered.

They had jumped into the cloud system with the Kammorrigan fleet jumping into the system as well. They were taking up positions around the cloud and were registering over a hundred ships with more coming in.

"Move us farther away and keep us in the dark," the Captain said to his Helmsman.

"Alright everyone, keep us quiet and remember our mission. We are to gather as much information as possible on these guys. All systems remain passive but I want readings on all electromagnetic emissions. It appears to me that our fleet is inside the phenomena so we can only hope there is a way out of it for them."

The *Nautilus* moved off away from the cloud phenomena and into the darkness of space where she blended in.

They waited for several hours while more Kammorrigan ships continued to appear and took up positions around the cloud. Over time fewer ships were jumping into the system.

After nearly a day of monitoring the situation the Kammorrigans started jumping away. The crew became very alert and almost agitated but the Captain and Executive Officer made their rounds to keep them calm. A few more hours saw nearly all of the Kammorrigans gone. Soon after her sensors picked up a nuclear detonation with a corresponding shockwave.

"Move us slowly around the phenomena and be ready with weapons," ordered the Captain.

The *Nautilus* began moving from her station seeking the cause of the shockwave.

CHAPTER 10

The Nautilus *came* around the cloud and found the Kammorrigan wrecked ship. Her sensors found an ion trail heading away from it. They set course and speed and began tracking it. Not too long after they left the wreckage; their screens picked up a flying disk with two of their fighters attached to the sides of it.

"Head for the disk," the Captain instructed, "Comms, send a priority message to that disk. Give her identification code and wait for a response."

"Admiral, it's the *Nautilus*. She is making contact with us."

The Admiral dropped his hand from his head and looked up.

"How much longer before the wreckage explodes?"

"Twenty minutes, we will be out of range of the shockwave," responded CAPT Lindsey.

"Alright, inform the *Nautilus* with instructions to meet us on our path but outside of the range of the explosion."

"Yes, Sir." She said and turned to her board to convey the information.

Twenty minutes later the Kammorrigan wreckage exploded hiding all traces of her being boarded by the humans.

The flag section came up beside the *Nautilus*.

"CAPT Strickland," the Admiral was radioing over to the *Nautilus*, "it is good to see you. I am curious why you didn't jump with the rest of the fleet."

"We must have been on the far side of the phenomena, Sir. We only read the enemy fleet departing the area."

"Alright, let's check your hull. We found tracers on our ships and that is how they tracked us. I am fairly confident that you don't have a tracker otherwise we would be knee deep in their ships. But check anyway to make sure."

"Affirmative, Sir, meanwhile is there some way we may assist you?"

"How much data can we transmit to you?"

After several minutes, "our holding storage is half full. We have been collecting a lot of information."

The Admiral considered his options.

"Alright, we will burn copies of what we have collected and transport them over to you. Meanwhile we either have to come up with a hyperspace drive for this disk, transfer all of us over to your ship or somehow connect the two ships and make the jump to Earth."

CAPT Strickland thought for a minute, "I will have my engineers look at the structural schematics of the ship and see if we can connect. I will also have them look into how we can assist with an engine for you."

"Thank you. Please coordinate with Dr. Vance. His team is working on it."

"Roger, Sir."

Dr. Vance was very concerned. His team had been exploring the entire section and they were not sure if it could handle hyperspace. The structure was sound and would support a normal space drive without any problems. They were running their calculations to see if the structure could handle a jump into and out of hyperspace. Even if it could handle the initial jumps, just how many could it handle? There were several jumps that had to be made prior to getting to Earth.

At least one thing was in their favor, the *Nautilus* didn't have any tracking devices on her. This was a plus; they had time to figure out the problem but how much time? They had rigged the shuttles to stay in hyperspace for five days before they would drop to normal space. Already the clock was ticking. They had to figure this problem out and fast.

Colonel Cole, the Fleet's CAG, entered the flag saucer section's dining hall. He went over and got himself a cup of coffee while scanning the facility. It was full of various members of the crew but he was only interested in two officers. He spotted Capt Hemming and 1st Lt Stanz sitting in one of the corners keeping to themselves. He approached them.

"Good afternoon, Gentlemen."

"Sir," they both responded and started to get up and the Colonel waived them to stay seated as he took a seat at the table with them. They both had the same look. Why am I still alive while all the others are dead?

The Colonel took a drink of his coffee. "Well, here we are. Eighteen of our Shipmates dead. They fought a good fight and yet here we are." Both men just stirred in their seats but kept their heads down.

"No good reason for you two to still be alive. You should be dead with them. What up with that?"

Both men gave a hard stare at the Colonel.

"Yes, you both believe you should have died out there. What in the world made you so special to be alive? Well, sometimes that is the way of things. No good explanation why one pilot makes it and another doesn't when facing such superior numbers of an enemy. But that is how it came about. You two made it. And that is good! From the Admiral to the shipmate, everyone is happy you are here. Now, I need you to step up and continue the work that all of us in one way or another sacrificed. Our comrades died for the here and now. You two are going to serve for the future."

With that the Colonel took another drink of his coffee while the two Pilots started thinking what he could mean.

"Colonel, what do you mean, Sir?" Asked the Lieutenant.

"First, you two will bunk with me. My quarters are being adjusted even now to accommodate you. Second, tomorrow at 0800, you will be in our ready room to go over every mission we have performed to date."

"Why do that? We have reviewed every mission after we have flown them." Asked Capt Hemming.

"To train our future pilots." Answered the Colonel, "When and yes, when we return to Earth, you two will be the few pilots that not only trained for space flight but to have engaged a multitude of enemies and survived. Your mission is now for the future. You will review all of our flight scenarios, missions, tactics, techniques and procedures. You're going to go over everything. Even now the flight recorders from your respective fighters are being downloaded so you can review this last fight. You are going to adjust our tactics and techniques to ensure future pilots can win which enables more to return home. You are going to set the standard of what makes an ace. You will be reviewing our respective enemies to see how they fought, both with fighters and their battle ships. We need to develop procedures on how to perform one on one fighter to full wings to taking down their battle ships."

The Lieutenant sat back in his chair showing some frustration. "That is a bit too soon, Sir. Maybe later but right now...." He trailed off on this thought.

"Frank, the best way to deal with this is to do the mission analysis and come up with better ways of battling the enemy. Besides, you may discover how and possibly why you survived. I have yet to review the flight logs to see what actually happened. We have been too busy. But you two may think your job is done. Well, it isn't. Your two fighters may become nothing but thrusters for this saucer or may still be fighters to protect this saucer. Either way you still have a job to do and that is to develop new and improved tactics. Understand?"

Both men nodded.

"Okay then, get some rest and a good meal tonight. I will see you in the ready room at 0800 tomorrow." As the Colonel was getting up the two Pilots nodded at him. When he reached the door to leave the dining hall, Colonel Cole turned back to see the two men talking to each other. This time they didn't seem to be asking why they lived rather how to proceed.

The engineers were sitting around the Admiral's conference table with all their calculations sorting through the numbers.

"Can we do it?"

"If we reinforce the superstructure, we can handle multiple jumps. We have the Marines and the other crew members already working on this. The issue is the design of this vessel. It doesn't quite support an engine for hyperspace. We can adjust the maneuvering jets and make them actual engines." Dr. Gregory Smith reported.

"What about shields and weapons?" asked Dr. Vance.

"No go, no way at all." Dr. Smith said, "This section was never designed to be a warcraft. I am not even sure why it was designed to separate in the first place. I mean I am glad that we all are alive to be worrying about this problem but it doesn't make a lot of sense."

"Okay, that leaves us with the option of attaching to the *Nautilus*. Can we do this?"

The engineers all looked at each other. "We are still waiting for the report from the *Nautilus* to see the feasibility of attaching to them. The flag section itself could be adopted to attach to a variety of ships but the *Nautilus* is such a different design that we are not sure. Amanda is working on a detail plan to attach the section but we need the *Nautilus* information first."

"Alright, I will tell the Admiral that the only real option is to attach to the *Nautilus* but we need time. He won't like the time part."

Dr. Vance got up to go to the Admiral's office.

CAPT Lindsey sipped her coffee while the Admiral checked his computer. Dr. Vance sat in his chair watching him. CAPT Lindsey picked up the report from the Section's Chief Engineer. She read it.

"I really believe that we have to get attached to the *Nautilus*. I don't see how she can have all these people onboard her. Besides we have too much of a collective intelligence and knowledge to make a choice of who goes and stays."

The Admiral looked up, "I agree, get started on attaching us to the *Nautilus*."

Kevin keyed his comm device, "I want CAPT Strickland." He flipped it off without waiting for a response. He looked at Dr. Vance.

"Get the design set and transferred over to *Nautilus*. I want to be attached and ready for our first jump within a day." He turned back to his computer. He would convey the urgency to CAPT Strickland and both crews would make it happen.

It was really an ugly contraption. The basic design of the *Nautilus* was a submarine with a sloping conning tower. Now it had the disk of the flag section attached just aft of the conning tower taking up the entire back end of the ship. The two fighters were attached to the disk. CAPT Strickland had insisted that the Admiral transfer his flag to the *Nautilus*. Vice Admiral Brannigan sat in his own command chair on his section. He was not about to transfer his flag to the *Nautilus* with so many of his crew going to ride these jumps out on the section. So, he stayed and thanked the Captain for his concern.

The *Nautilus* was moving on the general course towards Earth. Her engines were spooling up for the first jump. Her engineers kept going over the numbers ensuring everything was in order. The Captain was concerned about the stresses that were going to be put on their respective ships. It took them a day and a half to get the two ships joined. It was a hurry job but they really didn't know when the Kammorrigans would return. It was only a matter of time.

"Are you sure about these figures?" CAPT Strickland asked his Chief Engineer.

"Yes, Sir. The disk should remain attached to the *Nautilus*. I don't foresee any trouble with her. But the two fighters, I am afraid will be sheared off when we make the jump. I recommend we cut them lose and destroy them now."

The Captain thought about his options.

"We are already too far away from the wreckage for it to make any sense about their destruction." He scratched his chin. "Is there any way to bring them inside the *Nautilus*?"

The Cheng checked his hand device. "It wouldn't be stable and we could possibly cause damage to the hatch leading to the hold to attempt to bring them in."

"If they survive the shearing effect going into hyperspace, can we separate them and destroy them in hyperspace?"

"We could destabilize the hyperspace tunnel."

"Take them with us into the tunnel. If they survive great and we will deal with them there."

"Yes, Sir." The Cheng headed for his engine room.

The tension among the crews of two ships, now one, was high along with the eagerness of going home. They had several jumps to go to get home.

They jumped.

The well opened and the new ship jumped into the well. They began experiencing the vibrations right away. The joined ship bounced back and forth but continued traveling. The crews hung onto whatever they could find. Sickbay was getting calls for assistance due to injuries. All of which seemed to be minor. They couldn't afford to head out of sickbay to render aid until the shockwaves dissipated. The ship was beginning to list to the port side when the vibrations stopped. The Helmsman had to work to right the ship.

"Controls are sluggish Sir but I am able to right us now that these vibrations have stopped."

"Affirmative. Is the tunnel stable?"

The Helmsman checked his system and looked at the Astrogator who was checking his system. The Astrogator looked up and nodded at him.

"Sir, the tunnel is stable and we are progressing as planned."

"Systems check across the board and check on those fighters."

"Roger, Sir." The bridge crew ran their checks and each one reporting that all systems were green and somehow the fighters were still attached.

"How is the stress on the systems?"

"Sir, we are doing remarkably well," reported the Cheng. "I am glad to say that we are doing alright at this time. I will let you know the moment a problem occurs."

"Thank you." The Captain closed the intercom system and radioed for the Admiral. He came up on his center screen.

"Sir, all systems are online, the tunnel is stable and we are progressing as planned. We will check the readings to figure out why the disturbance upon entering hyperspace. I am sure it has to do with the change in our structure but we will see what we can do to compensate."

"I am sure it is. Very good, Captain, thank you for the update. Let me know about the injured at the earliest possible moment."

"Yes, Sir."

· · ·

The klaxons sounded onboard the *Chesty* as she came out of hyperspace around the mining planet that they had found. Soon after the klaxons sounded, the Watch Officer announced via the ship's intercom "General Quarters, General Quarters, all hands to their Battle Stations. General to the bridge."

MajGen Connington was in his cabin when the alarm sounded and he keyed his comm.

"What is happening?"

"Sir, we have picked up four ships in orbit over the mining operations. We have launched the alert fighters and all four ships have pulled up in battle formations. We still don't have the ships identified but are assuming them to be pirates."

"Good. I will be right there."

The General got up and headed for the bridge.

The remaining ships of the Strike Group had formed up with the *Chesty* as the anchor ship, the *Excalibur* and *Icarus* both took positions in front and to the left and right of the *Chesty*. The *Defiant* was in front of all the ships and slightly lower on the z axis to the *Chesty*. In this manner they could interlock all fire. Meanwhile the twenty-eight fighters launched. Eighteen fighters, in three ship v formations were heading for the alien ships while the remaining ten Marine fighters stayed with the Strike Group to provide fighter coverage.

The fighters were flying in fast with their weapon systems up. They were preparing for a fight anticipating the alien ships to open up on them at any moment. All the pilots were surprised when their comm system came online on an Earth frequency with English speaking at them.

"This is Orbital Defense Zeta. Incoming fighters stand down and identify yourself or we will fire upon you."

The voice was definitely human and the language was definitely English. The translator had not kicked in.

"Orbital Defense Zeta, this is EXPLORER Wing. Send IFF code at once lest we attack."

With the Identify Friend or Foe code the fighters would be able to confirm this was truly an Earth force or an enemy attempting to deceive them. The lead pilot had already engaged his IFF to verify the code. Within moments they received an Earth IFF and his system responded back.

"Welcome to Mining Operation Plymouth EXPLORER Wing. Welcome back."

"Thank you, Mining Operation Plymouth. We will convey your welcome to Strike Group EXPLORER."

The fighters turned and headed back to the fleet and signaled that the ships were from Earth.

MajGen Connington sat in the command chair on the flag bridge with the MEU Colonel standing next to him. They looked at each other slightly confused.

"Bring us closer and identify the ships ourselves. Do NOT stand down from General Quarters and keep our fighters in space. I want them on alert."

"Yes Sir," Responded the MEU Ops Officer who relayed the order.

"Alright bring us to the defense ships and let's see what there is to see."

The Strike Group did not break formation and the fighters formed up in front of them as they headed towards the planet. Within minutes they were able to bring the images of the ships onto their view screens. The ships were not built like the Strike Groups. These were more in the shape of a snub nose single hull configuration. The language used on the hull of the ships was English showing their hull number and names. The General looked at the Colonel and shrugged.

"Open up a channel," he told the Communications Officer.

"This is MajGen Connington, Commander of Strike Group EXPLORER."

"Welcome to Mining Operation Plymouth, we thought VADM Brannigan was in command."

MajGen Connington nodded his head in appreciation that they had their command structure.

"He is but is not currently with the Strike Group therefore I have command until his return," he only hoped that somehow the *Intrepid* would soon join them.

"How long have you been on the planet?"

"Plymouth has been here for three months now. As you see we have an orbital defense system. We are glad to see you since pirate activity still occurs in this region of space though we haven't seen them for several weeks now."

"Do you have any intelligence on their operating base in this region?" inquired the General, "if you do, we can eliminate them."

"Unfortunately, not," there was a moment of silence. "General, our Base Commander is inviting you and your key staff to dinner at the station here."

"I would be honored. We would like to catch up on news before we head for Earth."

"Dinner is at 1800 local time, Sir. We will send coordinates to your ship."

"Thank you. Explorer out," when the comm link was severed the General told them to stand down from General Quarters and asked the Colonel to prepare for planet side for dinner.

•   •   •

The *Chesty's* klaxons sounded. "General Quarters. General Quarters, all hands man your Battle Stations. General to the bridge," sounded the alarm system.

The General woke up at the sound of the klaxons and heard the announcement, what again he thought. He keyed his comm.

"Bridge, this is the General, what is it, pirates?"

"Not sure General," answered the Senior Watch Officer, "a ship has just jumped into the area. We are attempting to identify it. It is a strange configuration and we can't truly get a lock on it."

"Alright, launch the alert fighters I will be there shortly."

"Yes Sir, the fighters will be away shortly."

The General stepped onto the bridge.

"Report."

"Sir, the fighters are on their way, we cannot get a lock on the target however."

"What do you mean?" Asked the General.

"We are getting confusing readings. Sometimes we have a ship and other times we don't"

"Are we tracking a stealth ship or does it have a cloaking device?"

"I don't know, Sir," replied the Senior Watch Officer.

"Are all the ships at General Quarters?"

"Affirmative, Sir, to include the Orbital Defense ships."

"Good, how many fighters are heading for the contact?"

"Only five, we are keeping the other ones in the tubes at this point."

"Good, bring the *Excalibur* and *Defiant* around. I want them to head out to back up the fighters. Meanwhile get me the Commander of the Defense Force."

"General," called out the Communications Officer.

"What is it?"

"We are getting a transmission. It is the *Nautilus*, Sir."

The General looked at the screen. That would make sense he thought.

"Confirm IFF with them," called out the Senior Watch Officer.

"Yes sir," the Commo replied. She proceeded to send the IFF confirmation and then flipped on the internal bridge comm system.

"General Connington, this is Admiral Brannigan, come in." MajGen Connington looked over at the Comm Officer. She nodded back and gave a thumbs up for the IFF. He went ahead and flipped his own comm switch.

"Welcome back Admiral. We are having difficulty picking you up on sensors."

"That is good. I see you have gained some new ships."

"They are an Orbital Defense Force sent from Earth to guard this planet."

"Excellent, we should be joining you soon provided the *Excalibur*, *Defiant*, and the fighters don't fire upon us."

The General motioned for the Senior Watch Officer to stop them but he was already in motion to call them off.

"Admiral the *Nautilus* is welcome to come into orbit. What happened to the *Intrepid*?"

After a moment of silence, the response came over in a somber tone, "CAPT Smith and her brave crew gave their lives to destroy our enemy. Their bravery gave us the opportunity to escape the system undetected. The *Nautilus* will need to be relieved of her burden. Maybe the *Excalibur* or *Icarus* can take it from her. I will meet you onboard the *Chesty* soon."

"Yes, Sir, we will await your arrival. *Chesty* out."

"Make ready to receive, EXPLORER," called out MajGen Connington.

The two Fleet Commanders sat in the command cabin on the *Chesty*. Admiral Brannigan took a drink of his coffee.

"Good job, Paul, for bringing the Strike Group here. My thanks."

"No problem, Sir. I gather it wasn't too pleasant after we left."

"Losing the *Intrepid* and her brave crew and Captain was not at all pleasant. Their sacrifice was not in vain however. We downloaded the entire Kammorrigan database off that massive ship. Dr. Vance and team are analyzing it now."

"At least something worthwhile came from it. Wasn't there some way to save them?"

"Not after they separated the flag section from the ship. Captain Smith said that her hyperspace drive was a molten slag." Kevin shook his head. His remorse was deep and he felt the pain of the loss of two of his ships.

"I only wish she had not separated us. I have been thinking about it since we started the jumps. I really don't know if there was anything I could have done but she didn't give me that chance."

"Captain Smith was always strong headed once she made up her mind about things."

"Yes," said Admiral Brannigan, "once we have transferred the saucer to one of the other ships, we will get underway to Earth. It is good to see an Earth outpost here but we can't stay any longer. We must begin building a fleet that can take on these monsters."

"We should be able to get underway within a day or two."

"Good, let's not waste any time."

CHAPTER 11

Earth. She rotated around her father, Sol, the star of the system. If she had feelings, she would feel comfort having her brother, Mars, protecting her on one side and her sister, Venus, glowing with her passions on the other side. If she had feelings, she would feel comforted by having her companion, Lunar, the Moon in orbit around her. She would enjoy the life that dwelled on her. The various life forms lived their life to their pleasure, in one life form or another; however, she would have both pride and disappointment. That is if she could feel. That would be the crowning life form, man. She would be proud in their achievements, in their compassion to each other and the way they honored her. She would be disappointed in their cruelty towards each other, the other life forms and towards her.

Man had explored the various parts of her, Mother Earth. Now they were leaving her. A group had traveled to Lunar and began a colony there. They were digging into his surface. Another group was on her brother, Mars, setting up military and mining stations there. There was even a group out to her distant brother, Jupiter. They had built three main space stations, one around Mars and two near her. One of the stations in orbit around her was a command post. The other one would have reminded her of the ships they had built to cross her oceans, this one was building ships to cross the vast emptiness of space itself.

Yes, she could be proud of man that is if man would honor each other and her, that is if she could feel.

Major Glenn was the Senior Watch Officer onboard Mars station. It was two in the morning standard Earth time. They had not received any word from the mining colony on 237 Prime for over a month. Major Glenn had come on duty at 2300 and his section had been attempting to contact the colony with no success. He knew Space Command was about to send a strike group out with some Marines to see what was happening. They hoped the problem was only a communication one. The planet had a good defense system but without communications there were always concerns.

He took another drink of his coffee and placed the mug in the holder and turned to the message board. He nearly jumped out of his seat when the alarms went off loudly in the command room and all the watch standers were visibly startled as well.

"What is it?" he cried out. The only time the alarms go off is during a drill but none were scheduled.

"Don't know yet, Sir," came the response from the Scanning section.

"Alright, everyone calm down and run through the numbers. Check your systems and let's find out what triggered the alarm." Major Glenn turned to his board and started checking for updates.

"Sir," Airman Jones at deep sensors station called, "I have it. A group of ships jumped into our system past Saturn. I can't get a lock on them due to the lack of sensors in that sector. The only sensor out there picked up a group of ships but we can't get any resolution on them."

"Thank you," responded the Major, "Comms, contact Space Command and feed the telemetry to them."

"Yes, Sir."

"Sir, Mars station reports a group of ships jumping into sector 9. No resolution on them."

"Damn," CDR Stevenson breathed as he made a mental note to complain to higher authority about the lack of sensors in that sector. "Alright, launch a five-ship contact team to that sector. Let's get a read on them. Prepare Earth's defense system just in case. Get me all information on these ships and alert Moon base Alpha."

CDR Stevenson being the Senior Watch Officer at Current Operations onboard Space Command Orbital would have to report to the General this contact. He really hated not having enough information. With the mining colony at 237 Prime out of contact he had no way of knowing if these were Kammorrigans, pirates or some other alien contact. As far as he knew it was a shipment of the crystals coming in. So, all he could do was launch a partial squadron of fighters to investigate. Meanwhile he would have the new battleship prepare to launch in defense of the planet and bring the satellite system online for defense. When he had enough information, which would be in another minute, he would report out to the General on the situation.

"Major Glenn, sir," The Comm station called, "Space Command authorizes the launch of five fighters."

"Thank you. Contact Jupiter station to launch their ready alert."

"Yes, sir."

Jupiter station has a hanger with twenty fighters, living quarters for station and space craft maintenance crews, pilots, and a small team of scientists. They had two purposes; the scientists would study the planet and use their telescope to look at deep space. The other purpose was to house the fighters to be a first line of defense. When the Commander of the Station received the order from Mars station, he launched ten of his fighters. Five would go out to investigate the contact and five would take up a supporting position if required. Since they didn't have any data on the incoming contact he went ahead and placed the other ten fighters on alert. All ships were fully armed and fueled.

The fighters set off on an intercept course to the contact.

CDR Stevenson was watching the screens in the Command room while his watch standers updated it from their stations. He was used to having to wait for information to come in. Twenty years in the Navy serving on various command staffs aided in preparing a person for this lag of information. Nevertheless, it was still somewhat grating on his nerves. Unlike the navies on Earth where the U.S. Navy had intelligence on the other country's navies this contact was an unknown. Here a slight mistake could throw everyone into war or worse yet a defeat in their own system. He sat back in his chair and took a drink of his water.

The Communications Officer slapped his head with his open hand then shook his head and made a couple of adjustments to his board. This caught CDR Stevenson's attention.

"What is it, Comms?"

The Comms Officer shook his head again and made another adjustment to the board and read intently what was on the screen. He then turned around and reported, "Sir, the contact is the Strike Group EXPLORER."

The CDR just looked at him for a few minutes then, "How do you know?"

"We are receiving a communication but it wasn't on our standard channels for our own incoming ships. It kept bugging me so I ran it through a series of other channels and suddenly there it was."

The CDR started to get unhappy. "Have you confirmed the communication and the IFF?"

"No, Sir."

"Then do so and do it at once."

"Aye, aye, sir."

"And get me the Operations General."

"Yes, Sir."

The *Chesty* pulled slowly into her docking bay while the Admiral watched from his flag bridge now attached to the *Excalibur*. It was impressive watching the skilled crewmen both onboard the ship and the docking station handle her. Soon the Marines and crewmembers of the ships would begin their debriefings before being allowed leave to see their families. Everyone was excited. Vice Admiral Brannigan just sat in his chair watching the screen and occasionally taking in his own flag staff. He still had to finish his report for the President, Joint Chiefs of Staff, Space Force, and select members of Congress. He had been informed other country representatives would be at the briefings. He sighed; this would be a big to do and possibly a bit of an inquisition.

In fact, the whole affair would probably become a very accusatory inquisition by some of the other countries. Even though he had sailed with members from other countries, a lot of them were not let in on this flight. But the whole planet was now a space faring orb in space. He was surprised by the colonies on both Mars and the Moon and the outposts orbiting some of the other planets. The Mining Colony was the farthest outpost of Earth and he had already recommended that additional ships be sent to protect it. Already a fleet of ten ships were preparing to make the jump to the planet. At least the pirates would be battled and the Colony would be protected.

He rose and left the bridge to finish his report. In the morning he would be transported to Earth to make the briefing.

•   •   •

Ralph could see by the tense shoulders and back how angry the man in front of him was. He stood there quietly waiting. The two men were in an office. It was shaped much like a tunnel but not totally circular. The walls, floor and ceiling were curved, the ceiling and floor was elongated and the walls slightly shorter. It needed to be made this way to support the transparency at one end and the hatch at the other. The room could handle the stresses of the rotating station. The other man was looking out of the transparency at Mother Earth on the other side of the desk. He just stood there looking out the window at the planet while Ralph stood watching both him and the planet that they were Guardians of.

"Just who do they think they are?" Began the other man, obviously still quite angry, "Don't they realize I am supposed to retire?" He continued with his venting and Ralph just stood there waiting.

"Don't worry Kevin. This is your last assignment. We still need you."

"Bullshit! There are plenty of viable people for this job."

"Yes, but none with your experience."

"Bullshit. You know as well as I there are many bright and intelligent people dying for this job and they stick it with me. What did I do to deserve this?"

"You have always been successful."

With that the recently promoted four-star admiral, Admiral Brannigan spun about and glared at his old friend the four-star, Commander of Space Force, Admiral Nabum.

"You had something to do with this, admit it."

"What me?" Ralph tried to look all innocent.

"Come now, Kevin, you know you are the right man for this job and we still need you. You can't just fade away like you have been attempting to do for the past several years. You still have the job to prepare this fleet for the battle that is yet to come. We need you to prepare all the planet's defenses, the strike groups to include the Marines to take out this enemy of humanity and by your own report other races in the galaxy."

Kevin let out a growl and moved to the left side of the room towards the wet bar.

"What do you want to drink?"

"Just some whisky if you don't mind."

Kevin poured two glasses and handed one to Ralph who motioned him to sit. Ralph took the glass with a smile of thanks and sat down and watched his old friend as he took his seat behind the desk. It suited him. It was a command desk, after all Admiral Kevin Brannigan was just made Admiral of the Space Fleet. This was his command office. From here Kevin would be able to monitor every aspect of the fleet and two floors below him was his own Flag Plot to monitor the systems around the solar system. Ralph quietly smiled to himself while he took a drink. He had indeed been behind this assignment. He took a lot of time in designing this station with Kevin in mind and now he would finish his current job before moving on to the next. He looked up at Kevin who was still fuming. Mother Earth was slowly rotating out of the window as one of the space docks was coming into view.

"I don't like it, Ralph." Kevin was still pretty sore and Ralph knew he had to get him off the stew of being forced into this assignment and not to retirement.

"Who did you choose to captain the mission?" Ralph asked his old friend.

Kevin sighed changing his thoughts to this new mission. This would perhaps be the most important mission and the one with a lot of risk for both the planet and the brave crew. It was simply a reconnaissance mission but it had an intelligence aspect. The lone ship would go deep into their new enemy's territory to gather more information on the Kammorrigans. True they had the databases from the destroyed ship but there were other questions to be answered.

"The captain will be Commander Ortega who was the Executive Officer on the *Nautilus*. He knows what we are facing and has seen their might. He also performed quite well onboard the ship."

"They will be leaving soon?"

"Today as a matter of fact, we should be able to see the launch from the docks."

"I saw the ship's design. I see you have chosen the *Nautilus* form but with improvements."

"You are looking over my shoulder?"

Ralph smiled slightly and shook his head, "No but I am definitely interested in these projects. After all I have my own role in all of this."

"Yes, just what is that role?"

Ralph just took a sip of the whisky and looked up at the Admiral. Kevin took a sip of his and returned the look. Kevin let out a low growl when he realized Ralph was not going to answer him.

"As you know the database that my Strike Group recovered will tell us a lot about the Kammorrigans but this mission will let us see for ourselves how their fleet operates. Regarding the ship design, the *Sabachi* does follow the *Nautilus* design but with several upgrades. This new ship takes her lessons seriously," Kevin stated, "I have also chosen another officer from the *Nautilus* to be Commander Ortega's XO. And

I have given him a small contingent of SEALs and Marines, Recon types. I hope he won't need them but we don't know."

"I hope they don't give anything away," Ralph started. He didn't like this mission; sure, he knew the reason for it but he wanted Earth to remain hidden until she was strong enough to take on the Kammorrigans. But Kevin had pushed hard for this surveillance. "How will she communicate with us?"

"That is being worked on."

Ralph had been around long enough to know this line wasn't going anywhere; besides he was more concerned about the main fleet.

"How is the Control Room below? Does it meet your needs?"

Kevin took another sip of the whisky and thought about the question.

"Partly, I am having some modifications made to it."

Ralph smiled inwardly but looked hurtful towards his old friend.

"I'm sorry; I thought my team did a good job."

Kevin shook his head, finished his drink. He got up and went over and poured another one. "You want more?"

"No, this is good for me."

"You people want me to build a space fleet. A massive war fleet to take on an enemy that has been space farers a lot longer than we even thought about. The Control Room doesn't handle it in its present capacity. I need logistic ships; the war ships have to be logistic ships and then there is a question of Marines and the ability to transport soldiers for occupation."

"Occupation? I thought this would be a total naval or space battle, who said anything of occupation?" Ralph was shocked.

"Yes, take the Spanish-American war. We suddenly had colonies in the pacific. How many islands did the U.S. take? Well, we defeat the Kammorrigans just how many planets will fall into our control?"

Ralph looked up as Kevin walked back around the desk, took a look out the window then sat down.

"I didn't think of that but is that really necessary?"

"We have to think beyond the battle. I am already looking at how we will fight this fight. That is why I am sending that ship out there alone. She will get me information I need but, in the meantime, we have to build this fleet or rather fleets. I am planning on at least three. How many planet battles will there be? You and the others have only been thinking there will be one decisive space battle and the Kammorrigans will leave with their tail between their legs. Well, that has never happened in our history. There are always land troops after the naval battles and I mean battles. We will have to take some planets and make others uninhabitable. That is if we want victory. I must know which planets are which. So, no the Control Room didn't meet the needs. I have to train these ships' crews to behave in a way to gain victory. And oh, by the way who thinks I know what is best in this area? Because I went out there, this is space and the battles are in space."

"Who else is there? Yes, you were the one who went out there. I proposed you and you went. You went for diplomatic reasons but the way the Kammorrigans are; your military expertise is what enabled you to come back with the warning we needed. You have seen the space battles and know more about how to fight them than anyone else. That is why you are the Admiral of the Space Fleet and that of the world not just the U.S."

"Did you make this happen?"

"Hell no, but I am the one that lives with the decision and will support you as you need to accomplish the building of this fleet."

Kevin fixed him with a doubtful look. A light on his board caught his attention. He touched a button on his panel and read the screen. He motioned for Ralph to join him. They both stood at the window as the *Sabachi* left its dock on its mission to spy out the Kammorrigans. They watched it as it slipped into the darkness and lost from view.

"Are you really serious about occupying other worlds?"

"Of course, I am. There are many resources that we need and besides we have to build a defensive perimeter about the planet to protect her from all threats. The Kammorrigans are our immediate threat but there are pirates and slavers a lot closer to us than them. And we don't know who else is out there."

Ralph checked his watch, "Oh I need to go." Kevin nodded and Ralph put down his glass on his way out the door.

As he walked towards the lift that would take him to the shuttle bay, he thought to himself how easy it is to manipulate men like Kevin. Oh yes, he lied to him about his role in placing Kevin in this position. He was the central figure behind him both going out to meet the Kammorrigans and now to be the Admiral of the Space Fleet. He ensured no one else would get the job. Why? A simple reason: Admiral Brannigan was a responsible, honorable man that would ensure the right thing would be done. Such men are hard to come by and easy to manipulate for unscrupulous men like ADM Nabum. He smiled to himself as he touched the pad summoning the lift. His job was complete in making this adjustment. It was a good feeling knowing he had secured his planet at this time. He would allow himself just a bit of relaxation and then to the next phase of his scheming. At least he did it for Human kind.

·   ·   ·

Paul Connington was riding a shuttle from Earth to the Orbital Space Command. He was looking out the window as Earth sled slowly away. He shook his head. VADM Brannigan had sponsored his promotion. The President showed great pride pinning the third star on him. Now LtGen Connington was heading to see his new boss. He was surprised not to see VADM Brannigan at the promotion ceremony. Hell, he didn't even know where he was. But now Paul was finally a LtGen and heading up to the orbital for his new orders.

During the ride he thought back over the past six months. *Wow, it's already been six months since they had returned to Earth.* They came in to a welcome that they all could appreciate. Two weeks upon their return, he was transferred from the SESG to Space Force and assigned to the Planning Directorate. He was given only one week of leave and then back on the job. For five months he was assigned there. He was given ships' designs and personnel manifest to review. He wondered why a plans office would be reviewing ship designs. But there it was. Then he was told he was on leave for a month. What did that mean? Not a good sign but he enjoyed the time with his family. Been a long time since he had really seen them.

At the end of his leave, he returned to find he was no longer part of the Plans Directorate. ADM Nabum was now Chief of Space Operations and General Rodriquez was the Chairman of the Joint Chiefs. General Malcolm was now part of the State Department sitting on an international committee concerning space and how to govern it. ADM Nabum took Paul to see the President who pinned the third star on him. As they were leaving the White House the ADM handed him new orders to report to Space Fleet at the Orbital Space Command. Good luck he said and shook his hand and ordered the car to take Paul to the space port. And now here he is heading out to space.

The shuttle slid easily into the docking station. The hatch opened and Paul stepped out onto the hanger deck.

"Welcome to the Operational Space Station General, this way please" said the 1st Lt as she gestured towards some turbo lifts.

They approached the lift and the Lt keyed the pad for a car. They entered the car and the Lt keyed for the command deck. They stood in silence as the car moved upward in the station. When it stopped the doors opened and the Lt said her farewells as the General stepped through to see a Captain waiting for him.

"Sir, this way to the Space Fleet Commander." The Captain moved off with Paul following. Interesting this station. He had no idea what all the levels were or this meeting would be about. They approached a couple of doors and over them read Space Fleet Commander. The Captain opened the door for Paul who entered and the Captain said his farewell. The Secretary looked up from her screen, "Good morning,

Sir, he is expecting you." Then she touched a button and the inner doors opened and Paul went in to see his new boss.

He was a bit surprised. Of course, he recognized Kevin Brannigan, even with his back to him. He was pouring two glasses of Scotch as Paul approached.

"Good morning, Paul. Congratulations on the promotion. Please take a seat and here have this." Kevin handed him the glass as Paul was taking a seat and Kevin moved off behind the desk. Paul noticed a fourth star on Kevin's uniform.

"Thank you."

"Apologies for not being at the promotion. How was the leave?"

"Good, thank you, Sir. Congratulation to you on your star." They both raised their glasses and took a drink.

"I was wondering what happened to you after we returned. They buried me in the Plans Directorate."

"Yes, I know. I was able to get a couple of weeks of leave but not long. Damn, they had me up here shortly after that. I was going to retire but they wouldn't let me. Can you believe that?" They both softly laughed.

"So, what is this all about, Sir?"

Kevin finished his drink and put the glass down, he was staring at Paul straight on. He then stood up and walked over to his window and looked down at Mother Earth. That is what he always called the planet, Mother Earth. Paul sat there patiently. The Kammorrigan mission taught him about some of the Admiral's habits.

"Well Paul, we have to expand beyond our solar system. You and I discovered a lot of threats in space and we no longer can be confined to this system. We have to go out there." He waved his arm in an overarching motion. "That is why they put me in command of Space Fleet. What a stupid name. I'll get that changed. This should be Fleet Operations. Ralph is the Chief and it's his job and his staff to do Space Force." He sighed heavily then turned and went to a view screen and motioned Paul to follow him. At the screen he touched a key and a representation of the solar system, Alpha Centauri and Plymouth (237 Prime) came up.

"We are here now. We are actually building a space station here at Alpha Centauri." He pointed at the system.

"But that isn't sufficient. We are going to be discovered sooner or later. The Kammorrigans are looking for us, you can bet on that. But that isn't your problem."

Paul looked at him, "What is my job then?"

Kevin glanced at him with a mischievous grin and turned back to the screen.

"You recall that station we found and had to take down?"

Paul nodded as Kevin pushed another set of buttons and the screen expanded the view to include the station and with another touch it glowed and had a red circle about it.

"You are now Commander of a new strike force. No, not like EXPLORER was. This one is military designed for war. Yes, the ships will have science and engineering sections with a few labs but it is designed to neutralize threats. And it's yours."

Kevin keyed a few other items and the station grew to the center of the screen with a green line extending from it.

"Again, don't concern yourself about the Kammorrigans. Ralph is already constructing a fleet for them and I have a ship out already on that one. No, you are on a hunt for a different threat. You will proceed with your new strike group, which by the way you have spent the last five months reviewing the ship designs."

Paul quickly looked at him with surprise.

"That is right, Paul. We have been ensuring you would be familiar with your fleet and crews. Now is the time you will get to know them.

So, you will go by Plymouth. Everyone who leaves or comes to Earth must go through Plymouth. It is our check point to ensure hostiles are kept away from here. While you transit through them if they need aid with pirates, render it. But get underway quickly. You are to make for the station at best speed. Your engines are better than EXPLORER ships were thanks to the crystals. We have made significant improvements. Your ships already bristle with new weapons and shields. You ought to make quite a sight when you jump to the station. Reinforce our authority over them. After you have done that." Kevin then traced along the green line.

"Follow that transmission path and find out who or what is on the other end. Then neutralize the threat. By any means. That could mean diplomatic, a show of force or even obliterate them. Details of the mission and all coordinates are already onboard your flagship. Very detailed orders are on your personal system already. Any questions?"

With that Kevin returned to his desk. Paul stood there looking at the view screen.

"Wow. I didn't think this would be the job." Paul shook his head and returned to his seat and finished his drink.

"No, Sir. No questions about the mission. That is very clear. Just when do we depart and final leave for all hands?"

You will depart in four weeks. Enough time for you to get acquainted with your fleet, crew, and deployment leave. After that, get out of here and neutralize the threat."

"Yes, Sir. Well, if that is all, I best get going."

Kevin smiled. "Yes, my Secretary will ensure you are escorted to your command shuttle. Success Paul and I look forward to your return."

With that, they both stood up and shook hands. Paul turned and left the room. Kevin went over to the window and looked again at Mother Earth.

THE SAGA CONTINUES IN MINURVA